PERFECTLY POLITE

HILARI T. COHEN

Perfectly Polite is a novel. Any similarity to persons or events is purely coincidental.

Cover Art: KC Book Design

❀ Created with Vellum

For Alix and Jenn. Daughters of my heart...I am so lucky to have you both in my life!

Chapter One

JULIE PORTER WATCHED in amusement as her roommate and best friend stood in front of the open door of their stainless steel refrigerator, sighing. The two women had met at university and became inseparable ever since.

"Why is it," Caroline began, "that we never have anything good to eat in here?"

"There's lots to eat. You just don't like anything healthy!"

"Not true. I ate an apple the other day."

"Wasn't it covered in caramel?" Julie asked, sky blue eyes flashing, one perfectly shaped eyebrow raised.

"That's beside the point. The inside was all fruit." Caroline closed the door and leaned against the appliance.

"Why don't you try one of my yogurts? They have fruit in them too."

"Ugh. If it's not frozen from the Bloomingdale's counter, I don't eat yogurt!"

"How you stay so thin is beyond me," Julie replied. She tucked her always blunt cut, stick straight, shoulder length blonde hair behind her ears. The round, sapphire studs in her lobes accented the ocean blue of her eyes as they caught the light from the window, shooting a rainbow of reflection against the white walls of the kitchen.

"Oh wait!" Caroline said, her back to Julie once more, now digging around in the bottom freezer. "Here!" She triumphantly turned, holding a sleeve of Thin Mints in the air. "I knew I'd tucked these away for an emergency." Then, reopening the door to the refrigerator, she grabbed the almond milk. "At least this is somewhat palatable. Not like that oat crap you made me try." Pulling a glass out of the cabinet, she plopped herself down on a kitchen stool and tore into her snack.

"So happy for you, Ms. Montgomery," Julie said with a teasing tone. "And maybe when you're not so hangry we can go over the wording for your wedding invitations."

"Whatever you say," Caroline mumbled with her mouth full of cookie. "You're the expert."

Julie winced at the other woman's efforts to chew and speak at the same time. "I am, I suppose."

Caroline looked up, her amber eyes focused on her friend. "Jules. You wrote the book on this etiquette stuff. Literally. Whatever you say to do, Stephen and I will make happen. No questions asked."

Julie grimaced. It was true. She had actually written the most popular modern guide to how to do everything in the most proper way, with a chapter on weddings, from the correct engagement protocol to reception do's and don'ts. She had worked on *Practically Perfect* for well over three years while she toiled away as personal assistant to a very wealthy socialite on the Upper West Side of her adopted city. She learned a lot on that job, watching and soaking in all that she could of a lifestyle that up until that time had been foreign to her. It was that experience, observing every aspect of Mrs. Tassen's world, that gave her the confidence to be a full-time writer. The crazy part, the thing that amazed her most of all, was that the book was a hit from day one, remaining on the top of *The New York Times* bestseller list a year later, filling her bank account with the kind of money she'd only dreamed she'd have someday. The success of it shocked her still. She shook her head and smiled.

"Caroline. I'm just consulting as your BFF here. It's up to you and Stephen. Whatever you want goes, I'll just make sure it's done right."

"I'm sure you will, Ms. Control Freak," her friend said in a teasing tone as she took a large swig of her milk.

"No need for name calling. I'm protecting you, after all. Your wedding is a huge deal. One mistake can cost you everything."

"Now that's dramatic. I just design lingerie. I don't perform brain surgery." Caroline popped yet another cookie into her mouth.

"But your clients are watching. That's the part most people don't understand about the way of this digital world. Your customer is looking to you for guidance, that's why they check you out on your social media outlets. You have a high Q score, Caroline. Do you understand what that means? You're very recognizable to most of the world and your face is your brand. You've got to get this right or you'll lose credibility with your followers. Everyone loves to see someone at the top of their game stumble and fall."

Caroline chewed thoughtfully before responding. "I get it, believe me, and I'm thankful that you've got my back. There are so many ridiculous details to this wedding and I have to finish next spring's collection. That deadline won't wait. Besides, you know that all the social media crap overwhelms me on a good day. Quite frankly, I'm not all that interested in any of it. I wish that where my nuptials are concerned, it would all magically go away. I just want to marry Stephen. The rest of it I leave to you. And to my mother. Good luck with her, by the way."

"Angela isn't that difficult."

"For you maybe. She's not your mom. She's hyper-critical of me."

Julie felt a familiar pang at the mention of the word "mom". She didn't like to think about her own mother very much. She concentrated on what her friend had said and then responded. "Angela just has her opinions, that's all. She means well."

"Okay, but I'm still not sure why she is so insistent on this enormous black tie affair. It's like she's planning it just to spend my dad's money, as if she's got something to prove since the divorce. Stephen and I would have preferred to elope and we would have, if she didn't threaten to jump from the terrace of her apartment. She does live thirty stories above the city. That would have been quite the clean-up."

"*Caroline!*" Julie exclaimed. "Don't say that! Besides, you should be happy that she wants to celebrate you and Stephen in this way."

The other woman stood up and gave her friend a hug. "I'm sorry. I'm grateful for your help. And I don't mean to be so insensitive. I know you must wish that your mom was still here."

Julie shuddered and hoped that Caroline just assumed that the small tremor that moved through her body was sorrow. In fact, she prayed that it didn't betray her. Her mother was still alive. Instead, it was her own past and hidden identity that Julie wanted to remain buried. She'd kept that part of her life under tight wrap. No one knew the truth, not even Caroline. Julie intended to keep it that way. She knew she had to change the subject so that she didn't give herself away.

"Are you done eating, now? Blood sugar back to normal? Can you concentrate on this, please? We have work to do on the wording of these invitations. It's tricky when both sets of parents are divorced and now married to other people."

"Okay, okay. Let's do it. But afterward you have to try on my latest design. It's pure fantasy and you've always been my best model."

"Does it cover my nipples? That last number you had me try barely covered my boobs."

Caroline stood and put her hands on her hips. "So you have big knockers. Other women would kill for a shape like yours. Besides, that's the name of the game, Jules. Less coverage is more. It's a thing. It's popular to show off your assets these days. I mean, isn't that the true use of all that social media?"

"Not to me," Julie replied. "I think there is something to be said for a little bit of mystery."

"Well, the next time you meet a man worthy of you seeing you in one of my designs, please let me know." She shook her head. "But I won't hold my breath. You are too picky."

"I am not. I just don't see the point in hanging on to a guy that I know isn't for me."

"Right. That's why your last two relationships ended. That's why both of those men ended up proposing to the very next woman each one dated."

"Ouch!" Julie replied to the truth.

"I'm just stating the obvious. I'm not sure what you're looking for."

Julie sighed. "Me either. I'm just hoping that when I meet him, I'll know."

"You are really a hopeless romantic under that prim and proper exterior, aren't you?"

Caroline's words hit a nerve. Julie was a romantic. That's why she had little hope of finding the man who would tick off all of the boxes on her list of "must-haves". Opening her laptop, Julie said, "Enough about me. Let's wrangle these invitations and then maybe, if we complete our task, you can convince me to go out tonight for a drink. Sound like a deal?"

"Really? Oooh." Caroline's eyes widened. "You don't have to

ask me twice. You're on!"

※

JAMES CURRAN, CEO OF ONE OF THE LARGEST MEDIA
companies in the city sat at the head of the imposing, mahogany
conference table in his oversized meeting room, on the top floor
of his office building which soared above Fifth Avenue. His staff
had gathered for their weekly meeting, but as he looked around,
each member had his or her face buried in either their phone or
their tablet.

"Can I have everyone's attention? Devices down, please."

The group reluctantly relented, but that didn't stop the
continual sound of pings and bells, signaling notifications and
alerts.

"Sorry, boss," one of his editors said. "It's the nature of the
beast."

"I well understand that, Stu, but let's all try to have a face-to-
face conversation while we're here."

"Right," the chastened employee replied, turning his phone's
screen toward the highly polished table top.

"So what's our lead story?" James asked.

"We caught a break and have a nude photo of that hot young
female rapper, *Fizzy*. She was with some old guy on a yacht
docked off of Santorini," replied Gina, the senior editor of their
most popular publication, *Tell All*.

"Who is he?" James inquired.

"Some prince, I think," Gina answered.

"Full frontal?" Stu asked, leaning in.

"What do you think?" Gina replied, rolling her eyes.

"Let's verify the man's identity before printing that, okay?"
James interjected before a fight broke out between two highly
valued members of his staff.

"If you insist," Gina said, making notes on the tablet in front of her.

"What else?" James asked, looking around the table.

"The President's youngest son was caught sneaking out of the White House again. Last time it was a clandestine drug deal. Gotta assume the same again," Ron, one of the Washington correspondents offered.

"I'd like to be sure before you run with that. The kid is still underage, after all," James said.

"But boss," Ron began.

"No but boss, please. Besides, don't we have an agreement with the President? No more family exposés? Or at least not until Brandon turns twenty-one?" He thought back on the long discussion he'd had with the commander-in-chief after the last story ran about one of his offspring. They'd agreed to a truce on reporting any further family matters in exchange for a long and exclusive interview before the next election cycle. James wasn't about to renege. He wanted to move *Tell All* into a more serious type of journalism space instead of perpetuating his family's long tradition of gossip and innuendo in their bestselling supermarket rag. It would be a long climb, he knew, but was determined and single-minded in his approach. Small steps. A sit down with the most influential and powerful man in the world would be a true starting point.

He listened as his staff went around the room offering suggestions for this week's edition of *Tell All*. From paternity lawsuits to secret drug rehab for the rich and famous, they each had a story to tell. As the chatter swirled above his head, James silently ticked off all the ways he would inform his father about his ideas for a change in direction for the family business. Even though his dad had retired, leaving James at the helm, Benjamin Curran still expected to be kept in the loop when it came to any major decisions about his empire. Ben had created *Tell All* and carved its place into the mainstream, buying the building where they now sat with the first of the multiple millions in profits he'd made along the way. He brought his only son in as a partner right after James had completed university and then stayed on long enough to ensure that his legacy would live on. But then, once he stepped away from the day to day running of the business, he'd upped the stakes. Ben Curran wanted his only progeny to marry and produce an heir in his lifetime, refusing to turn over the control of the company's stock options until he had his way.

It didn't seem to matter that under James' influence, the tabloid had more than tripled their reader base around the world, as he modernized *Tell All* for the digital age, creating an App for readers to keep on top of all the lurid details of their favorite celebrities' lives, mishaps and missteps. He created a department that dealt exclusively with a variety of social media platforms, making sure that their subscribers received notifications as breaking news happened. He'd revamped the business model to stay ahead of the 24/7 news cycle, and by doing so, increased revenue exponentially. If he wanted to retire today at the ripe old age of thirty-two, he could. He'd made more money than he could spend in multiple lifetimes. But for James, it wasn't all about the dollars. It was more about controlling his own destiny. He desperately wanted to use his platform to reflect a more serious approach to the headlines, to the events that truly mattered in this ever-changing world, instead of the gossip and dirty little secrets the paper had been famous for since its inception. And in his opinion, none of that required him to have a wife or a child.

As the meeting wore on, James lifted his head and looked out one of the windows. From his seat at the head of the table, he had a magnificent view of the Flatiron building in the distance downtown from where he sat. There were a lot of stories outside his perch; he meant to uncover them all, but for now, he'd heard enough.

"I'm going to let you all get to it. I expect a rundown of this week's articles on my desk by the end of the day."

"Sure thing, James," Gina replied, wrangling control of the rowdy group.

He nodded in her direction and stood to leave. As he walked out of the room, multiple noisy conversations erupted around the table. To be heard over the din, he loudly said, "thanks, everyone."

The group briefly stopped talking over one another to acknowledge that he was leaving the gathering. As the glass door closed behind him, he heard the chatter resume at its deafening pitch once more.

James walked down the long hall toward his office, stopping at his assistant's desk for his messages. "Anything for me, Claire?" he asked the perky redhead.

"Mr. Braybern phoned. He said it was important, but he wouldn't leave me anything further. And your mother called as well."

"Great," he replied. "Would you mind getting me a coffee?"

"Regular, decaf or an espresso?"

"Actually an espresso sounds great. Thanks, Claire."

"No worries, boss," she said as she stood, pushed her chair back and went off in the direction of the lounge at the end of the hall.

James went into his own office. It sat in the corner of the building and had floor to ceiling windows on three sides. The furniture was modern, but masculine. His desk was glass, his chair made from a supple tan leather which matched the low slung couch on the opposite end of the room. His office was where he spent a majority of his time and the place where he had always felt the most comfortable. Just as sat down to review the files Claire had left for him, the cell phone in his pants pocket buzzed. He lifted it out and smiled at the number displayed. He tapped the screen.

"Ryan! Claire just told me you called. I was going to get back to you, I swear it. What's happening? Are you in New York?"

"Yes. I just got back into town. Meet me for a drink later?"

"Definitely. Just tell me where and when."

"How about that place near St. Marks? Rye and Rum? If I remember right, we had a great night out the last time we got together there."

"And if I remember right, you met that gorgeous brunette and left me sitting at the bar alone."

James heard his friend chuckle through the phone. "Right, I did. We'll get into that later. See you there at nine?"

"I'm intrigued! I'll be there, man."

James put the phone back in his pocket and smiled. He missed his old friend Ryan. They'd met as kids in elementary school and been close ever since. Ryan had pursued his own dream as a nature photographer and traveled all over the world in pursuit of habitats and species that faced extinction. James admired his friend's passion and the importance of his work to the world at large.

Sitting back against the soft leather of his chair, he realized that it had been a while since he'd been out. He could use a night of endless bourbon and male comradery. He began to shuffle through the papers that required his attention before his day was done just as Claire returned with his coffee. When she set it down on his desk she asked, "Need anything else?"

"Last month's new subscriber report. Thanks."

"Right away," she replied as she scurried to print out the information he requested.

As long as he had a few hours to kill before meeting his friend, he'd spend his time working. It's what he did best.

Chapter Two

JULIE HELD the shot glass in one hand, and stared at the sprinkling of salt stuck on her skin between her thumb and forefinger as she held a wedge of lime with the other.

"On three," Caroline said loudly over the roar of party-goers at the crowded bar.

"Okay, but this is it. No more for me after this one."

"C'mon, spoilsport. Let loose for once. It's Friday night. The weekend is upon us! We're two fabulous twenty-eight year-olds out for a girl's night. Let loose a little!"

"Famous last words."

Caroline scowled at Julie, then said, "One, two, three!" Downing her drink, she licked the salt on her hand before biting into the lime.

Julie grimaced but mimicked her friend's motions. She felt the warm sting of the tequila hit the back of her throat, burning a hot trail downward as it raced through her bloodstream. Despite herself, she could feel her muscles begin to relax.

"So freaking good!" Caroline said slamming her empty glass loudly on the bar. "When was the last time we did this?"

"It's been a while," Julie replied. "It's taken me this long to recover from that last crazy night." She glanced at Caroline, who was wearing a sheer kimono over a racy black corset. There were matching garters that were attached to a pair of opaque white stockings with a wide band of lace at the top, which circled her toned thighs. The outfit, which revealed every curve, was nothing short of outrageous. The look would not have been complete without the sky high red suede heels on Caroline's size seven feet. Only a fashion designer could get away with wearing what Julie considered to be intimate apparel out in public. But then again, her friend did have a specific image to maintain.

"Aren't you cold in that get-up?" Julie asked.

"Not if I keep downing this yummy tequila! Let's get another shot."

"No way. I told you. I'm over my limit. I have to work tomorrow. My editor is expecting three more chapters by the end of the week." She shrugged her shoulders. "Who can keep up with you and your wooden leg anyway?"

"C'mon, Jules. Just one. I promise," Caroline cajoled as she motioned to the young bartender for another round.

"You're impossible!" Julie replied, giving in just to keep Caroline happy.

"And if you want to talk about work, please! Look at you! You're dressed for the boardroom, not the bar!"

Julie looked down at the charcoal gray pencil skirt and lavender silk blouse she had worn. She had put on her highest, chic-est coordinating dove gray heels to mark the occasion of this impromptu girl's night out. "And here I was being nice by having one more drink with you. Sheesh!" She then stood up shakily, smoothed down her skirt and asked, "What's wrong with what I'm wearing?"

"You look like you just stepped out of a courtroom during a murder trial. As a matter of fact, you could star in one of those

SVU shows on television. How do you expect to meet a man if you don't put some effort in to what you put on your body when we go out?"

"I look fine! Besides, the only time I can wear these shoes is out for dinner or somewhere that doesn't require a whole lot of walking. They kill my feet!"

"Agreed. You went out on a limb with the footwear. But you're a writer, for cris'sakes. Can't you let loose once in a while and wear something fun?"

"Like what? Wear my intimate garments on the outside like you?" She shook her head. "I think not." She gesticulated with one hand around her friend's body. "You get away with this insanity because you designed it. I'd just look foolish." Julie nervously ran her hand through her hair. "Besides. I don't think I'd attract the type of man I'm interested in."

"What kind of man? The hot kind? Heaven forbid!" Caroline smacked her palm on her forehead for emphasis.

"Very funny."

"I'm serious. If you're not here looking for Mr. Right, at least look for a man who can offer you a fun night in bed."

"*Caroline! Really!*" Julie whispered, looking around to see if anyone else had heard her friend's words.

"Just saying," Caroline replied, rubbing a fresh wedge of lime on her wrist and then sprinkling salt over it. When the bartender re-appeared with more tequila, she gave him her very best smile in return. Julie watched as the younger man almost tripped over himself to please her friend.

"What else can I do for you ladies tonight?" he asked.

"I dunno," Caroline slurred a bit. "When are you done here? My buddy is in desperate need of a man such as yourself."

Julie felt a blush rise from her toes to her face as she reached in to take the tequila from him. "No, no, I'm fine, really. I don't need, um, I mean, she's just had a little too much to drink. Actually, I think it's time for us to go." She turned quickly, full shot glass still in her hand and whirled around on her spiky heels. She caught an edge of one of the uneven floorboards beneath her feet and the next thing she knew, she hit what felt like a brick wall.

Except it wasn't a brick wall at all. It was a man. A very good looking man, with brown eyes that crinkled up in the corners as he registered the effect of her actions. He had the slightest touch of silver threaded through his dark, well-trimmed sideburns and a fair amount of stubble on his chin. He put his big, warm hands on her shoulders to help her recapture her balance. When Julie realized that her drink had spilled down both the front of his crisply pressed white button down shirt and her own silk blouse, she silently cursed to herself.

"Are you okay? Did you twist your ankle?" a deep voice asked, his grip still holding her upright.

"It was the tequila, I think," she replied, turning quickly to grab a bunch of small square paper napkins from the bar and blotting them on his stained shirt. His chest was toned and muscular, and the more she touched him, the more flustered she became. "I'm so sorry. Please. Let me have your shirt dry cleaned for you. It's the least I can do." She stepped back, put the now wadded up and very wet napkins in a heap on the bar and fished around in her clutch for a business card. "Here," she said, finding what she searched for. She handed him the small slip of formality. "If you call me, I'll take care of that stain for you."

"Well, that's an original pick-up line," he said with a smile. "I admit, it's a new one for me."

"Pick-up line? What? No! I mean, I ruined your shirt. Let me pay to have it dry cleaned. Please. That would be the right thing to do."

She looked up at him and had the strangest sensation. It was as if he saw right through her, all her secrets revealed to his gaze.

She narrowed her own eyes a bit and stared back at him, holding on a minute longer than she dared, trying to determine what he was thinking.

"Do you always do the right thing, Ms..." He looked down at the card she'd handed him. "Porter?"

"Julie. It's Julie. And um, yes. I try to do the right thing whenever possible."

"Interesting, I'll take care of the shirt, though. It's not that big a deal, I assure you."

"I am so s-s-s-sorry," she stammered, her own words feeling awkward on her tongue. She was having trouble formulating a longer response, the tequila and his good looks combining to muddle her brain. Just then, Caroline came up behind her.

"Do you still want to leave?" she asked. "'Cause I could hang here for a bit. That bartender is kind of cute."

Julie turned to her friend. "And you're kind of engaged to Stephen and very drunk. That's a lethal combination. We should go." She linked her arm through Caroline's to help steer the other woman in the direction of the exit.

"Nice meeting you Ms. Porter," the man said, still standing in front of her.

She looked up and murmured, "I didn't catch your name."

"It's James," he said leaning in close, his spicy scent surrounding her, making her want to breathe deeply, to capture that one memory of him.

"Goodnight, James. I'll try not to spill anything else on you on my way out."

He smiled and stepped out of her way, allowing her steer her drunk roommate by him. All of a sudden, Julie wished that Caroline wasn't so tipsy. It might have been interesting to talk with that good looking stranger a little bit longer. Letting out a sigh, she helped her friend out to the street and called an Uber. The combination of the cool night air and her wet blouse made her shiver. Or at least that's what she told herself. It might have been more the recollection of her encounter with James that sent a thrill up her spine. *Too late now,* she thought as their ride appeared to take them home. *He was just another man in a city full of strangers, never to be seen again.*

JAMES PULLED THE WET FABRIC AWAY FROM HIS CHEST AND walked toward the back of the bar in search of Ryan. It didn't take long before he spotted his friend sitting alone, two glasses of bourbon already on the table in front of him.

"Hey! Good to see you buddy!" James said as he folded his long legs and sat down.

"You too! How'd you get wet?" Ryan asked, pointing to James' shirt.

"A slight accident at the bar." He smiled at the recollection. "It's fine. How was your last assignment? Take another Pulitzer Prize winning photo?" His friend's photojournalistic career catapulted him around the world and had earned him multiple, prestigious awards.

"I don't know. I mean, anything's possible. But this last job was somewhat tamer than usual. No wildlife. I was in Rome covering an archeological dig. A man who had been excavating a trench for some new plumbing in his bathroom uncovered an entire street buried below his house dating back to the 15th century. It was amazing, all these mosaic tiles with their original color intact. Pretty spectacular."

"Wow! I can't wait to see those pictures. Sounds interesting and a whole lot less dangerous than tracking that bunch of jaguars in the Amazon."

"Not a bunch," Ryan corrected him. "A shallow. And yeah, nowhere near as dangerous. What about you? Living on the edge? Did you speak to the old man yet?"

"No. But I'm close. I just have to find a way to bring up shifting the business model away from the one thing that made him rich and famous."

"Take him out to dinner and pose it outright? That's one way..."

"Nah. He'll just hound me about not being married yet. I don't want to hear it."

"He's just trying to insure the family bloodline doesn't end with you."

"Please. Me. With a kid? Not in the cards for guys like us. Am I right?" He raised his glass and clinked it against his friend's drink, taking a long sip of the smooth liquid before noticing that Ryan had not lifted his own glass.

"Well, that kind of brings me to what I wanted to tell you."

"Seriously? Did you bring a baby home in your carry-on?" James asked with a laugh.

"Not exactly. But...Daphne is pregnant."

"Daphne?"

"Yes. Daphne. The brunette I met in this very bar the last time we went out," Ryan replied, jogging James' memory. "We've been together ever since. Or at least when I'm around town, which apparently was just long enough for her to conceive."

"Oh, right, Daphne," James began, trying to hide his surprise. "I didn't realize that you two were a thing. I mean, that you were so serious about one another."

"If I'm being totally straight with you, neither did I, man, neither did I. But the more I think about it, the more comfortable I get. I mean, she's pretty terrific. She's beautiful and kind and I've really fallen for her. She tells me that she feels the same way. There's no good reason for us not to bring our relationship to the next level." He pulled a small black velvet box out of his pocket and put it on the table. "What do you think?"

James reached over and opened it. There was a very large

round diamond in an antique setting winking back at him. "That's some sparkler, buddy."

"I hope she likes it. She once mentioned that she likes more traditional things."

"How could she not? It's beautiful." He paused before passing the box back to his friend. "So, you're in love?" James asked.

"I think that I am," Ryan responded, nodding his head. "I can see my future. It's with Daphne."

"Are you sure about this? It's sudden, not to mention just the kind of commitment we've always avoided."

"True. But we're not getting any younger. I'm ready."

"What about your work, all the travel? Is she cool with it?"

"I'm thinking about cutting back some, if only for a short while. I've been at this grind for so long. I must have circled the world at least ten times. I could use a change. Hence, the more placid last assignment."

"Marriage and an infant is a big change alright." James drew in a deep breath. "But if you're happy, Ryan, then so am I." He downed the contents of his glass. "Let's celebrate. Next round is on me."

He got up and walked over to the bar to order two more drinks. Truth was, he needed a minute to process what Ryan had just told him. He couldn't imagine a life attached to one person forever. It just didn't seem like that sort of thing could ever work for him. He liked women. All different types of women. The one common denominator about those he chose to date was that they were most certainly not marriage material. They were all in it for the same thing was – a fun night out. Wild, uninhibited sex without strings attached. Not worrying about the future.

Scowling, he realized the truth. Up until now, he'd never even met a woman who would pass his father's scrutiny. As he reached into his pocket to pull out two twenty dollar bills to pay for their drinks, his hand grazed over the business card Julie Porter had given him earlier. He felt rooted to the floor as the most random thought came to mind: She was just the type of woman who would get his father's stamp of approval. Prim, proper, pretty. What did she say about herself? Something about wanting to dry clean his shirt, to do the right thing? Maybe in return for his ruined garment, she'd agree to have drinks with him. He could try to get to know her better, see if she would help him out, win his father over. He could just picture it now. If he showed up with a woman like that on his arm, maybe his father would relent. Nah. It must be the effect of the bourbon on his empty stomach. It's just a crazy thought. It would never be that easy.

Or would it?

Chapter Three

JULIE BROUGHT another full glass of ice water and two more
Advil into Caroline's bedroom. Her friend was strewn across her
mattress, a frozen eye mask covering her lids, both arms
extended over her head.

"Here. Take these," Julie said, dropping two oblong blue pills
into her friend's palm.

"No. Please let me die here. Tell Stephen I love him."

"Stop being so dramatic! You're just hungover. It will pass."

"Well, I know one thing for certain. No more tequila for me.
Ever."

"Ha! You say that every time we go out. You don't mean it."

"I mean it right now. I do." As Caroline sat up, the eye mask
fell onto the mattress. She took the pills from Julie and swallowed them down with a long sip of the water, handing the glass
back to her friend when she was done.

"I'm being kind." Julie motioned to the window. "See? I
didn't open the shade. It's a gorgeous June morning out there."

"Sunshine would end me. Leave it closed."

Julie smiled. "Will do. I'll be at my desk if you need me for anything. I'll make you some toast in a little while."

"You're the best friend a gal could ever ask for. Thanks for everything." Then Caroline lay back down, sinking deeply into her pillow.

Julie watched as her roomie burrowed even deeper under her blanket. She could only hope that the Advil did the trick; she knew that Caroline had a huge deadline looming and that she needed to be at the top of her game to finish the pieces of her collection for next year's spring line. Fashion designers worked an entire calendar year ahead, but Caroline was always toiling full-stop to try and beat the clock. Julie turned and closed the door to her friend's bedroom. Then she stepped into their kitchen and poured herself a cup of fresh coffee, taking it over to her laptop. She sat down at her desk to check her email, planning on getting started on Caroline and Stephen's invitation just after reviewing the chapters she owed her editor. She decided that the best option would be to work up a few drafts of the wedding invitation and have it all prepared so that her friend only needed to choose the one she liked best. As she waited for her computer screen to power on, she sat back in her chair and thought about the previous night's events. She had to admit that she'd had a good time, at least up to the point where she had spilled her drink all over that good-looking man. *James,* she reminded herself. That was his name. She glanced over at the blouse she'd worn to the bar, now resting on top of her purse, ready to be brought to the cleaners and wondered if she'd hear from him. She had been sincere in her offer of having his shirt washed and pressed but realized that what she'd experienced with the handsome stranger was a chance New York City encounter. There was nothing more to it.

Her screen sprang to life and she pressed the icon to open her mail. She blinked at the top of the list of new messages, not sure if what she saw there was real. He had actually emailed her! She jumped up and walked across the room to put some distance between herself and the computer, the subject line of his message glaring at her:

"Are you still wet?"

Whattttt?

Julie drew in a deep breath to try and stop her heart from racing. She wished that Caroline was awake and no longer hungover. She needed help. Did he mean to be pornographic? Was he that kind of asshole? Or was this a reference to her shirt? Should she open the email and read more? Or should she wait for Caroline? Holy crap. He wasn't even there and he was making her nervous! She walked back to the desk and lifted her coffee to her mouth with a shaky hand. After a few sips, she knew that she had to see the rest of what he'd written. Her curiosity was just too great. She put the mug down on the coaster she made at a pottery class, opened his missive and began to read:

DEAR MS. PORTER,

I'M OPTIMISTIC THAT YOU'VE RECOVERED FROM OUR FIRST MEETING and that your shirt has dried fully. Mine has and it's no worse for wear! I wish that you hadn't left the bar so quickly. I'm hoping that we can see each other again. Can you meet me for a drink later? Same place, same time as last night? I'd like to get to know you better...

JAMES CURRAN
  CEO, The Curran Media Group

. . .

JULIE SAT UP STRAIGHT IN HER CHAIR. THE CURRAN MEDIA Group? Holy crap! She knew that name well. They published that awful, gossipy tabloid, *Tell All*, the one she always tried to keep Caroline and her crazy antics out of. It was sold on every newsstand and at every grocery check-out in the city and as far as she was concerned, was the type of paper a person would use to wrap dishes when moving. It was not the kind of paper to read with any regularity. *Ugh!* Then, without a moment's hesitation, she did the one thing she knew she'd regret. She Googled him.

Her screen was immediately filled with pictures of James and a variety of beautiful women attending society parties and galas all over the city. There were numerous articles about him as well, from *The New York Times* and *Forbes* to *Page Six* and *The National Enquirer.* Not wanting to read the seedier stories about him, she stuck to the more reputable sources. Julie got a sense that he was a serious businessman in an industry that was rife with false-hoods and gossip. On further investigation she found out that he was clearly a trust fund baby; no amount of hard work could change the fact that his father had paid for an ivy league education and set him up in business. James Curran, she discovered, had lived an extremely charmed life. It was the polar opposite of her own experience. Julie slumped down into her chair. When she thought about her childhood, she shuddered, preferring to keep her memories at bay.

She had been raised by a single parent, dirt poor in Atlantic City, New Jersey. She had never really known her father. He drifted in and out of her life until she was ten; then he disappeared altogether. Her mom, Glenda Delgardio, worked at the Claridge casino as a cocktail waitress until it eventually shut down, taking her meager income along with it. Throughout college and while working her first job, Julie regularly sent her mother money to keep her afloat. It was somewhat easier now that she had a real income from her book sales, but it never seemed to be enough. She could barely afford to send a steady flow of dollars to her mother and live in New York City, but Julie scrimped where she had to. She had made it work. Living with Caroline had its perks; even though their taste in clothing was dramatically different, it did make it easier to borrow something when necessary, to share the cost of food and rent. However, Caroline and Stephen had already purchased a loft together in the West Village. They'd be moving at the end of the month, so Caroline either had to find a new roommate pronto or come up with a way to make more money to cover her increased expenses. The landlord had just sent Julie a new lease and she had to decide if she was going to sign it on her own. Plus, she knew that while her first book was a hit, that didn't guarantee her income if the second one flopped.

Worst of all, Julie still never lost the deeply rooted fear that somehow she'd find herself back in a place where the electricity was often turned off, or cockroaches crawled out from the cracks in the walls. As a child she was always hungry because they didn't have enough to eat. Growing up, Julie often fed herself a dinner of unheated canned soup with saltines and peanut butter if her mom had actually gone to the grocery store, or nothing at all if she'd been too drunk or high after her shift and had not. Now living in a trailer park on the outskirts of the seedy tourist town, her mother was quietly using who knew what drugs and drinking herself to death on Julie's dime. It was not a pretty picture, one that Julie avoided bringing to mind as best as she possibly could.

Julie had created a life for herself, even changing her name and was happier to leave her mother out of it entirely. That's why she told people that her mother was dead. It was less painful than admitting the truth, that her origin story was better forgotten than revealed. She had put herself on the path to lift herself out of poverty, out of the cycle of single parenthood by default. She'd attended a local community college for two years in a work/study program before transferring to Columbia University in Manhattan on a full scholarship to obtain her degree, avoiding the nightmare of student loan debt. On the Greyhound bus ride that autumn all those years ago, somewhere between the New Jersey Turnpike and the Lincoln Tunnel, she had made up her mind to never return to her mother's home ever again. Caroline was already set up in the dorm room Julie had been assigned to and they hit it off immediately, becoming close friends and exploring Manhattan together. Once she graduated, Julie took the job as a personal assistant which fully altered the course of her life and she never looked back. Deep down she knew it was better that way.

Now, surrounded by the blue glare of her computer screen, Julie realized that she was faced with a dilemma. She was curious about this good looking stranger. There was a light in his deep brown eyes that she'd seen the night before, something that she wanted to explore further. He'd reached out, so clearly he was interested in her as well. But he represented a large, noisy, gossip machine. Anyone he went out with was going to be the subject of intense scrutiny and research. She could be found out and exposed for the truth of where she truly came from, who she really was. She'd worked so hard to leave that identity buried. Was he worth it? Would she be willing to take the risk on a man she'd barely spoken to? A man she didn't know at all?

Julie sat there behind the screen longer than she realized, scrolling through the articles about James and reading every one until Caroline stepped into the room, her curly chestnut hair sticking out in every direction, her boy shorts and tank top as wrinkled as her bedsheets. For as much as she designed expensive lingerie, Caroline still preferred to shop at Target for her own sleep comfort.

"I'm alive," she said dryly, "In case you were wondering."

Julie pushed back from her desk as she closed the lid of her laptop. "I had no doubt," she replied. "Can you handle some toast now?"

"I think so," her friend responded.

Julie got up and went into the kitchen, filled another glass with water and put it on the counter. Caroline followed and plopped down on a stool to wait for her breakfast, lifted the drink and sipped at it.

"You might not believe this," Julie began, "but that guy from last night emailed me."

"What guy? The bartender?"

"No! Don't you remember? I spilled my tequila on a random man as we were leaving? I drenched his shirt and mine?"

"Hmm. Wait. Maybe some of that is coming back to me." Caroline paused, then shook her head. "No. Not really. Tell me again what happened."

Julie put two slices of whole wheat bread into the toaster, then reached into the refrigerator to grab the jar of raspberry jam. She turned and pulled a plate out of the cabinet and opened a drawer to find a knife to use once the bread was ready.

"You were being way too friendly with the bartender. I wanted to get us out of there before something really bad happened. When I turned to leave, I lost my footing. I spilled my tequila all over this guy, so I gave him my card in case he wanted me to pay for the dry cleaning. He got in touch and asked me out for drinks tonight."

Caroline's eyes widened. "You're going, right?"

The toast popped up and Julie placed it on the plate, carefully covering each inch of both slices in jam before placing it in front of her roommate. Then she grabbed a linen napkin and handed the breakfast to Caroline. "I'm not sure if I want to go."

"Why the hell not? It's a night out and he might be interesting. Take a chance."

Julie tried not to frown. "He's kind of famous."

"Who cares? So are you," her friend said, biting into the toast. "You're a bestselling author," she added, her mouth full.

"He's much more recognizable than me," Julie winced at both her roommate's table manners and her reaction.

"Would I know him? Is he a movie star? Or on tv? Is he the cute guy from *This Is Us?*"

"No, nothing like that. It's James Curran."

"Who?"

"The CEO of Curran Media? You know, *Tell All?*"

Julie watched as Caroline's brain slowly processed the information.

"Oh," was all her friend said.

"So you see? I can't go."

Caroline put another bite of her toast into her mouth and licked her fingers. "No. I don't see. He's just a successful businessman. Nothing more."

"Really? It's a whole lot more. He goes out all the time, with lots of women. I don't want to be another notch on his headboard."

"It's just a night out. Have one drink."

"I don't think so. I don't want to end up in his rag of a paper. You know, shielding my face from one of his damned paparazzi photographers."

"You are being dramatic! If you ask me, he's just what you need right now. So far out of your comfort zone. Show me a picture."

"Nope. I'm not going."

Caroline stood up, went into her bedroom and came back holding her phone in her hand. "No worries. I'll look him up myself."

Julie watched as her friend tapped through a series of screens until she found what she was looking for.

"He is damned good looking! I love a man with a little gray in his hair. You have to go."

"I don't have to do anything other than finish up the wording for your invitations. That's my plan for today."

"C'mon, Julie. Do it for me," her friend implored. "You need a suitable plus one for my wedding. He'll do just fine."

Julie sighed. "No. Not going."

"Okay. Just tell me. Where did he want to meet you tonight?"

"Rye and Rum. Same bar as last night's fiasco."

"Cute. A return to the scene of the crime," Caroline replied. Julie could see the other woman's brain churning and knew she was working on a plan. "He put some thought into this. He knows you've been there, so he's sure that you must be comfortable in those familiar surroundings."

"Don't try to change my mind, Caroline. I've decided not to go."

"Uh huh. I hear you. I'm just not convinced that I can't get you to go anyway."

Julie rolled her eyes. "Really? How?"

"Well," she began, "you must be somewhat interested, or you would have never told me that he emailed you."

"That's not true," Julie replied. "I was just a little surprised that he reached out, that's--"

"Hold on. Let me finish," Caroline said. "I can tell that this guy is intriguing to you, despite his occupation."

"But—"

"I think that deep down you want to see him again. You're just afraid. Maybe you were attracted to him, maybe he made you feel something that scared you." Her roommate nodded her head up and down. "Yes. That's it. He made your heart beat a little faster, didn't he?"

"Don't be ridiculous," Julie said turning away so that Caroline could no longer see the expression on her face. Her friend had struck a nerve.

"One night, Jules, that's all it is. And if you're uncomfortable, you pick yourself up and leave. Besides, it's not exactly a secluded place. You won't be alone. It's a bar full of other people. No big deal."

"You just don't get it," Julie started to say before Caroline interrupted her.

"I don't understand what it is I need to get." She turned her phone screen around so that it faced Julie. "This is a successful and good looking man. Unless you've decided to join a convent and take a vow of celibacy without mentioning it to me before today, I see no good reason for you not to see James Curran again." She put her hands on her hips. "Now let's go figure out what you're going to wear. I have some thoughts..."

Chapter Four

JULIE STOOD in the center of her bedroom. Her entire closet had been emptied out in an explosion of black, white, and gray fabric. Slacks, dresses, skirts, and blouses were tossed onto every available surface, her roommate responsible for most of the mess.

"Don't you have anything with color in here?" Caroline asked, a black wool skirt in one hand and a gray cashmere cardigan in the other.

"I wore my lavender silk blouse last night."

"That's it? One pastel colored frock?"

"I'm not like you, Caroline. I don't like to be noticed. I prefer to just blend in. Besides, when I worked for Mrs. Tassen, she made it clear that a lady wears tailored, subtle clothing. Nothing flashy. Ever."

"Oh boy. That's fricking ridiculous. You need some party clothes. Let's go into my room."

"I'm not wearing your crazy lingerie outside of this apartment. Not going to happen."

"I own more clothing than my own designs, you know. Let's just go look."

"Or let's forget the whole thing. Anyway, I never emailed James back. He probably thinks I'm not interested."

Caroline started to toss clothing off of Julie's bed in an attempt to find her friend's phone. Three layers later, she held it out in her hand. "It's not too late. Tell him you'll be there."

"I really don't want to do this, Caroline," Julie said, taking her iPhone back. "I think it's a bad idea."

"What's a better idea? Having one drink with a good looking stranger, or staying here in your room rehanging all of this?" She motioned to the piles of garments strewn in every direction. "I'll make a deal with you. Go for an hour and I'll put away every last boring skirt and blouse." She walked over to Julie and took her hand. "And as a bonus, I promise to loan you something to wear that isn't as outrageous as you think."

Julie drew in a deep breath. She was intrigued by James, but more than that, she knew that if she didn't go her friend would torment her for weeks to come. She'd go, she decided, but just for an hour.

"Okay, okay," she relented. "One drink with him."

Caroline squeezed Julie's hand. "I knew you'd come around. Now," she said, leading Julie down the hall and into her own bedroom. "Answer him."

"What should I say?"

"Nothing fancy. Just say that you'll be there."

Julie lifted her phone and unlocked the screen. She scrolled through her mail until she found his message. As she opened it, she felt her hands begin to shake. "Should I just say that I'll be there? Or should I thank him for inviting me out?"

"Wow. You've been out of the game longer than I realized," Caroline replied. "Give me your phone, will you please?"

Julie nervously handed the device over to the other woman and watched as she quickly responded to the email for her. She heard the familiar sound of the missive being dispatched before making its way to him and froze. "You sent it? Without showing me what you wrote?"

"Of course I did. Time's ticking here and you're not dressed."

"But what did you say?"

"Just that you'd be delighted to see him tonight. Look," she motioned to the phone.

IT WAS SO NICE TO HEAR FROM YOU. I WAS HOPING YOU'D REACH *out. I'll be there at 9.*

"THAT'S IT?" JULIE ASKED.

"What else is there to say? Anyway, the rest is up to you. Now, let's figure out what you're going to wear!"

Julie had to admit that she was amazed by Caroline's ease with the world of dating. Her friend seemed so comfortable responding to this total stranger, so sure that he was someone that Julie might want to get to know better. It all seemed foreign to Julie, like being in a country where she didn't speak the language. She realized just then that she didn't speak the dialect of dating at all. Sure. After college she found herself in a few relationships that lasted as long as a year at a time, but whenever it reached the point of the man wanting to take things to the next level, to introduce her to his family, she backed off. She didn't want to answer questions about herself, her personal history. She would always end things before they got too serious. For the past four years, she hadn't dated at all. She'd been busy writing and then promoting her book. She was too long out of the game and the more she thought about it, James was so far out of her league that the mere notion of meeting him later was causing her stomach to do major back flips. It was unnerving, to say the least.

Caroline, on the other hand, seemed not to notice Julie's discomfort. She was chattering away, pulling brightly colored pieces of clothing out of her closet and dresser drawers. Julie forced herself to focus.

"Nothing too revealing, Caroline. I'm not wearing anything that's either boobalicious or micro-mini short."

"You think I don't know my customer? I make a living understanding exactly how to dress all types of women. Now," she said, holding up a red, lacy camisole. "I'll let you wear your own black trousers, the ones with the wide leg, and that pretty white silk blouse with the peter pan collar. But you've got to wear this underneath. Just the top of the trim will show. It gives the illusion of sexiness without him being slapped in the face by those curves of yours."

"I don't know. Red? I'm not a red girl."

"That's the point. Shake things up."

"That's crazy."

Caroline was already pulling at the black silk sweater that Julie had put on earlier that day, trying to yank it up over her head. "Take this off. We need to get you put together."

"Alright already. Let me do it," Julie replied impatiently as Caroline turned and started rifling through her dresser drawers again. Julie lifted the garment off and folded it neatly before placing it down on the bed. Her friend swung back around and her eyes shot wide open.

"Is that a bra or a red cross bandage?" she asked disdainfully, reaching over and pulling on the elastic band under Julie's right breast. "You must be kidding with that thing."

"Why? It serves its purpose just fine," Julie responded. She looked down at her sensible, white cotton sports bra.

"You do realize that you live with someone who has made a career out of making women's undergarments look good as well as being fully functional, right?"

"So?" Julie asked, wide-eyed.

"So don't embarrass me or my brand." She grabbed her own cell phone out of her pocket and hit a button.

"Deena? I have a crisis here at home. Can you messenger over a set from the Serafina collection right now? A 38C and the matching bottoms in a small, please?" She cocked her head to one side while her assistant responded something that Julie couldn't hear. Then she said, "No. Not the garters. I think that would be a step over the edge. At least for now. Thanks." She disconnected the call and dropped the phone back down onto the mattress. "Problem solved," she said with a sigh of relief.

"I didn't realize that I was a problem," Julie said, her feelings hurt by Caroline's assessment of her.

"Well, if you think that I would have you meet a man like James Curran tonight wearing that plain piece of cotton across your boobs, you would be wrong!" her friend said emphatically, crossing her arms over her chest.

"It's not like he's going to see what I have on underneath my clothing. Really. Not going to happen."

"Too bad!" Caroline began, "But not the point."

"What is the point? Please, enlighten me."

Caroline shook her head signaling her dismay. "What you have on against your skin should make you feel something. Strong. Empowered. It doesn't matter if you're the only one who knows about what your undergarments look like, or if no one ever sees you in them. What matters is that you know what's there. It's your personal secret. A lovely piece of lingerie should make you feel courageous. That's my whole business model. I'm kind of hurt to realize that you never knew that before."

Julie walked over and grabbed onto Caroline's shoulders,

pulling her in for a hug. "I am so sorry. I didn't mean to insult you. Never. It's just that this date has me twisted into knots. Just know that I've always considered you to be a creative genius. Really."

"Well, that's better." Caroline stepped back and looked directly at Julie before saying, "I'll forgive you if you wear the lingerie set that should be delivered here in less than an hour. And the red camisole. I promise that it will help to change your life."

"I surrender," Julie replied. "I have no strength left to argue."

Caroline smiled. "That was my devious plan all along." She turned back to her closet. "Now. Let's talk about your shoes. . ."

AT 8:45 THAT EVENING, JULIE WAS FINALLY READY TO GET into the Uber that was waiting outside of her building. She was clothed in the outfit that Caroline had picked for her, right down to the skimpy black bra, red camisole and matching black panties that had arrived from her friend's showroom late that afternoon. The set was made of the softest silk, with an intricate pattern of fine Italian lace set by hand along the edges. As soon as Julie put it on, she understood exactly what Caroline had meant. As they lay against her skin, the feel of the intricate garments helped to bolster her own courage for the evening ahead.

Her blouse was open just enough for the wispy detail of the camisole to peek through a tiny bit, making her feel more self-conscious than usual, if that were even possible. But it was too late to back out now. She was well on her way downtown to Rye and Rum and the very handsome James Curran. She had to admit that she was more than a little curious about the good looking stranger. Besides, it was just one drink. She was fully resolved. She would not have more than one.

She lifted her head and looked out the window of the Uber. Park Avenue was ablaze with hundreds of colorful tulips, blooming in pots along the median which divided the car lanes into opposite directions for travel. Even though the sun sunk low on the horizon, the delicate head of each flower was visible, seemingly waving at her as she made her way to the bar. Before she knew it, the driver slowed down and crawled to a stop outside of his destination. She thanked him, stepped out of the Uber and into the night. Squaring her shoulders, she walked inside.

The music was pumping, swirling around her head as she made her way over to the bar. She searched the room, looking for James and for the briefest moment, thought he might not be there yet. But then he appeared in front of her and her heart beat even faster in her chest. He was wearing another crisp, white button down shirt, this time with a more informal pair of khaki slacks. When he saw her, a broad smile crossed his face.

"Julie," he said, bending in close to her ear so that she could hear him over the loud music. "I'm so happy that you were able to meet me tonight."

She nodded, not trusting her own response enough to speak yet.

"Come with me," he reached out to take her hand. "I have a table reserved where we can actually hear each other."

She felt his fingers tighten around hers. A shot of liquid warmth traveled up her spine and settled low down, right beneath her belly button. She drew in a deep breath and let him lead her deep into the back of the bar. It was quieter and more intimate there as well, with high backed wooden booths that offered a bit more privacy. James motioned to the padded cushion and said, "Please." He waited for her to be seated before folding his legs under the table and setting himself down across from her.

Just then a waiter came by with a silver ice bucket. Inside rested a bottle of Casamigos, and on his tray sat two glasses each filled with perfectly made, square frozen cubes. In a separate dish, there were wedges of fresh lime. He also left them with a small ramekin of olives and another bowl brimming with warm almonds. When he turned to walk away, James said, "I hope you don't mind that I ordered for us. I do know you like tequila, after all." He smiled at her.

Julie felt herself blush. "Well, you would know after last night's fiasco."

"I don't see it as a fiasco. It was more of an opportunity. Now we have the chance to get to know one another."

He lifted the wet bottle out of the bucket. "Can I pour you some of this?"

She nodded and watched as his hands deftly dispensed two drinks, dropping more ice into each one, his long fingers wrapping around each glass easily as he worked. Once he was done, he handed one to her.

"What should we drink to?" she found herself asking.

"To new friends," he answered, his brown eyes warm and inviting.

"Yes," she murmured. "Of course." She lifted the glass to her lips and took a sip. The liquid was cold and smooth on her tongue and she immediately felt a familiar sensation begin to spread through her blood, loosening her limbs and her mind. "This is delicious. Much better than what we were drinking last night."

"Good. By the way. How is your friend? Bad headache?"

"She's fine. Rocky start to the morning, but she powered through."

"Glad to hear it. And you, Julie. How was your day?"

Julie thought back on the course of the last few hours, the

craziness in preparing for this date and just said, "Fine. Productive."

"Productive? That's an interesting word. Are you working on something specific?

Julie smiled. *Yes,* she thought. *Myself!* Instead, she answered, "I have a couple of projects in the works. Not the least of which is creating the invitation for my roommate's Caroline's wedding. She's the friend who was here with me last night."

He nodded in understanding as if he were filling out a spread sheet with all the pertinent information about her life that he needed to know. "Is that something you do professionally? Are you a wedding planner?"

"Wedding planner? No, nothing like that. I am involved in a segment of the industry, though." *I guess he didn't Google me!* Her inner monologue was running wild now. *He must not know about my book. Why would he? It's not exactly a topic most men found to be compelling. Should I mention it? No. That would be too... wait. He's talking again... Concentrate, damn it!*

"Well," James continued. "I'm not too familiar with that sort of business. Do you find the work interesting?"

"Yes." She decided to go for it. "Actually, I wrote a book that contains a chapter about it."

"A writer? Now that I find fascinating! I'm in the publishing business myself. Newspapers, not books."

"I surmised that from your last name," she replied. *And from Google,* she thought. *Lots and lots of Google.*

His gaze caught her own just then and she wondered if she'd given herself away.

"You look beautiful tonight, by the way. I didn't want to miss the opportunity to tell you that," he said, switching gears before continuing.

"Thank you. I was feeling so foolish for spilling my drink on you. I'm not generally that clumsy."

"You don't seem so. In fact, I think you look damned graceful. I'm very attracted to graceful."

"Oh," was all she could say. Then she picked up her glass and
finished the contents a little too quickly. Forget the one drink
limit. She was in it now.

Chapter Five

James could not take his eyes off of the woman sitting across from him. She was more beautiful than he'd remembered, her shiny blonde hair just grazing her shoulder, her deep blue eyes warm and inviting. She had an air of dignity that he found shockingly sexy, so much so that he was beginning to feel uncomfortable from the growing erection under the zipper of his pants.

"I know this sounds like a cliché, but do you come here often? This bar, I mean?"

She smiled and shook her head back and forth. "No, not really. Last night was an anomaly. My roommate, Caroline? I had to bribe her with a night out so that we could finally finish the last of the wording for her wedding invitations."

"I see. So it was more a work and reward situation, not a girl's night."

"I guess you can say that. Although, she's always trying to get me to go out more. I'm sort of a homebody."

"Really? I would think that you'd have men lined up to spend some time with you."

"I'm too much of a workaholic for that sort of thing. And the whole bar vibe isn't my favorite way to spend an evening anyway."

"Oh? What is?" he asked, making notes in his head as she answered.

"I guess a quiet dinner in a nice restaurant, or maybe a movie. I don't see how you can really get to know someone if you're shouting over the music of a bad cover band."

He smiled. "I agree," he answered.

"If I'm being totally honest, I wasn't too sure that I wanted to meet you here tonight."

"Really?"

"Yes. I mean, you seem nice enough, but you're a complete stranger who I drenched in tequila last night. Right now I'm fully out of my comfort zone."

"Well, I'd never have guessed," he said, lifting his glass to her and taking a sip of the smooth liquor.

She smiled at him, the corners of her eyes lifting and reflecting the dim light in the space, making him feel warm from head to toe. That was the moment James was sure that he was right about the woman sitting across from him. Julie Porter was the answer to his prayers and exactly what he needed to bring home to his father. James knew that Julie would absolutely charm the old man. With her by his side, his dad would finally have to hand him the keys to the kingdom, of that James was certain.

She was beautiful, but she was also so much more than just that. She was clearly smart and had a properness about her that had been lacking in the other women he'd dated. The way she sat, her back straight and leaning away from the seat of the booth, the regal way she held her head and truly listened to what he was saying before formulating a thoughtful response, all of it combined to make her absolutely ideal for what he had in mind.

Now, he just had to convince the beauty sitting across from him to agree to help him without scaring her off.

☙❧

THREE HOURS AND A GOOD AMOUNT OF TEQUILA LATER, THEY were still there, in that booth. They had spoken about the kind of things that went way beneath the surface of banal chatter. She was so well informed on a variety of topics and he found her easy to talk to. It was as if the world had shifted away, leaving them together in a small bubble, alone.

James knew that had to come up with a way to ask her for a second date. He had to ease her into his scheme. He didn't want to frighten her away and he knew that he felt emboldened, having consumed a good deal of the liquor in the bottle that sat between them. She had sipped at her drink, barely finishing her second one and he realized that he had far more tequila than she had. In fact, James had to control his desire to touch the fine red lace that peeked demurely from her blouse. He was desperate to know the feel of the skin that lay beneath that alluring material. He wanted to taste the soft curve of her collar-bone, to dip lower and caress the swell of her breasts. He knew that she wasn't the type of woman who would allow him to be so forward, so soon. Just by sitting across from him, she was affecting him in a way that he'd not experienced before. He silently took stock. He'd dated a lot of women. She was so different than the rest that she was actually making him nervous.

Get yourself under control! His mind screamed as he tried to clear the fog of alcohol that he'd allowed to descend and crowd around him. Then a thought formed in his tequila addled brain. *Now. Do it now. Ask her for a second date...*

"Since you're also involved in publishing," he began, "I

wonder if you'd accompany me to my company's annual advertisers' gala?"

He watched her eyes widen in surprise. *Oh no,* he thought. *She's going to turn me down.*

"When is it?" she asked.

"Next Saturday night. I can have my assistant send you the details." He watched as she processed his words. *Be convincing!* His inner monologue went into overdrive. *Give her a good reason to attend...* "I think you'll find it interesting. There are plenty of industry people who will be there and as I'm sure you realize; the publishing business is all about connections. A project is only as good as its ability to be considered by someone with the means to make it happen."

She smiled at him just then, and to his surprise, her genuine reaction made him feel warm all over.

"Send me the information, James. I'll let you know if I can make it."

"I hope you will," he replied, thinking about his next move. He glanced down at his Patek wristwatch, a gift from his father. The hours they'd spent together had flown by and it was getting late. "Can I offer you a ride home? It's almost midnight."

"That's not necessary. I can arrange for an Uber," she said, lifting her phone from her small handbag.

"I insist," he replied. "I'll call my driver. He'll be here soon."

She looked directly into his eyes before deciding. "Alright," she responded, gifting him with another beautiful smile before tucking her phone away.

Surprised at just how happy he felt at the thought that he'd have her alone for a little bit longer, James texted Charlie and asked him to bring the car around to the bar in ten minutes.

"Done!" he exclaimed and then asked, "What are you working on now? A follow-up, or something completely different?"

"Well, I'm still doing a lot of press for my first book. We're thick into wedding season, so I think it makes a great features piece. I've gotten a ton of calls for both print and television interviews."

"Interesting. Maybe I should have one of my editors reach out."

"I don't think I'm your reader's exact demographic," she said shyly.

"Wow," he teased. "You must not think too highly of our readers then."

"It's not that," she began. "I'm pretty sure that your audience is more involved in splashy celebrity weddings than the small details it takes to set things in their proper order."

"This just gets worse." He watched as she blushed and tried to backtrack over her words.

"I don't mean to be rude, James. I tend to think that your readers might find what I do to be stuffy and boring. I can obsess over the tiniest detail. I truly can. I don't think the *Tell All* consumer cares at all for what font a wedding invitation is printed in, but I do. Little things matter."

"Do the little things insure that a relationship lasts? That the wedding couple makes it to their first anniversary?"

He watched as she smiled easily at his question.

"Maybe," she replied. "I'd like to think so."

"How exactly?"

"I believe that if you spend the time to do things right, to put in the effort and consider every small decision with as much importance as you do the big ones, it says something. It's meaningful to let your partner know that you've thought long and hard about the commitment you've made to each other." She leaned in just then. "It signals that you're serious."

He considered her words for a moment before responding. "I guess I hadn't thought much about it before."

"A classic commitment-phobe thing to say," she challenged.

Then she reached for her purse, which he took as a signal that she was ready to leave. He had to think fast.

"Not really," he countered, looking her straight in the eye and holding her gaze. "I'm not opposed to marriage. I think it's more that I haven't met the right person. Yet."

"Maybe," she said, after a bit. "Well, when you do, you have my card. I can help set all the details straight for you."

She was all business now. *Oh Miss Porter,* he thought. *Wait until you hear what I have planned for you. There will be plenty of details for you to juggle, if you accept my offer. I have ways to keep you very, very busy...*

James stood up and politely offered her his arm. "The car should be waiting outside. Shall we go?" He watched as she gracefully rose from her seat and lifted her purse from the table, accepting his offer to keep her steady on her feet. Once she touched him, he felt a strange and unexpected warmth spread through his body. He inhaled her sweet scent as it rose with her, vanilla and honeysuckle. It was as if she made him hyper-aware that this was the way he was supposed to feel but never did: calm, comfortable and grounded. In that moment as they touched, he knew that this woman was about to change his world.

James kept hold of her hand as they exited the bar and he opened the door of the waiting town car, having to let go of her so that she could get in, even though he didn't want to break their brief, physical connection. As soon as he sat down next to her, he wordlessly reached for her hand again, this time interlacing their fingers together.

"Good evening Mr. Curran," Charlie turned around from the driver's seat and greeted him. "Ma'am." He tipped his cap. "Where can I take you tonight?"

Julie leaned forward. "Third Avenue and 78th Street, please."

"Sure thing," Charlie replied as he looked forward and put the car into gear.

Damn. James realized that this ride was to be short. He had to make the most of it.

"I had fun tonight. I've never been so happy to have had a drink spilled on me before. I mean, if you hadn't bumped into me, we wouldn't have met."

She smiled. "I guess it's one way of introducing myself, although I hope never to do that again. I was truly mortified."

"It just makes you as human as the rest of us. And it led us here, to right now." Instinct took over in that moment and he leaned in and kissed her. Her lips were impossibly soft against his own, eagerly parting when he teased her with his tongue. Her reaction made him bold; he pulled her in even closer and ran his free hand up and down her leg, finally resting it on her upper thigh. He could only think that he wished she'd worn a skirt so that he could feel the skin there as well, instead of the fine wool fabric of her trousers. As he deepened the kiss even more, she let out a soft moan and he knew that she was experiencing the same reaction to him as he was to her; it was electric.

He felt the motion of the car slow and knew that they were nearing their destination.

"Julie," he whispered, resting his forehead on hers. "That was really nice."

She said nothing, but he could see that she was as clearly shaken as he was by what had just transpired between them. He could feel her erratic breath on his cheek and knew that if he placed his hand on her chest her heart would be pounding as quickly as his own.

"Can I walk you upstairs?"

She shook her head. "No. Thank you for the offer, but there's no need. We have a doorman, and Caroline will be awake." She looked up at him sincerely. "I'll spare you the inquisition."

He could sense that she was trying to gain control of herself. He had to make a bold move to try and keep her off-balance.

"Julie, please," he whispered. "don't go upstairs. Stay with me tonight. You won't regret it. I promise..."

The car stopped.

She smiled at him, and ignoring his last comment said, "Thanks for the tequila. I had a good time."

Accepting defeat, he opened the door and stepped onto the sidewalk, then turned and offered her his hand to help her out as well.

"Goodnight, then, Julie."

"Goodnight James."

He watched her disappear inside the lobby of her building, hoping she'd turn around, but she didn't. Once she was out of his line of sight, he got back into the town car.

"You can take me home now, Charlie," he said to the driver. As they eased back into traffic, he began to process the details of the night, but kept coming back to the same thing: how could he keep this woman in his life? Not just as a pretense to get his father to turn the business over to him, either. He was intrigued by Julie. *When was the last time you made out in the back seat of a car? High School? Damn!*

And just like high school, James knew one thing for certain. He was heading for a shower once he got home. He needed some relief from the hormones coursing through him from that kiss, and he knew that for tonight, the colder the water, the better.

Chapter Six

When Julie opened the door to their apartment, Caroline was sitting cross-legged on the couch wearing a robe trimmed in brightly dyed ostrich feathers. There was a large bowl of popcorn perched on her lap.

"I waited up. Tell me everything!" her roommate exclaimed.

"Wow. Can I take these pumps off first? My feet are killing me."

"Ok. But then I want every last detail."

Julie pulled the heels off and wriggled her toes. "So. Much. Better." She walked over to where her friend waited and sat down, shoes in hand. "I had a surprisingly good time." *And an amazing kiss in the backseat of his car,* she thought to herself.

Caroline arched one meticulously groomed brow. "Oh no you don't. That will not do. When I say details, I mean it. Tell me everything, from the moment you walked out of the Uber."

Julie watched as Caroline put a large handful of popcorn into her mouth. "Am I your evening's entertainment?" she asked with a smile.

"Well, sort of. I mean, as an engaged person, I will never have another first date. So, yes. I want to know all about yours."

"I walked into the bar and found him immediately," Julie began. "He had already gotten us a table in the back and ordered a whole bottle of tequila."

"Do you have a wooden leg all of a sudden? You seem pretty sober to me," Caroline asked.

"I had one full drink. Then I just sipped at the second. I didn't want to have too much. I needed to keep my senses intact."

"Of course you did. Such self-control," Caroline teased. "So opposite of me!"

Julie continued. "We talked. For hours. I got to know him a little better."

"And?"

"And I was surprised at how much I liked him."

"Really? You were surprised?" Caroline's eyes widened for a moment. "I'm not. Let me spell it out for you. He's handsome and rich. What's not to like?"

"He could have been an arrogant ass, but he wasn't." Julie's voice trailed off, reliving that moment in the backseat again. "Here's another thing you're probably wondering about. He's a great kisser!"

Caroline dropped a handful of popcorn back into the bowl. "How'd you find that out?"

"He gave me a ride home and we may have made out in the back seat," Julie answered.

"Wait. How'd you end up in his backseat?"

"His driver picked us up."

Caroline's mouth formed into the shaped of an "O", but no words came out at first. She recovered quickly. "His driver. Very fancy."

"I guess it's just part of his lifestyle to have someone else transport him around Manhattan. Easier than trying to park on the street, right?"

"You mean like the rest of us mere mortals? Sure." She paused for emphasis, then asked, "so after the kiss in the back-seat, what happened?"

"I came upstairs."

"That's it? What's your plan? Are you going to see him again?"

"He asked me to go to some advertisers' gala with him next weekend."

"Whoa. I assume you said yes."

"I said I'd think about it."

Caroline jumped up then, scattering popcorn all over the rug, "What?!? Are you kidding me? You have to go!"

"I don't have to go. I might want to go, I mean, I'm intrigued and all, but I haven't decided."

"What's there to think about? He's hot, he's into you and you like him. You said you had a good time tonight."

"All true. But an event like that? I barely know him."

"What does that have to do with it? He wouldn't have asked if he didn't want to continue to explore a relationship with you."

Julie sighed. "I think he goes out with lots of women, Caroline. I don't want to be another in a long line of notches on his headboard. I'm not looking for that." *And that's the kind of event that will be covered by his tabloid. What happens if they start digging into my past?* The thoughts swirled in her head, causing it to ache. She rubbed her temples and stood up. "I'm going to bed. It's been a long day and I just want to lay down."

"This conversation is not over. I'll still be here in the morning and we'll pick it up then," Caroline said emphatically.

"I'll count on that," Julie sarcastically replied as she walked into her room and shut the door. As she undressed for bed, she couldn't help but think about James. She did like him more than she ever could have imagined. He was easy to talk to and she felt as though he was truly interested in what she had to say. And that kiss! Thinking about it made her skin tingle. It was just such a big chance to attend a public event with him, one she didn't know if she was willing to take.

She had stripped down to just the camisole and frilly bottoms that had come with the set from Caroline's collection and hesitated before deciding to wear the silky undergarments to bed. Darting quietly into the shared bathroom in the hall, she washed her face and brushed her teeth, swallowing down two Advil before returning to her own room and slipping between her soft cotton sheets. Once she closed her eyes, the last thing she remembered was the way he smiled when he looked at her as she sat across the table from him earlier that night. She was surprised at the soothing effect that had on her as she drifted into sleep.

THE NEXT MORNING, JULIE ROSE TO THE DELICIOUS SCENT OF coffee brewing. She pushed her blanket away, grabbed her robe and went into the kitchen. She found Caroline, already awake, watching as the glass pot was filling up with the strong, dark liquid.

"I can't believe you're up before me. When does that ever happen?" Julie asked.

"Didn't you hear the intercom buzz? Look what was delivered. Curtis just brought this up and left it outside our door."

Curtis was the daytime doorman of their building. He had a crush on Caroline and looked for any excuse to bring packages to her, just for a glimpse of her smile.

Julie looked over at their small café table set for two in the kitchen and saw a beautiful basket of muffins and croissants from Lafayette Bakery downtown. "Who sent that to you? A grateful customer?"

"It's not for me, silly. It's a gift for you."

"What?"

"Check the card."

Julie held up the small, handwritten note:

I HOPED YOU MIGHT TRY A DIFFERENT SORT OF BREAKFAST...START your day off with sweet thoughts and please consider joining me at the gala. Check your email. Everything you need to know is there. I'll be in touch,

James

SHE LOOKED BACK DOWN AT THE BASKET. ASIDE FROM THE delectable pastries, there was a jar of homemade cherry jam and a container of freshly made sweet butter. "This is incredible," she said.

"Fresh croissants? This guy does know how to get my attention, if that matters," Caroline said. "Do you mind if I help myself?"

"Are you kidding? Please, eat something. I'm not sure if I can just yet. I think I need coffee first." She walked over to the pot and filled a mug with the steaming liquid.

Julie watched as her roommate chose a pastry, breaking off a small piece and popping it into her mouth.

"Mmmm. It's almond," she said as she enjoyed her first bite." Caroline pulled the flaky croissant apart and held a corner of it up. "Try this. It's so damned good."

"Maybe in a minute," Julie replied. Her stomach was doing flips at the mere thought of James arranging to have this lavish breakfast sent to her this morning.

"Caroline," she began, "you don't think that he actually went down to this bakery today and chose all of this, do you? I mean, he has an assistant. He probably sent her, right?"

"I guess so, but who cares? It's the thought alone that counts," she replied as she piled jam high onto her next bite. "And, it must mean that he's thinking of you. He must have enjoyed that kiss as much as you did."

"Very funny," Julie replied wryly. "He just wants a date for that damned gala. He thinks he can charm me into going with him."

"Well, at this rate, if you don't go, I will! Who knows what other interesting gifts he has in mind? I like this guy," she continued to speak with her mouth full of croissant, "besides, it wouldn't be the worst idea in the world for you to go with him. You might meet some fascinating people, make a connection or two. You never know. Just check your phone for his email, will you please?"

Julie watched her roommate lick the jam off of her thumb. "I really don't think it's a good idea." She paused to take a sip of her coffee, hoping it gave her some courage. She did want to see him again. She just didn't want to take the risk of her past coming out in the tabloids. It would ruin the reputation she'd so carefully curated. Then she made the ultimate mistake. She opened her phone and scrolled through to find the email from his assistant. She clicked on it and began to read:

GOOD MORNING, MS. PORTER,

Mr. Curran asked that I send you the details for next Saturday's event. It will be a dinner dance to be held at Cipriani, the downtown location. A car will be in front of your building promptly at seven pm. The dress is black tie. Please let me know if you plan to attend.

Regards,

Claire Dawson

SHE PUT HER PHONE DOWN ON THE TABLE AND CAROLINE turned it around so that she could read it as well. "Cipriani, huh? Very fancy."

"Forget it, I'm not going," Julie replied, "Besides. What would I wear?"

"There it is! A crack in the old armor! That's all I needed to hear. And as far as your outfit for this soirée, I am sure we can figure something out. Between our two closets and some of my industry contacts, I can have you primped and ready in under an hour."

"I have nothing suitable in my wardrobe, I know it. I have cocktail-type dresses, nothing floor-length."

"Who says you need to wear a gown? I think you'd stand out more in my black tuxedo jumpsuit. It's fashion forward."

"It's backless! Forget it."

"Just try it on. Let me live vicariously through you. Please? I'm not even married yet and my social life is so boring. Stephen's always working, trying to get his new business off the ground. Besides, this will be fun." Caroline walked over to the sink to rinse her hands, then quickly dried them on a yellow dish towel. "Meet me in my room," she said, a skip in her step as she walked off.

Julie was torn. She liked James. A lot. Clearly, he felt something about her as well, or he wouldn't be pushing so hard for her to attend this party with him, of that she was certain. But was it worth the risk? She'd been so careful, so guarded up until now. She almost wished that she could at least tell Caroline the truth, but she was afraid. She was a *New York Times* bestselling author with a book at the top of the charts based on the rules of proper etiquette. If people knew the truth, that she was raised by a woman who currently lived in a dilapidated RV in a seedy trailer park in south Jersey, her perfectly crafted persona would be blown to pieces.

Julie Porter wasn't even her real name, but no one would take advice from someone named Julie Delgardio. It was too South Jersey. She had once read about a private school in Connecticut called Miss Porter's where wealthy young girls learned how to navigate through high society, to do things the proper way, so she adopted that last name. It seemed more staid, more simple. She worked hard to lose the regional accent that marked her as someone who was not native to a more upper class way of life and when she went to work for Mrs. Tassen she observed absolutely everything. Thinking back, her time working for that woman was the most important part of her education. Having a degree from an Ivy league school was nice, but it wasn't everything. It was what she learned from Mrs. Tassen that had made it possible for Julie to have the success with her book that she enjoyed today.

She shook herself out of her memories. Decision made. No. She could not go to the gala. She could not take that leap of faith, that all would work out and be fine. She'd send him an email and decline.

Julie picked up her phone and was about to write a short note to James when Caroline called out, "C'mon. No time like the present. Just try on the jumpsuit." She put the device back down. If she said no, he'd probably never want to see her again. The memory of the kiss in the car, the way it made her feel, his bold invitation to stay the night, and the promise that it held was all a mystery, swirling with intrigue and desire. Maybe she could do this one thing. She thought of him and felt a strong pull. She could tell a bit of the truth, that she was camera shy and didn't want her photo snapped. She might be able to get

James to agree to that in exchange for her attending the gala at his side. It had to be worth a try.

Leaving her phone next to her coffee cup, she pushed away from the table and walked into Caroline's room, having every expectation that she was opening a window that she might not be able to close. Summoning the last of her inner resolve, she braced herself for whatever was to happen next.

Chapter Seven

BY THE TIME Julie had tirelessly tried every combination of formal wear that Caroline had in her closet, they had finally reached consensus. She would wear the jumpsuit with a double-breasted black silk jacket over it. The front of the garment was thankfully unrevealing. It gathered at her collarbone, a silk cord threaded through the neckline and tied, the long tails trailing lightly down her naked back. If she kept the jacket on, no one would know that the garment dipped so low that the top of her rear end was nearly visible. Caroline insisted that it would be spectacular to wear this jumpsuit the way it had been designed, but Julie couldn't imagine exposing that much skin to a roomful of strangers so she planned to keep the jacket on all night. Her roommate completed the look for Julie by lending her a sky-high pair of black patent strappy sandals and a small, intricately beaded evening bag.

"He's not going to be able to control himself around you!" Caroline said, clasping her hands together in glee.

"If I go, it's only to, how did you put it? 'Grow my brand'? I'm not going for anything else."

"Okay, sure. I mean, it's true, you might make some valuable contacts in a room like that. But, let's be honest and call it what it really is—a second date with that hottie."

"Sheesh, Caroline, you're relentless."

Her roommate shrugged her shoulders and said, "I know you better than you know yourself. There's a large part of you that wants to go. You're attracted to James, don't deny it."

Julie looked at her friend and felt her prior resolve melt away. "You're right. I do find him interesting and very sexy. But he lives in a world that I want to avoid. It's filled with lies and scandals. How can that be good for my reputation as an expert on what's proper and polite in our society?"

"That's the whole point. It's sensational. The press will love it and you'll have a ton of exposure. You'll put a whole new spin on what you do and maybe, just maybe have the chance to make a positive change on the way people think about all the rudeness out there. Perhaps you can convince some nasty people to reconsider their behavior. Wouldn't that be something amazing?"

"C'mon, Caroline. That's a stretch. I don't think the readers of *All That* care about proper place settings and invitation wording. We couldn't be farther apart on that whole issue."

"I disagree," her roommate said with an air of authority. "You might have more influence than you think. People are naturally curious. There will be a portion of James' readers who will want to know more about you and one way to do that is to buy your book. I predict a giant spike in sales after Saturday night's event."

"Something tells me that they will be hugely disappointed when they discover that I'm not the person they think I am."

"What?" Caroline asked with mock surprise. "You are the most polite and proper person I've ever known! Do you have a dark secret I know nothing about? Do you use a salad fork for dessert? Heaven forbid!" She smacked her own forehead with the palm of her hand for emphasis.

Oh, if you only knew the truth, Julie thought, her stomach churning with anxiety. *I wish I had the courage to tell you.*

"So it's settled. You're going in this gorgeous outfit and we'll figure out what to do with your hair. I'm thinking a high pony-tail, so that just in case you take off the jacket there will be nothing in the way of the statement the back of that jumpsuit makes. And you'll wear my crystal chandelier earrings, no other jewelry. No need to gild the lily. It's already sheer perfection."

"Gild the lily? Did you actually say that?"

Caroline smiled. "Yes. Just trying to see if you were paying attention. In any event, my work here is done. I'm going to have more coffee and maybe another pastry. Wanna join me in the kitchen?"

"In a minute. I'm going to change out of this first," she motioned up and down at the clothing she had on. "And I have to let James know I plan on attending with him."

"Great, but don't dawdle. I'm going to take one bite from each piece of the baked goods he sent you until I find the one I love the most."

"Ugh, really? Are you kidding?" She looked straight into Caroline's eyes and knew that her friend was serious. "Use a knife at the very least, please."

"Better hurry!" Caroline said as she left the room.

Julie reached around and untied the cord of the jumpsuit. The silky fabric fell away and pooled at her feet, leaving her standing in just the lacy black thong her roommate insisted she wear. She knew that the outfit was out of her comfort zone, partially because she had to go basically naked underneath. It felt somewhat reckless and dangerous, but the fabric did feel good against her skin. She hadn't given much thought to the way her clothing reflected exactly who she was, or what she presented to the world with her wardrobe choices before this. It was almost ironic to be friends with a lingerie designer, someone who knew exactly how to make the most of the soft curves of a woman's body and not experiment herself by wearing one or two of her friend's racy pieces of lace and satin. It was just that Julie felt so awkward with the idea of flaunting her figure. Looking in the full-length mirror, she knew that despite the size of her breasts, she could get away without wearing a bra, and while she owned a few thongs from Caroline's collection, she rarely wore one. She just never considered how it would make her feel. Maybe she really did need to take a page from her roommate's book and let loose every now and then. She stepped back, still wearing the sky-high heels. What would James think when he saw her on Saturday night? Would he be excited?

James! She had to let him know that she would attend the gala with him. She kicked off the shoes, grabbed her robe and slipped it on. Then she began to compose an email to send to his assistant:

Dear Ms. Dawson,

Please let Mr. Curran know that I will be attending the gala on Saturday.

Thank you,

Julie Porter

Short and to the point. She hit send before she had to chance to change her mind and walked toward the kitchen in search of some more caffeine. She could use a loaded shot of liquid courage.

FOR THE REST OF THE WEEK LEADING UP TO THE EVENT, JULIE was consumed by a growing apprehension. She wasn't sure which was worse; her fear of being exposed or her undeniable desire to see James again. Now, sitting in the plush leather backseat of the town car he'd sent for her, Julie felt her heart pounding under the thin fabric of the borrowed jumpsuit she wore. As the car joined a line of other vehicles discharging formally dressed party-goers onto a red carpet in front of the venue, she felt as though she might faint. She was about to ask the driver to turn around and take her back home when the passenger door opened. James was there. He reached into the car offered her his hand. He looked incredibly handsome in his bespoke black tuxedo and crisply pressed dress shirt. His bow tie was perfectly perched right under his Adam's apple. He was simply stunning. She slipped her palm into his and despite the height of her heels, gracefully stepped onto the sidewalk. Then, what felt like a sudden storm of bright light almost blinded her and she realized that it was, in fact, dozens of camera flashes all firing at the same time. So much for keeping a low profile.

"You look beautiful," he said as he drew her into his embrace, shielding her from the aggressive paparazzi. "Don't let the press scare you. I won't let them bite."

He smelled both clean and spicy and she tried her best to get the right words organized in her mind and put them in the proper order so that she could respond. Instead, she just gripped his hand tighter.

"By the way, thank you for being here and for being my date tonight. I really appreciate this. I owe you one." He smiled at her and she felt her stomach do a somersault that took her by surprise. "Are you ready?" he asked.

Julie nodded. His strong fingers held her own tightly, guiding her down the carpet toward the ornate entrance of the building. She could not even begin to calculate how many snapshots had been taken of the two of them as they made their way inside, but she knew it was more than she wanted to think about. She took a deep breath to try and calm herself and once she regulated her fluttering heart into something less annoying than the rapid tin drumbeat she'd been feeling, she was able to take in her surroundings.

The building where the gala was being held was an old bank, built in the late 1800's. It had soaring ceilings painted with beautiful frescoes and moldings trimmed in gold. On the far end of the immense chamber was the original safe, a very large and wide cavernous-like steel box that was lit from within, rows and rows of string lights twinkling over what appeared to be a bar. There was a stage off to one side with a multi-pieced band playing cocktail music and a highly polished wood dance floor in the middle of the space. Beautifully set tables, covered with sharply starched linen tablecloths, gleaming crystal stemware and sparkling white china rimmed the room. This was a formal business party on the verge of becoming "the event" of the society season.

Just then a server appeared with a tray of filled champagne flutes. "Would you like one of these?" James asked, lifting two glasses and handing her one.

"Yes, thank you," Julie replied, watching the waitress' face as awareness dawned and she recognized James. He appeared to be immune to the other woman's reaction as he took his filled flute and raised it to Julie.

"To you. And to many more evenings spent together."

She smiled and carefully brought the glass to her lips, grateful for the chance to have a sip and catch her breath. As she swallowed some down, she recognized that it was an expensive champagne. It was icy cold and very smooth.

"This is delicious," she said to James.

"Nothing but the best for this crowd," he replied. "We're

here to make friends and influence spending. We aim to make a good impression with the people who help fund what we do."

She nodded. "I understand. I've been on both sides of this type of equation. There was a bidding war for my book and I was wined and dined for a bit by most of the big publishing houses. It's really something to be treated this well."

"Julie. You deserve all this and more, believe me." He leaned in and whispered in her ear, "I'd love to share the 'more' with you later tonight."

There it was again. Her stomach flipped and she suddenly felt warm all over. He had a remarkable way of making her feel both off kilter and alive in a way that she hadn't experienced before. She took another sip of her champagne, hoping that it would make her feel calm. She was undeniably attracted to him but didn't want to let her guard down. At least not yet. Before Julie had a chance to reply, they were interrupted by a woman who clearly knew her date.

"James! There you are!" Julie heard a throaty voice from behind where they stood. When she turned around she saw a vision of gold brocade tightly spun into a slinky evening gown on a waif-like woman leaning in to kiss James on both cheeks.

"Delilah. How are you? Looking ravishing, as always," he said, then continued, "meet Ms. Julie Porter. Julie, this is Delilah Murray."

She felt the perfectly coiffed blonde's piercing amber eyes on her, as the other woman quickly accessed Julie's hair, her make-up, her outfit, silently deciding if she was important enough to be on James' arm. In a different century, the woman would be a solider wearing metal armor poised for battle, instead of the designer couture she sported tonight.

"Porter? Any relation to the Porters of Newport?" Delilah asked.

Julie smiled. "None."

"Oh," the impossibly thin blonde responded curtly, dismissing Julie before turning her attention to James. "I saw your father earlier. He invited me to come out for cocktails next weekend. I assume you'll be there as well?"

"I hadn't planned on it, but now that you mention it, maybe Julie and I would like to get out on the ocean for a bit. We'll see." He scanned the room for a minute, then said, "Excuse us, Delilah. I see my father now and I'd like to introduce him to my beautiful date." He grabbed Julie's hand and began to walk across the vast space. Julie glanced back to see Delilah still in the same spot, her mouth slightly open at the shock of having been so quickly left standing alone. Halfway there, he stopped. "Sorry about Delilah. Our fathers think that if we united, they'd have more than just two families connecting. It would be a huge business merger as well. Her father owns paper mills and before we were digitized, *Tell All* was their biggest client. She set her sights on me years ago, but believe me, she's not my type."

That was a lot of information, Julie realized. All she asked was, "You have a type?"

"I do," he replied, holding her gaze and squeezing her hand. "More about that later when we're done with all of this. And let me also apologize in advance for whatever my father might say to you. He's quite the character. He has absolutely no filter."

Well, the apple doesn't fall far from that tree, was all she could think before she found herself standing in front of the man who had created the one thing that could light the spark to set her whole world up in flames. *Tell All.*

Julie immediately realized that Benjamin Curran was clearly holding court, surrounded by a dazzling array of men and women dressed to the nines and hanging on his every word. He was tall, like his son, with perfectly combed grey hair and a classically styled tuxedo that fit him like a glove. Ben was an imposing figure to be sure and Julie felt a heightened sense of unease from

James as they approached the older man. James seemed to be on edge, which in turn, was unsettling to her. She was just here tonight doing him a favor, nothing more. They barely knew one another. Why should he seem so concerned about introducing her to his father?

She did not have a lot of time to ruminate on it because all at once she was standing in front of the man. She heard James speak.

"Good evening, dad. Let me introduce you to my date, Julie Porter."

"A pleasure, Ms. Porter," Ben replied, his eyebrows raised in surprise. Without letting on too much of what he thought of the woman standing with his son, he turned back to the group around him. "Excuse us, one and all. It's not often that my son introduces me to one of his female friends. I'd like to get to know this young lady a little better." Then he turned to Julie and slipped his arm around her bent one, linking them. "Come with me. Let's have a drink and a chat."

She looked up at James. If she knew him better, she would be sure that what she saw looked like a tiny bit of panic in his eyes. Turning back to his father, she said with more confidence than she felt, "I think I'd enjoy that. Shall we?" She leaned into Ben and together, they crossed the dance floor to the small group of intimate tables near the bar as if they were the only two people in the room.

Chapter Eight

BEN PULLED the chair out from a small cocktail table and Julie sat down. He motioned to a waiter who seemed to appear out of nowhere and barked, "Champagne for the lady. I'll have a Jameson. Neat."

To Julie it sounded more like a command than a drink order and the server scurried away quickly leaving her to hope that the young man could deliver their cocktails quickly without spilling a drop. She was pretty sure that Benjamin Curran would not tolerate any mishap.

"So, Ms. Porter," he began.

She interrupted him. "Please. Call me Julie." *Maybe that will soften him some,* she thought.

"Julie," he continued, "it's not often that I get to meet a woman that my son is seeing. He hasn't introduced me to a date since his high school prom. Tell me. How do you know James?"

Wow. He didn't mince his words. Right down to it. Her mind raced to provide a suitable answer to the same question she'd asked herself ever since James' email invitation.

"Actually, sir, we met not that long ago. He knows that I'm a writer and that perhaps I'd be able to make some valuable contacts here."

She watched as he sat back in his chair, his eyebrows raised.

"Are you a journalist?" he asked.

"No. But I do write non-fiction. I have a book currently on the bestseller list. *Practically Perfect.* Maybe you've heard of it?"

The older man shook his head, signaling that he did not recognize her work "Topic?"

"Proper etiquette."

Ben let out a roar of laughter so loud that some of his guests turned their heads toward the sharp sound. "Etiquette? Really? That's wonderful. A dying art, to be sure."

The very nervous waiter returned with their drinks, carefully placing each one on the table between them before rushing away.

She felt the need to defend herself. "Honestly, Mr. Curran, I think that we need rules in our society more now than ever, so I hope that good manners are not a 'dying art', as you said. The constant barrage of social media has changed us. People hide in their homes, behind their screens typing whatever hurtful untruths they concoct in their own minds. I believe that there needs to be a line drawn now, before the damage is irreversible." She paused and looked directly at him then added, "We need to be nicer to one another. If we had some sort of unified guide, maybe it would help. That's why I wrote the book. It mainly covers an overview of polite behavior but my editor has asked me to write another volume, this time focusing on wedding etiquette. Apparently, there's a great need for an entire book on how to host a large party without any major gaffes or impropriety."

Ben's sharp blue eyes focused on hers. "You do know what my family does, how I made my fortune, right?" he asked before taking a large sip of the tawny liquid in the heavily cut crystal glass in his hand.

"If you mean *Tell All,* then yes."

"Have you ever read a copy?"

Julie knew better than to directly answer that very loaded question. It was a trap. She kept her legs crossed at the ankle and her posture straight, not allowing herself to lean back against the cushion of her chair. She took a small sip of her own drink, placing the glass down carefully before responding, giving herself a chance to compose her best response. "I did extensive research before I began to write my first book, sir. I'm always exposing myself to new materials, to different ideas. That would include how not to have the bright light of public scrutiny constantly shine on you, how to avoid the social media traps that so many young people seem to fall prey to today."

She watched Ben's face as he listened and was surprised when he smiled. It was so unexpected in the moment, that all Julie could was smile back.

"Interesting," he murmured as he leaned in closer to her. "You're different, Julie. You seem to have a very unique perspective. Smart, beautiful...an extreme departure from the flighty empty-headed types that I've seen my son photographed with previously. I dare say, I approve."

She looked away for a moment, trying to find James in the crowd, her mind racing. *Approve?!? Did James bring me here for this? To introduce me to his father and gain his approval? Why would he do that? Was he even attracted to me at all? How could I have ever thought that he was after meeting someone like Delilah?*

She didn't realize that James was waiting silently behind her until Ben said, "This young woman is charming. Why didn't you bring her around before?"

James drew in a breath, clearly trying to say something that would appease this man without leaving room for any further discussion. "I was too interested in keeping her all to myself. Now, may I have my date back, please?"

Sensing the growing tension between the two men, and feeling disgusted by them both at the moment, she remarked, "Actually, gentlemen, I think I'm going to get some air. If you'll excuse me, please."

Julie stood up and with one sharp glance at James, left the men standing alone in her wake. She made her way across the room to the open doors leading to a balcony that looked out over a small private garden. It seemed so serene there, much more inviting than the scene inside the lavish party where she felt so out of her element.

She walked over to the short staircase that accessed the manicured lawn and could smell the jasmine that wound around the elaborate brass scroll design of the railing as she held tightly to the cool banister. She drew in a deep breath, the perfume from the flowers calming her down somewhat. Finding a stone bench, she sat, and continued to drink in the heady scent of the delicate blooms, allowing herself a moment alone to compose her thoughts. *Coming here tonight was a mistake. James clearly had a motive other than introducing me to some industry bigwigs. He needed me to meet his father. But why...*

She didn't have to stay, she knew that, yet something was keeping her from bolting to the street and into a car that would bring her home. She wanted to know, wanted James to tell her his real reasons for bringing her here tonight. She deserved the truth. As she sat in the warm night air, she felt herself grow steadier, more assured. Just as she was about to go back inside to find him and demand some answers, he came looking for her.

He cleared his throat and then asked, "May I sit here with you?"

"I don't want to keep you from your very important guests,

Delilah among them." She could not keep the sarcasm out of her voice and quickly added, "I'm fine. No need to rescue me."

He looked at her for a moment before saying, "I'm sorry about what just happened in there, Julie. I am."

"Which part? Delilah judging me for not being from a family line she recognizes? Or your father deciding whether or not I'm worthy of being here with you tonight?"

"You're angry," he replied, but quickly followed with, "I guess I deserve that."

"I have to apologize as well," she responded. "I should have known better than to think you really wanted anything to do with me. I clearly don't fit in with the crowd in that room."

"Yes you do. More than you know," he replied. "They are no better than anyone else, especially not someone like you."

"Why did you bring me here tonight, James?" she asked boldly. "Why was it so important for me to meet your father?"

"I'd like to answer that, Julie, I would. But not here. Is it too much of me to ask you if we can continue our evening elsewhere?"

"What?" she asked in surprise. "Don't you need to be inside that room, making nice with your advertisers?"

"It's more important to me to try and set things right with you. I owe you that at the very least."

He looked so sincere that Julie felt some of the breath leave her body. And for as much as she wanted to know what he could possibly say, she responded, "I don't think that's such a great idea. It would be better for us to just part ways and pretend this whole night never happened."

"I don't know if I can do that. You're pretty unforgettable." He reached for her hand. "Please, give me the chance to explain myself. And if you want to never see me again after that, I promise to leave you alone."

She felt her resolve waiver. She did want the truth. Julie realized that her silence was giving him the opening that he needed.

"We don't even have to go back inside. We can walk out around the garden. It will take us down the block away from the photographers. I can have my driver pick us up there. No one will even realize that we're gone."

"Won't your father be looking for you?"

"Not while he's in that crowd, he won't. Besides, he's three drinks in already. One more and we'll be the last thing on his mind."

"And the advertisers? What about them?"

"I have a whole staff of people who know exactly what to do in my absence. It will be fine."

"Where would we go, dressed like this, where we won't be noticed?"

"Really? This is New York City. No one will give us a second glance. But I do have the perfect spot in mind. How do you feel about having dinner with me, alone? No prying eyes."

She couldn't help but be curious about where he might take her and what he might tell her. "Okay, James. But believe me. This is your last chance. Whatever you plan on revealing better be good."

He let out a visible sigh of relief. "Oh. It is. I promise." With those words, he took her hand and like a pair of cat burglars, they snuck off together through the darkness into the night.

⁂

THIRTY MINUTES LATER, THEY WERE SEATED AT A SMALL TABLE at James' private club. A trio of low candles cast soft shadows on the pristine linen cloth and the heavy silverware gleamed in the low light. He was right about one thing: when they exited that garden onto the crowded street in their formal attire, no one even noticed. The car was waiting exactly where it was supposed to be and they got inside quickly, Julie's heart beating faster as she sat closely next to him, their legs touching for the entirety of their quick ride to their destination, the heat between them palpable.

They stopped at a non-descript townhouse on the upper east side of the city, exited the car and climbed the stone staircase to the entrance. James was greeted by the doorman and they stepped inside. It was all dark wood and leather furniture, somewhat imposing on first glance. It smelled expensive. Julie reminded herself of something her old employer had told her: fitting in to a place that feels intimidating is only a matter of convincing yourself that you belong. Once you do that, other people will assume the same about you.

There was no menu, just a series of delicious courses that were delivered with precision by a team of well-trained and discreet servers. They shared a bottle of 2006 Scarecrow cabernet, which tasted earthy with a distinct flavor of black cherries. When the most perfect plate of petit fours arrived to signal the end of the meal, she said, "This is so much better than whatever they were going to serve at that function tonight. Thank you."

"No, Julie, thank you for letting me do this for you. I'm am truly sorry about earlier."

She looked directly at him and drew in a breath. "So, James. Time to put your cards on the table. Why did you invite me to the gala?"

"It's complicated, but...here it is. I wanted my father to believe that we're the real deal. A couple in love, with a bright future ahead of us."

Julie shook her head, not sure of her hearing. What he just said made absolutely no sense. "What exactly does that mean?"

"It means that he has to think that you're the woman I'm

going to marry and start a family with, someone grounded and real."

"What? We hardly know each other! You can't be serious!" she replied.

"I know, I know. Please, don't hate me. It's a long story."

"Well, James," she said, lifting her wine glass. "I suggest you start talking to me."

"Okay." He sat up straighter. "The truth of the matter is that I want to take *Tell All* in a different direction, to true journalism, honest, impactful reporting. I can't do that until my father lets loose of the reins entirely. He's made it very clear to me that he won't do that until I'm settled down with a family of my own."

"And I'm involved in that decision? How? We're not in a relationship, we met by chance, in a bar, just a week ago." She stumbled over her words, barely getting them out of her mouth coherently.

"I know, Julie. But I'm hoping to change that. I'm hoping you'd be willing to play along."

"Play along?"

"Yes. Let my father believe that we in love, that we have a future together. In return, I'll deposit a million dollars in the bank account of your choosing."

Julie's eyes widened. "Please tell me that you did not just offer to pay me to be your girlfriend. I believe that's called prostitution."

He quickly replied, "I disagree. To be precise, it's only prostitution if there's sex involved. But then again…"

Julie saw the raw desire in his eyes and had to fight the impulse to let herself drown in those steamy depths. "No. Don't make a joke of this," she said, shaking her head. "And to be clear, the answer is never. Goodnight, James." She leaned in, wanting to make sure he heard her next words. "Please. Don't contact me again." Julie then picked up her evening bag, the one Caroline had lent her when the night still seemed full of promise, and stood, hoping that her quaking knees wouldn't betray her. For as much as she said no to him, a small part of her really wanted to say yes...

"Okay, okay," he said, quickly getting to his feet and reaching for her hand. "Wait. That was obviously a poor attempt at humor. It was a mistake. I shouldn't have said that about prostitution. It was just plain stupid. Please, Julie, please. Don't go."

"James," she looked straight into his soft, brown eyes and tried to sound convincing. "Best of luck with your plans. I hope you find a woman more suitable than me to spend the rest of your perfect, prescribed life with. Someone who will make your father happy." With that, she turned and walked out of the club and didn't even wait to call for an Uber. She hailed a yellow taxi on the street instead.

As she settled into the backseat for the drive home, all Julie could hope for was that Caroline was asleep. She didn't want to rehash her evening with her roommate. At least not until she had the chance to set things straight in her own mind first.

How could I have ever thought that someone like James Curran would be interested in me? We couldn't be more different, in every way...

Her mind drifted back to the car ride to his club, their legs resting against one another, the heat that radiated between them. She couldn't deny that she felt a pull toward him, something so primal and unexpected that it truly took her breath away. More than that, she was pretty sure that he felt it too. But his proposition? That she could not forgive. To offer her that kind of money in an attempt to trick his father into believing that they were planning a future together and truly in love? No chance she'd agree to something like that, even if that kind of money would go a huge distance to getting her mother into a quality rehab to deal with her addiction. Then, just for a minute, Julie let her mind wander. A million dollars would mean that she could move her mother out of her awful trailer and into a small, clean apartment. She could have food delivered regularly and put her mom on the path to better health. Maybe, just maybe, her mother could regain some semblance of a life.

No! Julie shuddered. She could never accept an offer like the one James proposed. When she married, she would do it for love, not money. She shook her head as if the motion would clear her mind of her thoughts. It didn't help. When she looked out the window of the taxi, she could see the familiar storefronts of her neighborhood. She was almost home where she could hide until the remnants of this night faded away with the sunrise.

Luckily, when she stepped inside of the apartment, it was dark. Caroline was either out or asleep. Julie didn't care which it was, as long as she could make it into her bed undisturbed. She quickly undressed, hanging Caroline's clothing carefully and emptying out the contents of the evening bag. She'd return everything in the morning. After she washed her face and brushed her teeth, she slipped between the cool sheets of her bed and closed her eyes. She tossed and turned for what seemed like an eternity before falling into a fitful sleep, images of James plaguing her, the feel of his lips against hers, the rock hard chest she knew she'd find under that fine dress shirt. She was better off without him.

Why then, did the mere thought of him ravage her dreams and leave her more confused than she ever could have imagined possible?

Chapter Nine

JAMES SAT ALONE at the table until the last candle burned itself out. He had been drinking steadily ever since Julie turned away from him and walked out of his club. *How could I have ever thought that someone like her would bend to my will? That an offer of an enormous sum of money would convince her to help me with my plan to change the trajectory of my life?*

He silently sipped at the remnants of his drink. Any number of women would have agreed to play along with his deception. Not Julie. She had too much character, she was way too honest. Much to his own chagrin, he had unknowingly been drawn those very traits about her in a way that made him uneasy. He could not get her out of his mind, despite finishing the wine from dinner and moving on to drink half of a bottle of Glenlivet. As a matter of fact, the alcohol intensified what he already knew: he had to do something to change her mind. Even if he had to give up on the notion of a sham of a marriage, there was something about her that he had to have, something he knew he desperately needed. For all the women he'd known, for all the women he'd taken to his bed, Julie had gotten to him in a way no one had done ever before and he knew why. She was too good for him. She would make him a better man. That was the simple truth. The question rattling around his liquor-addled mind was clear: how could he convince her that he could make her happy? What did he have to do?

James lifted his head and looked around the now empty room He immediately realized that he should leave and let the staff finish up and go home, but was unsure about his ability to make it out to the car on his own. It was worth a try. He stood, gained his balance and began to walk out, nodding to the maître d' as he concentrated on trying to remain upright. In the foggy wine and whiskey fueled haze that swirled around in his head, he had a random thought. *Ryan.* His friend might have some constructive ideas on what to do next. Now if he could only remember to call him in the morning, maybe Ryan would have some sage words of advice that would help. Heaven knew how much he needed assistance.

৩১৯

THE NEXT MORNING DAWNED BRIGHTLY, A FACT THAT JAMES was all too aware of as the sun's rays made their way across his pillow, resting on his still closed lids, reminding him that he was too drunk the night before to have thought to close the blinds in his bedroom. His head was pounding and the inside of his mouth felt like it was covered in some sort of furry material. He finally dared to open his eyes. That only made matters worse as the room seemed to swirl and bend to his vision.

"Damn," he said aloud to no one.

He carefully sat up and waited for the immediate surge of dizziness to pass. After a few minutes, when he was pretty sure that his legs would hold him, he pushed himself up off of the mattress and carefully stood, dodging the landmine of his hastily discarded shoes and clothing, making his way gingerly into the bathroom for a much needed shower. He let the water heat up to the highest temperature he could tolerate and then stepped into the spray. Opening the cap of his body wash, he rubbed a good handful of it all over his chest and legs, suds covering every inch of him, washing away the remains of the night. It took a good while before he could even think of moving out of that steamy stall; his movements were slow and deliberate. Once he turned off the water, he reached onto the warming rack for a clean, plush towel and was grateful that his housekeeper, Mariella, kept him in good supply.

He dried off, put on a pair of soft sweatpants and a tee shirt before padding barefoot into the kitchen to make himself some very strong coffee. He popped a pod into the complex machine, slipped a mug underneath the spout and pressed the appropriate buttons to fire it all up. He knew that it would only be a matter of minutes before it was prepared, but the wait seemed interminable. He needed help clearing his mind and setting himself back on course to win Julie over. Glancing up at the digital clock on his stainless steel microwave, he saw that it was only 8 o'clock. Too soon to reach out to Ryan on a Sunday morning. Once the coffee was done brewing, he reached for it and brought the steaming liquid to his lips. Just the first sip began to work wonders. He added two Advil, downing them with the next gulp and went to sit on one of the low grey leather couches in the living room.

From his seat he could see out the large window overlooking Manhattan. Even on a sleepy weekend morning, there was plenty of activity. Yellow cabs cruised up and down the wide expanse of Fifth Avenue, couples walked hand-in-hand, perhaps on their way to an early brunch or maybe even a picnic in Central Park. He loved his home, his city and never felt alone. But for the very first time ever, he was thinking that maybe he'd like to share all of it with someone special.

Julie. Was she still sleeping? he wondered.

He could not stop his mind from imagining what exactly it was that she wore to bed, if anything at all. He took another sip of coffee. The thought of her naked was incredibly arousing, despite his hungover state. He had to reel himself in before he needed to take another shower, this one ice cold. Just then he felt his cell phone vibrate. He had slipped it into the pocket of his pants when he got dressed. He looked at the screen and the familiar number registered. Reluctantly, he knew he had to take the call.

"Good morning Dad," he said. "You're up early."

"I could say the same for you. Where did you disappear to last night? Did it have anything to do with that delightful woman you brought along with you? Is she still there?"

"No. She's not here. But we did leave the gala together. Turns out it just wasn't the kind of event she was comfortable attending."

"Well, then, bring her around to the house. We can have a longer conversation, a chance to get to know each other better. Let's say drinks next weekend?"

"I don't think that will be possible. She made it clear that she didn't want to see me again."

"And when has that small detail stopped you before? You're charming, I'm sure. Figure it out. I liked that one. I can see potential there for her to set you on the road to the life and family you deserve."

"It's not that simple. I don't even think that she'll take my call."

"That sounds ominous. What the hell did you do to make her feel that way?"

James sighed. With the level of deception he'd planned, the

way he meant to fool the older man, there would be hell to pay if the truth came out. He had to think fast.

"We just aren't meant for each other. She was somewhat intimidated by the opulence of the gala. Delilah didn't help. She made it clear to Julie that she did not fit in."

"Since when did it matter what Delilah thinks? I know you aren't interested in her. But Ms. Porter? Well, simply put, I liked her. A lot. She had smarts, looks and moxie. She didn't back down when I challenged her. That's just the type of woman you need in your life, not another one of those vapid models you always seem to have on your arm."

"Dad! There is just no way," he began, "she made her feelings very clear—"

His father interrupted him. "Oh, yes, there is. You have to find it. I will see you both at the house next weekend."

The line went dead.

Great, just great, James thought to himself. *How the hell can I convince Julie to give me another chance?*

He lifted his coffee but the contents of the mug were now cold. He got up to make another and decided that waking Ryan for help was his only option. He hoped that his friend would have the solution that James so badly needed.

He forced himself to wait an hour before dialing the familiar number. Two more cups of coffee and he was finally feeling steadier on his feet. After three rings, the other man picked up the call.

"Hello," Ryan mumbled, whispering.

"Ry. It's James. I need a favor." He leaned back against the cool concrete counter.

"At 9:30 on a Sunday morning? Hang on."

James could hear a muffled female voice and his friend moving around on the other end of the call. When he spoke again, Ryan sounded fully awake. "This better be important," he teased. "You woke Daphne up, and as she reminds me, she's sleeping for two."

"It is, but it's much too detailed to go over like this. Can you meet me for brunch?"

"I guess so. Daphne has plans with her mother this morning. Something about choosing baby clothes. How hard could that be? An infant doesn't care what its wearing, right?"

"Way over my paygrade, buddy. See you at Sadelle's in an hour?"

"Okay pal, but you're buying. That smoked fish is pricey and I'm saving my pennies for a college fund."

James smiled. "Sounds good. See you there."

"Right."

The call disconnected. James turned and put his now empty mug into the deep kitchen sink and went into his bedroom to put on some real clothes before heading out to meet his friend, hoping that Ryan had some good ideas and was just the lifeline he needed to work his way out of this mess.

WHEN JAMES ARRIVED AT THE RESTAURANT, RYAN WAS already seated. There were two tall Bloody Mary's, both elaborately decorated with spears of olives and lemon wedges in each on the table. James' stomach turned at the sight of more alcohol.

"Good morning. Thanks for coming out to meet me," he said, gingerly slipping into the vacant chair.

"Yeah, no worries. I've gotten us started with your favorite brunch beverage."

"I see. I think I'll pass today." He moved his glass toward his friend.

"Tough night at the gala?"

"Did I tell you that I was attending the gala last night? It's a long story and I had way too much to drink. So much, in fact, that I don't even remember mentioning it to you."

"Oh, you didn't. But the photos are all over *Tell All, People* and this morning's *New York Times*." He picked up his phone, unlocked the screen and started scrolling.

James closed his eyes and imagined how upset Julie would be when she found the evidence of last night's debacle. He opened them again and his friend had turned his device around so that James could see for himself. He took the phone from Ryan and began to go through each picture. There were actually some good shots, especially the one where he helped Julie out of the town car when she first arrived. The photographer had captured the expression of anticipation on her face, wide-eyed and innocent. She looked lovely.

"Ugh. That was only the beginning of the night. Before it all went to shit."

"What do you mean?"

"It's a long story." He pointed at the drinks on the table in front of his friend. "And you're going to need these when I explain it all to you."

Ryan leaned in. "That sounds ominous." He lifted his own glass and took a long swallow. "I'm ready now. Begin."

James recounted the events of the previous night, including the interaction Julie had with his father at the gala and the proposition he made to her at his club afterward.

Ryan listened intently. James watched as his friend quietly continued to sip at his Bloody Mary until the glass was empty. Then he switched over to the second one. When the waiter came by for their order, Ryan sent him away, fully engrossed in James' tale of woe.

"So let me see if I fully understand you," Ryan began. "Once this woman finished telling you that she felt awkward in the crowd you inhabit, you then offered her money to pretend to be

your girlfriend? Can I get some of the drugs were you taking?"
He shook his head. "In what universe did you ever think she'd
agree to something so absurd?"

"Well, when you put it that way..."

"What other way can it be put?"

"I know, it sounds so bad. But if I'm being honest with you
now, I guess the real problem is that I genuinely like this woman.
There's something about her that I can't get shake. She's attrac-
tive on a level that goes much deeper than just being a beautiful
face. She's smart and funny. And she's sexy as hell."

"She seemed to make it clear to you that she has no interest
in your scheme. What part of that did you not understand?"

"I know. I was a total ass. But I want to fix it. Can you help
me or not?"

"James. I think you have to accept defeat here."

"I can't. She's all I can think about. I have to get her to know
me better. I have to get her to give me a second chance."

"Then tell her it was all a mistake. Apologize. Send flowers.
Do something for her that comes from a place of truth, buddy. If
you really are attracted to this woman you're going to need to
forget what she can do for you, for your quest to revamp *Tell All*.
If you want her, you're going to have to do something special for
her."

"I don't think flowers will cut it," James said, shaking his
head.

"It's a start. But I agree, you need a larger gesture."

"But what?" James asked.

At that moment, Ryan gestured to the waiter. "I need some
food if I'm going to think about this. Let's order. Maybe on a full
stomach, we can come up with something."

After they ordered, James let out a sigh of relief. Perhaps
there was hope, after all. There had to be, because he wasn't
about to give up yet. Not by a long shot. Then he had the most

random thought. Julie had a roommate. Maybe the best way to win her over was through her friend, the one who was so drunk the night they first met. But how? He turned to Ryan with renewed energy.

"I think I might have an idea. Julie lives with a friend. If I can impress that woman, perhaps I'll get another chance with Julie."

"Interesting," Ryan replied. "You may be on to something there."

A few minutes later, the waiter delivered their food, placing it down with a flourish.

"Perfect," Ryan said looking down at his plate. "I'm starving."

"All of a sudden I am too," James replied, lifting a fork.

Ryan nodded, finished chewing a bite of bagel and said, "Everything always looks better on a full stomach. Let's eat."

Chapter Ten

JULIE HAD to force herself out of bed on Sunday morning, steeling herself for the barrage of questions she knew she was about to face from Caroline. She was going to have to explain to the other woman why she didn't plan on ever speaking or seeing James again and was really not in the mood to rehash the previous night's events. She pulled out a pair of yoga pants and a tee shirt. Maybe if she told Caroline that she was going out to an aerobics class she could delay the inevitable. Caroline hated to exercise.

She followed the scent of brewed coffee into the kitchen, where she found her roommate firmly planted on a stool, apparently waiting for Julie to spill the tea about James and her evening.

"Finally, you're up!" Caroline exclaimed. "It feels like I've been waiting for you all day already!"

Julie glanced up at the clock, and with one eyebrow lifted said, "Hardly. It's only 9:30."

"You know what I mean, smart ass." She leaned against the counter. "Give me all of the details. I've been so patient."

Julie blew out a sigh. "I was thinking of going to the gym. Want to come with me?"

"Since when do I ever choose to go to the gym? No. Don't change the subject. I want you to tell me everything about the gala. Who was there? How was the food? What happened with James? Did you guys kiss again on the ride home?"

Julie stood up straight. She was going to have to say something. "It was a disaster. End of story. I told you I didn't want to go, and I should have followed my instincts. I'll put the jumpsuit back in your closet when I get home later, and please, let's not discuss this topic again."

Caroline jumped off of the stool, planted her hands on her hips and said, "Oh no. No you don't. You're not shutting this conversation down like this. Don't leave me hanging!"

Julie knew when she was defeated and decided to make this a quick recap. "Really. It's not worth rehashing the story. We just didn't hit it off. I found the gala to be overwhelming to say the least. It was over the top, extremely opulent. And I met James' father, Ben. He was plain old scary."

"You met Benjamin Curran? Wow!"

"Oh, I did. We had a chat. He's a real charmer."

"That's sarcasm I'm hearing?"

"To say the least. He's very imposing and I think that James is intimidated by him. Anyway, that's the story, nothing more." She was not in the mind to disclose the rest of the evening's activity, especially not James' proposition. Julie walked past where Caroline still stood, hands on hips, and went to grab a mug from the cabinet over the coffee pot. Once she had if firmly in hand, she filled it with the steamy liquid and sat down, motioning her friend to do the same.

"But you and James seemed to hit it off when you had drinks together last week. What changed?" Caroline sat back down on her stool.

Julie hesitated for a moment, then chose her words carefully. "I think he needed a date last night, that's all."

"Something is just not making sense, here, Julie. I mean, when I saw the way you looked up at him when you arrived there last night..."

"What are you talking about? You weren't there, were you? Were you hiding in the bushes?" Julie asked with a shaky laugh.

"Wow. You really need to step into this century, doll." Caroline pulled her phone out of the pocket of her denim shorts. "Get a look at this!"

Julie took the device from Caroline and could not believe what she saw. Photo after photo, almost in stop action. There she was, stepping out of the car and taking James' hand. It was the two of them, walking each inch of the red carpet together. There was even a grainy shot of them in the garden. It was naïve of her to believe that this wouldn't have happened. It was her own fault; she knew the paparazzi was there. She had given James too much credit to think that he could have prevented this disaster at all.

"Just great," she said, handing the phone back to Caroline.

Her friend scrolled back to the first picture. "C'mon, Julie. Even you have to admit that in this photo, you look absolutely smitten." She held it up again.

Julie knew that she couldn't argue. In that first shot, when she emerged from the car holding onto James' hand, she was still in the glow of the moment, thinking that he was special. That was well before the hammer was lowered and he made that disgusting proposal to her. "Yes, well, as it turned out, we just weren't meant for each other. End of story."

"You mean short story, huh?" Caroline asked with a sigh. "I had high hopes for this one."

"So sorry to disappoint you. Now, if you don't mind, I'm going to head out to try and clear my head with some exercise."

"If you say so," Caroline responded, taking a sip of her coffee. "I'll be here when you get back. Stephen is coming over and we're going to try to finalize the guest list."

"Great. Then we can have an idea of how many invitations to order." Julie took one last gulp of the contents in her mug. It tasted bitter in her mouth. For today, at least, the idea of weddings was one she could live without.

⚜

ONE SWEATY HOUR LATER, AFTER AN INTENSE BOOT CAMP workout, Julie felt somewhat better. No one in the class said a word to her about the pictures on the internet so she tried to convince herself that it couldn't have been that big a deal. *People scroll through that crap every day*, she thought to herself on the walk back home. *They don't pay all that much attention to it anymore; unless it was someone like JLo or Beyonce, no one noticed.* She ducked into her building and smiled at the doorman.

"I just brought a delivery upstairs for you Miss Julie," Curtis said, tipping his hat.

"On a Sunday? Something was sent on a Sunday?" She felt her stomach drop. It wasn't a package from her publisher if it came on the weekend, and the only other person who might think to send her something was the man she wanted to forget.

"Yes. Miss Caroline has it for you, safe and sound," he answered as he walked her to the elevator and pressed the button. The doors opened immediately.

She stepped inside.

"Have a nice day, Miss Julie."

"You too, Curtis," she replied absentmindedly, her anxiety building as the car ascended to her floor. When she reached her destination, she stepped out onto the carpet and slowly walked to her apartment, the key in her shaky hand, her breathing shallow. As she turned the lock and opened the door, she was greeted by the heady scent of flowers.

"What the..." The words got caught in her throat when she saw the immense floral arrangement, jasmine wound around thick stems of hydrangea and dozens of miniature roses in the softest baby pink.

"Well, Julie. You may be done with James Curran, but apparently, he's not done with you. The guy sure does send some inspired gifts," Caroline's voice floated in the air from somewhere behind the overly generous presentation of flowers.

"I don't know what to say," Julie replied.

Her roommate appeared and responded, "Then let me do the talking. This guy is interested in you. For whatever your reason, for whatever offended you, he's letting you know that he's sorry."

"I don't agree. He's just used to getting what he wants and he believes that I possess something that suits his purpose. Flowers are not going to sway me or my decision not to see him again."

"Will you at least read the card?"

"Why? I'm telling you, it's not going to change my mind. Nothing can do that."

Caroline walked over to the giant bloom-filled crystal vase and pulled the little card out from between the stems. "Please?" She implored. Julie took it from her, cleared her throat and began to read:

JULIE. I KNOW THAT I OVERSTEPPED LAST NIGHT, THAT I *shouldn't have proposed what I did. It was wrong and I could not be more sorry. I want to make it up to you, I want to make this better. Please, give me one more chance to prove that I'm not the person you think I am. I am better than that, I promise. Would you consider one more date? This time, bring your roommate and her fiancé for a ride around Manhattan on my sailboat. There's safety in numbers, right?*

I hope you'll consider this offer. I promise never to make you feel uncomfortable again.

*J*AMES

JULIE STOOD STILL, HOLDING THE SMALL WHITE CARD AND RE-reading it over and over, seeing the words but not truly comprehending them. How could he even think that she would try again after last night? She had to stand up for herself and say no, or better yet, not answer him at all.

"What does the note say?" Caroline asked after what seemed like a long pause.

"It's a weak attempt at an apology," Julie said as she passed the card to her friend so that she could read it for herself.

Caroline scanned the note quickly and asked, "Well, you left that piece out of the story before. What proposal? Is that what he had to apologize for?"

Julie looked up at her roommate's face. She knew that now she had no choice but to explain herself.

"He made me a very inappropriate offer. He needs to convince his father that he's got a serious girlfriend, someone who he might be the one to make him settle down. He thinks that I could fill that spot, work alongside him to deceive his dad. I said no." She left out the cash offer part. Caroline didn't need to know that much. *Or maybe she should. Maybe then she'd understand why I can't to see this man again.* Then Julie had an even more uncomfortable thought. *Or maybe I'm protecting James from Caroline's ultimate wrath. But why?*

Deep down, she knew why and let out a long sigh. She was, despite the events of the prior night, still attracted to him. She just didn't want to have to act on it.

Caroline replied softly, "Wow. That's a lot to handle."

"Exactly. That's why this boat ride isn't going to happen."

"Wait a minute, wait a minute," Caroline began. "Let's not be hasty. The man apologized, which means that he knows what he did was wrong. He's asking you for another chance."

"I realize that, but –"

"But what? He wants to prove that he's better than whatever he said to you last night. And you'd have me and Stephen there with you. Let me meet this guy for myself. You know that I'm a better judge of people than you are."

Julie had to agree. Caroline always seemed to be able to size up a person after just one conversation, and she had an excellent track record. She was almost always right. *But James can be very charming. Could he possibly fool her friend?*

"You're just in it for the private boat ride around the city, right?" Julie teased.

"Well, that's part of it. I mean, how do you pass something like that up? I'd like to see just how the other half lives."

"I had a glimpse of it last night, Caroline. It's definitely not all its touted to be."

"I think that as my best friend, you should let me find out for myself." She went over to the vase and drew in a deep breath. "That jasmine smells so good."

Jasmine. The garden. James had clearly thought about which flowers to send this morning. This was not a random arrangement put together by his assistant. This was a bouquet meant to give her pause, give her something to think about. Her brain felt jumbled and disorganized. She did not know what she wanted to do. A large part of her wanted to turn away and never contact him again. But there was a small piece of her that couldn't deny the physical attraction she had for him, the desire to be kissed by him again. And again.

Shaking her head in an attempt to clear it of any further

thoughts of James for the moment, she turned to Caroline and said, "I'm going to take a shower. I need a break. We can talk about this later."

"Okay. Just keep an open mind. It might be fun and if I think, after meeting James, that he's not for you, I swear to never mention his name again."

"Right. You know better than to make me that sort of promise. You won't be able to keep it and I'll be upset with you instead of with him."

"Challenge accepted. I'll be here, literally smelling the roses, when you are done."

Julie walked off to her room, stripped out of her sweaty exercise clothing and threw on her robe, leaving her phone on the bed. Then she went into the bathroom, turned the water to its hottest setting and stepped into the stall. The stinging spray felt good on her tired muscles and after she washed, she switched to a cold rinse which went a long way toward clearing her mind from her dizzying morning. By the time she dried off and put on a pair of jeans and a clean white tee shirt, she felt much better. She picked up her phone and glanced at the screen, her knees going weak at the message that was displayed there:

GOOD MORNING DAUGHTER. LOOKS LIKE YOU'RE DOING WELL FOR *yourself. I saw the picture of you in Tell All on the arm of that rich guy. I think it's time for you to increase in my allowance seeing as you must be flush with cash. Simply put: Share the wealth and I'll leave you alone.*

Mom

THIS DAY HAD JUST GONE FROM BAD TO WORSE. JULIE STOOD alone in her bedroom, still as she could be for a long minute. So much for thinking that no one saw those pictures on the internet. All of a sudden James' offer of money took on new meaning. It shifted the power away from her and gave it back to the woman whose very existence could destroy the life Julie so carefully created for herself. It wasn't fair, but she knew right away exactly what she had to do and she didn't like it at all. She was going to have to see James again and possibly accept his offer. She'd keep it all business, perhaps draw up a simple contract with terms she could live with, something that made sense and suited both their needs. With that thought, she threw herself down on her bed, buried her head in her pillow and tried to block out the world on the other side of her bedroom door. She'd worked so hard to make a life for herself. This would be a set-back, for sure, but she'd make it through in one piece. She would not lose herself, or worse yet, lose her heart to a man who offered her money to play act alongside him and deceive his own father.

Truth be told, she was worth much more than he could ever pay her. She knew that deep down in her soul. Now if she could only remember that the next time she saw him. He was charming, all right. But she was smart. That had to count for something.

Chapter Eleven

JAMES SAT BACK on the sofa in his apartment late that afternoon, advertising reports spread out on the coffee table in front of him and waited. He had confirmation that the flowers had been delivered. Now it was Julie's move. He prayed that she would change her mind and that he would hear from her.

He and Ryan had chiseled out a plan. Hopefully, the flowers would soften Julie just enough for James to get a second chance. He thought about her, how wonderful her lips felt against his own, how sweet she smelled, how she fit so perfectly in his arms. He had been with a lot of women, yet none of them had gotten under his skin the way Julie had. It was unnerving.

Could I have been a bigger idiot? he asked himself. *Why did I ever think that she'd go for the money?*

Of course, there was still the issue of his father. It was only a matter of time before he had to tell the old man that he couldn't bring Julie to the house the following weekend because she wanted nothing more to do with him. James could picture it all now. His dad, shaking his head, once again disappointed by something that James had done. It was somewhat understandable. As a boy, he had given his parents a very hard time. He'd been kicked out of one school after another until they finally sent him away to a strict boarding institution that prided itself on discipline as a core course and part of a young man's education. By the time he was ready to graduate, James had finally pulled himself together enough to attend university and experience the newspaper business from the bottom up. As a college student, James worked at the lowest level of *Tell All*. Ben had him learn the hard way—starting with the proper procedure for how to run a delivery route, to understanding the basic layout of the paper, deciding what was important enough to print, to selling ad space and writing copy, and for all of it, James proved himself to be an eager student and a fast learner.

What James discovered after his training was done was that he'd surprised his father. He realized that the other man kept waiting for the second shoe to drop, and when it didn't his dad reacted in the only way he knew how. He doubled down. Under Ben's watchful eye, James had soaked in every detail and subtlety of the business and quickly climbed the corporate ladder until he deserved the corner office he now occupied. It hadn't been easy, but it had been worth it. Along with his success came a long line of women who were all too happy to be seen on James' arm, to enjoy the fast life and to willingly warm his bed, fulfilling his every desire. Until he met Julie, he didn't realize just how empty his life was, how he had become as predictable as the damned celebrities *Tell All* covered. There was nothing real in his life, nothing at all. Except for Julie. In the brief time he'd known her, she had made it impossible for him to go back to the way things had been for him.

He felt his phone vibrate in his pocket. Reaching in, he pulled out the device and stared at the screen. *She had sent him a text!* He quickly read it:

. . .

James. Thank you for your thoughtful gift. I don't know if it will change anything between us, but I'm willing to give this one more try. A Friday night boat ride with Caroline and Stephen sounds good. Please let me know where we should meet you.
   Julie

James could not believe the words were actually there on the screen, so he re-read her short message again. She was going to give him another chance! Holy shit! He jumped up off the couch, feeling rejuvenated. There was hope in his heart as he thought about the proper words to text back in response:

Julie. I'm so happy that you've agreed to try again. My driver will be waiting for you and your friends outside of your apartment building promptly at 7:15 on Friday evening. I'm looking forward to all of us getting better acquainted. I promise, you won't regret this.
   James

Short and sweet. He absolutely didn't want to do anything to scare her off again, so he hit the send button and waited for a response.

James,
   Let's hope not.
   Julie

He read her brief response and smiled. Now all he had to do was let his father know that he'd be taking his boat out for a sail with Julie and her friends, that she'd agreed to see him again. That would have to be enough to appease the old man, at least for now. He considered texting, but decided to hold off and speak to his father instead to explain. However, that conversation could wait. He went back to the reports in front of him with a fresh outlook, feeling hopeful that his second chance with Julie would be the magic he so desperately needed.

❧

THE NEXT DAY JAMES SAT AT THE DESK IN HIS OFFICE AND punched the familiar number onto the screen. He had spent the better part of the prior evening deciding what he'd say and he was determined to set his plan in motion without having his father throw a wrench in the works. Once the phone connected, he said, "Hello, dad."

"James. What can I do for you?"

"Just wanted you to know that I will be seeing Julie again on Friday night. I offered her a ride on my sailboat. She's bringing some friends."

"Hmm. Well. I guess I should be pleased that she forgave you for whatever transgression you committed at the gala. I'll give you a pass this time. But I do want you to bring her around the house. Your mother would like to meet her."

"Let's see what happens after the boat ride, dad. No promises."

"James, I think that you know I'm serious about not loosening the reins on *Tell All* until you settle down some. I'm not going anywhere until you show me that you're done leading the life of a rogue run-around."

"That's hardly who I am and you know it."

"No. I really don't. Prove it and we'll see what happens after that. You're on the clock, son. Really." The line went dead.

James looked at his phone in disbelief. His father was not giving in any time soon. Despite all of his success running the family business, he still needed to prove himself to the old man. Not just him, either. James needed a rock solid plan to impress Julie and her friends, to make her feel confident that he was worthy of her, not the fool he'd been with her before. He needed to take them somewhere fun, comfortable and not too over the top. That's when inspiration hit. He opened his phone and scrolled through the list of contacts, pressing the name he'd been searching for. He waited until he heard the familiar voice on the other end pick up.

"Kelly's Marina. How can I help you?"

James smiled at the sound of the thick Irish brogue on the other end of the call. "Liam! Good to hear your voice. It's James Curran."

"James! It's been too long. How the hell are you?"

"Great, man. Hope you are too. I'd like to take *Isabel* out on Friday night. Can you have her ready?"

"Of course! I'll have her sparkling clean and set to go. What time?"

"I'll be at the dock at 7:00 and some friends will join me shortly thereafter. Is that all right with you?"

"Yes, it's good. Should I stock the fridge? Is this a dinner cruise?"

"Um, no. Just a cheese plate would be great. I think we'll eat at Mac's after we get back. I'll bring along the rest of what I need this time."

"Sounds great. See you then," Liam replied.

"Can't wait," James responded, then ended the call. He sat back in his chair and smiled.

Just then Claire walked into his office with a cup of coffee which she placed on his desk in front of him. "What's gotten into you?" she asked, noting his expression.

"What do you mean?"

"You're smiling. That's the first time all day."

"Is it?" He shuffled some papers, not wanting to explain himself to his assistant and added, "The ad revenue is up. That's all."

He watched as she looked at him suspiciously.

"Whatever you say, boss." She turned to leave.

"One more thing. Could you make a reservation in my name at Mac's on Friday night? Four people at 9."

She nodded on her way out the door. "Of course."

"Thanks," he said before turning his chair to look out the window. This was a solid plan. Now, if it only worked.

⁂

THE REST OF THE WEEK SEEMED TO CRAWL BY AT A SNAIL'S pace. As he sat at his desk on Thursday afternoon, James considered his options for what they would drink before dinner while he took his passengers on a ride around the city. He wanted to have a chilled champagne ready, it was just a matter of which one to choose. Something light and not too intimidating. He ran a list of the options in his head when a lightbulb went off. He'd pick up a bottle of Perrier-Jouet Bell Epoque. Perhaps the flowers painted on the bottle would make Julie think of the garden outside of the gala. He wanted desperately to go back to the time before he'd made that rude proposition to her later that very same night. Satisfied with his selection, James went back to work.

BY THE TIME FRIDAY ROLLED AROUND, JAMES COULD BARELY contain his excitement. He would be seeing Julie again in a few short hours and he had a lovely bottle of champagne chilling in his refrigerator at home, just waiting to be brought to the dock. By late afternoon, he could no longer concentrate on the work that he knew could actually keep until the following week. He quickly shuffled the papers into a neat pile and walked out of his office, letting Claire know that he was leaving and giving her the rest of the day off as well.

"Thanks, boss!" was all she said as she shut down her computer and grabbed her purse. "It is a beautiful afternoon out there."

"I hope you do something that allows you to enjoy it," was his response as they made their way together into the waiting elevator. The ride to the ground floor was short, and at the first moment she could exit, Claire quickly turned to him and said, "See you Monday!" Then she was gone, disappearing into the crowded lobby. He smiled to himself. Maybe he should consider letting the staff work half days on Fridays in the summertime. It was an easy perk to offer, and the rewards might be worth it. Happy employees made for a better work environment for him, too. He pushed his way through the set of revolving doors and stepped into the bright sunshine. Charlie sat waiting for him in the car.

"Good afternoon," James said to his driver. "I'm going home for a bit, then I'll be heading to Williamsburg. We'll leave for Kelly's Marina at 6:45 tonight. After you drop me off, I'd like you to pick up some friends and bring them over as well."

"Of course, Mr. Curran. Just send me the address."

"You've actually been there. It's Ms. Porter's apartment building."

"Oh, yes. No worries, sir. I've got this handled." Charlie smiled knowingly, then turned and steered the car into traffic. It was a Friday afternoon in the city and it seemed to James that everyone was headed out to be somewhere else. The stop and go motion made him feel sleepy and he closed his eyes, drifting off to thoughts of Julie and second chances.

A FEW HOURS LATER, FRESHLY SHOWERED WITH A BOTTLE OF chilled champagne in hand, James stepped out of the car once again, this time waterside in Brooklyn. It was perfect weather for a boat ride and James could not wait to take Julie out to watch the sunset. He felt as if the evening ahead was full of possibilities. He walked down to the dock where he saw Liam waiting for him.

"James," the burly man shouted out his greeting.

"Liam. It's great to see you!" James replied, grasping the other man's hand in his own, warmly shaking it.

"What a night you've got here. It's lovely out on the river. Barely a ripple of a wave."

"I'm looking forward to it. I don't think I'll raise the sails though. Not enough wind. I'll stick with the motor for now."

"Agreed. You'd be better off to raise the sails when you're out on open waters anyway. Just a short sightseeing cruise, I'm guessing?" Liam asked with a smile.

"Exactly what I had in mind. But I'll be back, soon I hope, for a longer ride."

"Sounds good. Just let me know when you want to go out again and I'll have her ready for you. Text when you return tonight and I'll be sure to tighten her down until the next time." He turned to go.

"Thanks again."

"Of course," Liam said as he headed back toward the marina's office.

James stepped aboard the *Isabel*. He'd named the boat after his maternal grandmother, who he fondly remembered as the only person who truly understood him when he was young. His grandma Isabel was fun-loving and adventurous. She used to take him for long walks in Central Park where they'd pretend to be on a search for wild animals. Even though they never saw anything bigger than a raccoon, his grandmother would spin stories that made him believe that anything was possible. Lions? Tigers? Zebras? All of those animals and more made appearances in Grandma Isabel's tales. James used to look forward to spending time with her, until his father put an end to what he termed "frivolous activities" all together once James was shipped off to boarding school. When she died, James was sure that the happiest, most carefree days of his life were behind him. But then he met Julie. He only wished, in this moment, that his grandmother could have met her too.

He glanced at his watch. It was almost time for Charlie to return with his passengers. James went below deck. There was a bedroom, a bathroom and kitchen on the lower level of the ship. It was comfortable enough to spend some real time here traveling around the east coast. He'd once sailed all the way to the Bahamas with a wild group of women. James shook his head. He was pretty sure those boisterous days were now behind him. He grabbed the ice bucket and four champagne flutes and found the cheese plate and bunches of grapes that Liam had left for them in the squat fridge. Carefully juggling the small pre-dinner snack, he brought everything up on deck to the small table on the port side of the stern. There was one more short set of stairs that up led to the steering and navigation equipment at the helm of the ship. The mainsail sat midway between where he stood the bow. Even though the brightly striped canvas was currently stowed away, the mast still stood tall and looked majestic. The boat's hull was made of fiberglass and the trim was teak, polished to a gleaming finish by none other than Liam himself. This boat was

James' pride and joy and he couldn't wait to share it with Julie. Just then he heard a car door slam shut. James drew in a deep breath, counted to ten to calm his nerves and then went to greet his guests.

Chapter Twelve

"Julie," James said, his smile just as spectacular as she remembered, "Welcome aboard the *Isabel*."

She reached out and put her own hand in his outstretched one and immediately felt that now familiar warm shot of electricity at the contact.

"You look lovely tonight, Julie," he whispered as he helped her board his boat. She had worn a simple emerald green jersey wrap dress and a pair of wedged sandals, hoping to look casual yet polished. His compliment made her feel warm all over. She took a deep calming breath and then said, "Thank you. And thanks for having us here. This is my roommate Caroline Montgomery, and her fiancé, Stephen Millson."

"A pleasure to have you all aboard," James said warmly. "Let me get you settled on deck before we get underway." He brought them to the comfortable seating area at the back of the ship. Julie couldn't help but be amazed at her surroundings. This was not a little fishing boat; it was more a luxury yacht for the rich and famous, both of which were an apt description of their host. She watched as James effortlessly and immediately charmed

Caroline by complimenting her on her nautical outfit: a pair of wide bottomed navy sailor pants topped with a striped boat necked shirt sporting a three-quarter length bell sleeve. He engaged Stephen in an animated conversation about the slumping New York Yankees. James had made two new friends in a matter of minutes. All of that was before he'd actually even poured them a glass of what appeared to be an expensive champagne, the pretty painted bottle dripping water from the ice bath it had been nestled in.

"I thought we'd take a quick tour of lower Manhattan, slip back down and around the Statue of Liberty and then have dinner at one of my favorite seafood spots at the marina. How does that sound?" he asked the assembled group.

"I'd say it sounds great!" Caroline clapped her hands together almost spilling the contents of the glass James had just handed her.

"If I time this right, the sun should just about be setting as we tie up and dock back here. So please. Have something to eat, enjoy the wine and I'll get us underway."

Julie watched as he smoothly climbed the short set of stairs that led up to what looked like a large steering wheel and a whole lot of complicated electronic equipment.

"Julie," Caroline hissed. "Go. Get up there. Keep James company."

"I don't want to distract him from what he's doing," she replied, her eyes never leaving his form as he flipped a bunch of switches and then motioned to a marina worker to untie the ship from the dock.

"Are you nuts? He looks like a natural up there. Very capable. Something tells me that he can steer and chew gum at the same time. Go!"

Julie looked at Caroline's imploring stare and knew that her friend was right. She took a large sip of her champagne and carefully walked up the steps. Just as she reached where James stood, the boat picked up some speed as he navigated into deeper waters. She listed to one side before falling into him.

He reached out to catch her, drawing her close against the length of him. "We've got to stop meeting like this," he teased, clearly referencing the night when she tripped and spilled her drink all over his shirt.

She put her hand on his chest to steady herself, once again feeling the rock hard strength there. She couldn't stop her next thought, that this was a place she wished that she could explore further without the material between them. *Oh boy*, she mused. *If I go down this road there will be no coming back for me. I have to keep myself on track. Make a business arrangement, that's all.*

"I'm okay now," Julie said, stepping back, breathing a bit more quickly than normal. "I just needed to get my sea legs." His eyes burned brightly back at her, signaling that he was as affected as she was from the brief contact. She knew it would be best to change the subject. Looking out at the view in front of her, Julie exclaimed, "Wow! There's the Freedom Tower."

"Yes," he responded. "It's quite beautiful. I think of it as a sentinel, guarding the tip of Manhattan, along with the rest of the financial district. It's remarkable how much has been rebuilt down here since 9/11. Hell, it's amazing what's been restored from all the flooding when Hurricane Sandy hit us hard."

"Did the boat get badly damaged with all the rising water?" she asked.

"I was lucky. I didn't have the *Isabel* then. She probably would have been lost in that storm."

Julie shook her head. "I was uptown at school when that hurricane hit. It was pretty bad there, but no real flooding. Just no power for days on end. And then it got so cold, remember?"

"Yeah, I do. Too bad we didn't know each other back then. I could have taken you out to my parent's place. They didn't suffer at all – they have a whole house back-up generator. Hot coffee, hot water and heat were never an issue for them," he remarked.

"They were lucky," she answered.

"Or exceptionally privileged."

"Well, James, look around." She motioned to the fancy equipment in front of them. "I think that word applies here as well."

"True," he replied. "Believe me. I worked hard to get this far. I know it looks different from the outside, but I did work my way up the ladder of my father's business. He didn't make it easy and I didn't get anything without a whole lot of sweat equity. I appreciate everything that I have."

He looked so sincere that she wanted to believe him. "I'm sure you've worked hard, James. It's just that you had doors open for you because of your last name, too. It does make a difference."

"Is my name a problem for you, Julie?" he asked quietly.

She hesitated a moment before shaking her head. "No. It isn't. I guess that what I'm trying to say is that I'm not used to the public nature of your business or the media attention that follows you around. I'm a private person. I really didn't love seeing those pictures of us from the gala all over the tabloids and the internet." *And it caught my mother's eye. That's the reason that I'm out with you this evening.*

Or at least that's what she told herself. Standing here now, so close to James that she could smell his spicy scent made her wonder if she didn't have a dual purpose for accepting his invitation tonight. She could not deny the attraction she felt; it was palpable and she knew he was experiencing the same feeling. Her breath caught in her chest and she could hear her heart drumming an uneven beat in her ears. Her stomach tightened and she felt a serious sense of desire begin to pool there, dipping down lower until her legs felt as though they might not hold her upright for very much longer.

"Do you mind if I sit in your chair?" she asked, a bit out of breath.

"Please do," he said, helping her into the captain's seat.

He leaned in and with his arms on either side of her, he turned the wheel of the ship and they headed out of the East River into the Upper New York Bay as he maneuvered the *Isabel* toward the Statue. When he was set on course, he started to point out various navigational buoys and markers in the waters ahead of them. Julie could tell that James was very comfortable out on the water and that he truly enjoyed sharing this passion for boating with her. It felt almost a bit too natural to have him this close to her; he fit around her like a caress and she wanted to stay in his warmth for as long as she could.

"If you'd like, you can take over," he murmured into her ear.

"Really?" she asked, turning her face toward his. Her eyes burned with excitement.

"Of course. I'm right behind you if you need help."

He lifted his hands off of the steering wheel and placed hers there instead. "Steady as she goes, captain," he teased. "Just keep us heading toward Lady Liberty."

Julie turned back toward her target and felt the rumble of the ship's motor as she held tightly onto the cool metal. She could not believe how powerful she felt, bringing them ever closer to the custodian of the harbor ahead. The statue loomed large as they drew near. She really was a spectacular sight to see.

"This is really special, James. Thank you for letting us come out on the water with you tonight."

He leaned in close to her ear and whispered, "I really wanted to see you again."

She turned around and looked into James' deep brown eyes. She saw her own desire mirrored there and was not at all surprised when he kissed her. It was soft and tentative at first, but then he dipped his tongue in her mouth to explore her further and she could feel her insides liquify instantly. This was not an ordinary date and James was not an ordinary man. Despite the fact that she was wary of him, his wealth and his lifestyle, she could not control her own body's reaction to his nearness; she matched his passion with her own. They tangled their tongues even deeper, igniting a flame between them that Julie knew was going to be hard to douse. He pulled away first, glanced up at the horizon and immediately put his hands over hers on the wheel.

"Time to turn this ship around," was all he said.

For a minute she wondered if he meant their relationship. Their kiss was hanging in the air between them, leaving them both a bit unsteady on their feet. In that moment, Julie realized that it was way too late for her to return to her delusion that this was just going to be a business transaction between them. She was actually falling for this guy and she didn't know how to stop herself from drowning.

❦

ONCE JAMES NAVIGATED THEM BACK TO LAND, HE QUICKLY jumped onto the dock and tied the boat with precise knots onto the small metal posts that served to secure it safely. He then helped both Julie and Caroline out, lifting each one of the women over the side of the *Isabel* with ease. Stephen was able to make it out on his own.

"That was really wonderful, James. Thanks so much for the tour," Caroline said sweetly.

"Well, I hope you'll all come back out for a day trip sometime this summer. We can hit the open water and actually use the sail. It's a lot of fun."

"I would love that," Caroline responded.

James turned to Julie. "I've made reservations for the four of us for dinner. It's a short walk. Is that good with you?"

"Of course," she replied as she watched Caroline's eyes widen in agreement.

He offered her his arm. "Right this way," he said, leading the group to a seafood restaurant at the base of the pier.

It was a cozy spot, with small, sparkly lights hanging across a patio filled with an informal, summertime crowd. Each wooden table had a bucket filled with plastic bibs, nut crackers, mallets and extra napkins. There was a blackboard over the lively outdoor bar with a list of fresh seafood available that night, as well as the names of the local beers on tap. It was so different than the private club he'd taken her to after the gala.

"This place looks great!" Stephen exclaimed. "I love the vibe here."

"I've been coming here since Mac opened it. He serves the freshest seafood around. Everything is caught on the east coast, some of it locally, delivered daily and always delicious. If you like a lobster roll, you're in the right spot."

"Who doesn't love that?" Caroline asked.

Just then the waiter came by and took their drink orders. The group decided to try a pitcher of a local ale as well as a dark porter. A few moments later, frosty glasses appeared, were filled and comparisons were made and discussed at length.

This is fun, Julie thought. She fought the impulse to allow images of her mother to ruin her evening. She would figure it all out, but not tonight. For right now, she would give herself permission to enjoy this precious break from her biggest problems. As they drank the contents of the pitchers and had them refilled one more time, the conversation flowed. Caroline told James all about the lingerie business, probably more details than he ever needed to know; James and Stephen bonded over a shared love of both New York sports teams and deep sea fishing.

Right before dinner was to be brought out to their table, the effects of multiple glasses of beer took a toll on Julie's bladder. She excused herself for a quick trip to the ladies' room and Caroline took the opportunity to join her.

"Julie," her friend exclaimed, grabbing onto her arm when they were out of the men's earshot. "James is great. I don't know what you were so nervous about. He seems to really like you. What gives?"

Julie pushed open the bathroom door and pulled the other woman inside with her. "I know. It's just that –"

"Don't you even start making excuses for why you can't be involved. That's what you always do. This guy is the real deal." Caroline stepped into a stall and shut the door. Julie did the same, but over the thin plastic wall, Caroline continued to lecture her. "There is no good reason, no reason at all, why you shouldn't follow through on this. He made a mistake at the gala, but surely tonight makes up for that, right?"

Julie thought back to the kiss they just shared on the *Isabel*. "I suppose," she replied.

"Good. Then it's settled. He can be your plus one at our wedding."

Julie heard the flush of the toilet, finished peeing and did the same thing. She met Caroline out by the sinks where her friend was already washing her hands.

"Here's what's going to happen. After dinner, I'll claim exhaustion. Stephen and I will leave. You stay. Have another drink. Let the rest of your night develop, however it does. I won't be expecting you home until much later. If at all."

"That's crazy. Nothing is going to happen."

"You're so wrong. I know what I know. You've both got it bad."

"Got it bad?"

"Yeah. Lust. It's written all over your faces. Stop fighting the feeling, Julie, and for once in your life, don't do the proper thing. Just have some fun."

· "Easier said than done, Caroline. It's complicated."

"How? We're out with two handsome men and we're about to eat lobster. What's left to discuss?"

For once, the way Caroline summed it all up was true. And Julie could not find the words or the strength to summon an argument.

AFTER A DELICIOUS MEAL CAPPED OFF WITH A RIDICULOUSLY large, shared hot fudge sundae, Caroline put her spoon down and exclaimed, "I'm so full. I need to go home and lie down."

Julie stifled a laugh. "Are you sure you don't want one more drink?"

"No. We should go."

Julie watched as the other woman shot her fiancé a look that meant business.

James stood. "It was really nice to meet you both. We have to do this again soon."

"Absolutely. And we'll make it out to Yankee Stadium for a game, too," Stephen added.

"Sounds good, man," James replied. He shook Stephen's hand and leaned over to put a chaste kiss on Caroline's cheek. "Safe home you two. Charlie will take you and then circle back for us."

Julie watched as Stephen put his arm around Caroline and led toward the street. Then she turned her attention to James.

"Thank you for a lovely evening. I had a really nice time."

"Can I convince you to have one more drink with me?" he asked, signaling the waiter. Once the young man appeared, he asked, "May I have the check, please?"

"Oh," Julie said, confused. "I thought you wanted another drink."

"I do. But not here," he replied. "I thought we could have it on the deck of the *Isabel.* I just want to be sure that she's all tucked in."

"Doesn't the marina handle that for you?" she asked.

"Most of the time. I could text Liam and ask him but we're so close by, I can just take care of it myself. It's such a nice night. I promise, it won't take me long."

"Okay," she replied, her mind beginning to race. *Keep it together, Julie. It's just one drink under the stars. What could possibly happen?*

Chapter Thirteen

THE SHORT WALK back to the boat was uneventful enough, despite the fact that James took her hand in his and held it until they were back onboard. The friction she felt as he wound his fingers around her own made her heart beat a bit faster in anticipation. He sat her down on the comfortable couch at the bow of the ship then said, "Don't move. I'll be right back." He disappeared down the short flight of steps to the cabin below to find them something to drink.

Looking around, Julie noticed that the *Isabel* looked pretty tucked in already, and she realized that Liam had already been here, cleaning up after them. *So James just wanted to extend our evening.* She craned her neck to see if he was on his way back up yet, but when he didn't seem to be, she turned her gaze skyward. It was moonless night, chockful of stars. Tilting her head fully back against the cushions, Julie couldn't help but marvel at the softness of the warm summer air against her skin and the beauty of her surroundings. She tried to take it all in, to be in the moment, and to breathe. That's when James returned with a glass of red wine for each of them. She smiled as she took the drink from him. He sat down next to her.

"Thank you," she said.

"You're most welcome. Star gazing? Are you an amateur astronomer?" he asked with a smile that made her feel woozy.

"No. Not at all," she replied. "It's just that I haven't seen a sky like this in a long while. Living in the city, you never see stars. Too many streetlights. It's darker here at the marina."

"This is nothing. You have to come out onto the ocean with me one night. It's magical."

I can only imagine, she thought. *Dreamy, in fact.*

"I'm sure it is," she responded.

He cleared his throat. "Listen, Julie. I hope that you'll forgive me now for what happened after the gala. What I proposed to you was completely inappropriate. Please, forget I ever said it. You had every right never to speak to me again, but here's the thing. I like you. I really do. And I'd like to keep seeing you, if you'll let me."

A thrill shot up her spine at the same time that her brain processed the information. *Does this mean that his offer is off the table? If it is, what am I going to about my mother's threats? Damn it!* She realized she had to answer him and her brain scrambled for a coherent response.

"I like you, too, James. We all make mistakes. I'll forgive you for last week, but please try to understand that your world, your lifestyle, it's... well it's a lot. More than that, I'm not comfortable with all the media attention. I like my privacy."

Sh watched as he let out a breath and said, "I get it, Julie, I do. That's why we're here, on the *Isabel*. It's just us. No reporters, no cameras. And you have no idea just how much I appreciate you accepting my apology. If it's okay, we can enjoy this wine and get a little better acquainted. Tell me something about you, something I don't know already. Where did you grow up? Were you a tomboy or a Barbie sort of girl? Do your parents still live in your hometown?"

Ugh. Just the subject I want to avoid. Think fast.

She skirted the topic as artfully as she could. "New Jersey. Near Philly. But I'm a New Yorker now. I have been living here for a number of years," she hesitated, but then said, "my parents are gone."

"Oh, Julie. I'm so sorry to hear that. Is that a recent thing or –"

"No," she answered abruptly cutting off the line of conversation. "It happened a long time ago. I don't like to talk about it."

She felt herself digging an even deeper hole of deceit. She could see that he was uncomfortable with her abrupt answer and was glad when in the next breath he switched gears to safer territory.

"Do you like living in the city?"

"I do. How about you?"

"I like knowing I can leave when I want to unwind. It's true, what they say, you know. New York never sleeps. Sometimes I just want to go somewhere else, somewhere quiet."

"Really? Because you seem to like the nightlife. I mean, I've seen photos of you out and about..."

He smiled. "I do a lot of that for business. I prefer being here, on this ship." Then he leaned in and said, "I really love that you're here with me. I don't share this experience with very many other people."

Julie could feel a warm flush travel through her body. She took a small sip of her drink trying to think of the perfect reply, but his nearness made her brain feel fuzzy. It was maddening. She struggled to keep the glass she still held in her hand upright and not spill any of the deep ruby liquid onto the deck as the heat of his body next to her own made her feel shaky. She could tell that he sensed that she was uncomfortable when he gracefully took the wine from her hand and put it on the small table in front of them. She felt a sudden jolt when his fingers grazed her own, a magnetism that charged the air between them that she could not ignore.

Before Julie could say anything, he moved even closer and put his lips on hers, kissing her gently. She could not stop him or help herself. The combination of his touch, his proximity, and his scent threw her senses into overload. She wanted more. She kissed him back and tasted the alcohol on his tongue as it teased her own. Then he turned and shifted his attention to her neck, nipping and gently grazing his mouth downward toward her collarbone. Despite the now cool night air, she felt warmth pooling between her legs. Her body could not deny what her brain wanted to forget: he was incredibly sexy and she wanted him. All of him.

"Julie," he whispered in her ear. "Come below deck with me. There's a bedroom..."

"Isn't Charlie on his way back to get us?" she asked breathlessly.

He looked at her and smiled. "I'm the boss. I can give him the rest of the night off."

The air between them was crackling with electricity, the energy between them was palpable.

Her eyes widened and she said nothing. He stood and reached for her hand, pulling her up against the length of him. "I want you. What do you want, Julie?"

Instead of overthinking or coming up with a smart answer, she decided to go with her body's reaction to him. She ran her fingers along the fabric of his shirt, finding her way to the buttons and slowly undoing the top few so that she could feel the skin beneath. She heard the sharp intake of his breath as she bowed her head a bit to touch her lips to his exposed chest.

"I like that," he said. "I want more..." James then lifted her into his arms and carried her down the steps to the cabin below, walking past the small living area into the sleeping quarters at the bow. It was a small space dominated by a king size bed that stretched almost from one wall to the other. Narrow night tables were the only other furniture in the room. James placed her carefully down in front of the bed and reached for the tie that secured her dress to her body. Then he slowly pulled on it and it released, the garment falling open, exposing her to his gaze. For once she was happy that she'd given into Caroline's request that she wear the same lingerie she'd worn on her first date with him at the bar. The black, lacy set made her feel empowered, just like her friend had promised.

James released a sharp breath as he urged the dress off of her shoulders and watched it pool to the floor in a puddle of green fabric. "You. Are. So. Beautiful."

Julie quickly stepped out of her shoes and kicked them into a corner. Then she finished unbuttoning his shirt, slipping the soft cotton down off of his arms until his chest was fully exposed. She lightly ran her fingers over his finely chiseled muscles and could feel the strength of him beneath his skin. He was sexy and strong and she felt the overwhelming need to see the rest of him naked as well. She reached for his belt but he put his hand over hers.

"Wait," he murmured. "I want to see all of you first."

Her heart beat faster at his bold statement, her blood coursing through her body, drumming incessantly in her thighs, her stomach, her core. She reached around to undo her bra but he stopped her.

"Let me," was all he said.

Her breathing became shallow as his fingers lightly caressed her back. He deftly unclasped the small hooks there until the lace fell away, exposing her breasts to the night air. She felt her nipples grow taut immediately and she thrust herself forward. She ached to have him touch her.

When he did, it was with his lips and tongue and she thought that she might combust with the thrill of it all. He was gentle yet insistent; the warmth of his mouth bathed her in sensation until she thought she could bear it no more. She needed him. Now. Julie reached for his belt once again and this time he did not stop her. She fumbled with the buckle, finally releasing it and undoing the top button and fly zipper so that she could pull down the garment and have all of him for herself. She'd forgotten his shoes however, and he laughed at her impatience.

"I'll get those," he smirked, kicking off his loafers and removing his pants in one swift motion.

She gasped at his erection clearly peeking out from behind his boxers. She watched as he slowly removed those as well, now standing fully naked before her.

"Your turn," he said, his eyes holding her gaze. Then his fingers lightly grazed her skin as he inched down the tiny lace thong. He got to his knees and kissed her there and her world shrunk to the space where all of her body's awareness originated. No man had ever worshipped her in this way; she could barely keep herself upright and on her feet.

He must have sensed that she was overcome by this amount of stimulation because he briefly stopped and laid her back on the mattress against the large pillows resting on the headboard. "Protection? Birth control?" he asked.

"I've got us covered," she replied breathlessly. "I promise."

Finding his place once again, his tongue magically worked and ignited every fiber of her being. Julie felt overcome with desire for him and despite being near the precipice of pleasure, said, "James, please. I want you inside of me. Now."

In one quick moment he was, slowly at first, stretching her to her limits with the length and width of him. Once he was fully seated within her, they began to move in a rhythm all their own. She felt everything; every ridge and inch of him pulsing as he thrust forward and filled her with powerful waves of energy. As her own orgasm rolled over her she was left breathless, clinging to him in an effort to stay rooted to the moment. She may have been with other men before James, but he had just made it incredibly difficult for her to imagine giving herself to another ever again in the future. This felt like some sort of magic.

"Julie," he whispered. "Open your eyes."

When she did, she saw her own expression mirrored in his and she knew one thing for sure. She was headed for trouble. There would be no avoiding it. Her carefully curated image, the polite and proper persona she tried so hard to maintain, it all just fell away. There, in his arms, she felt like a fully different person. Someone awake and alive. Her problems: where she was going to find a cheaper place to live, her next book project, her mother's sudden reemergence, all of it, just faded into the background. She wanted to stay here, with James, in this gently rocking ship in the dark of night, never to leave this cocoon of warmth and serenity.

"How do you feel?" he asked, interrupting her own inner monologue, his fingers gently running up and down her back.

"Good," she murmured. "Really good."

"Julie, that was..."

"Shhh," was all she said, as she drifted off into a very peaceful sleep.

WHEN JULIE WOKE THE NEXT MORNING SHE WAS FULLY disoriented. Unsure of where she was and unable to place the gentle sway of the room she was in, she felt something heavy resting on her stomach. She looked around and saw James' bare chest exposed as he lay next to her, his arm splayed out on her mid-section. The memory of the night before came rushing back to her and she struggled to sit up, not wanting to disturb him but desperately needing to pee. She gently moved his appendage and slowly crept out of the bed in search of the bathroom. She really didn't want to think about the mechanics of the toilet as she was sure that there must be some sort of tank system for waste, but as she sat down she just felt grateful to be able to relieve herself while tied to the dock.

The night before had been more than amazing, but nothing had truly changed. She really liked James. She just didn't know what she was going to do about it. After she finished and washed her hands, she tiptoed into the bedroom, picked his discarded shirt up off of the floor and threw it over her naked body. She stepped back into the small living area and found her purse. She lifted out her phone. Despite the low battery warning, she saw at least a dozen texts from Caroline the night before:

WILL YOU BE COMING HOME LATER?
 Are you still with James?
 Having fun yet?
 You're okay, right?
 Right?!?

INSTEAD OF HAVING TO GO INTO A LONG EXPLANATION OVER the phone, she made the quick decision to fill her friend in once she was back home. With a sigh, Julie dropped the device into her bag and returned to the bathroom to wash her face. The woman staring back at her had wild sex hair and mascara under her eyes. She hurried to do as much damage control as she could, even finding a tube of toothpaste, spreading some on her forefinger and rubbing it over her teeth. She was almost done rinsing out her mouth when a very naked James appeared in the small doorway.

"Good morning, Julie." He flashed her his megawatt smile. "How are you feeling today?"

Startled, she squeaked out, "Fine. You?"

"I feel great!" he replied, squeezing behind her, his rapid response to seeing her standing there apparent. "Just give me a minute and I'll show you what I mean."

"Oh, of course," she fumbled her way out of the bathroom, leaving him in privacy to complete whatever it was he planned on doing. A minute later, he returned.

"My shirt looks even better on you than it did on me," he teased.

She pulled it closer to her body. "I hope you don't mind. It was the only thing I could find to put on."

"Mind? No, of course not. I'd just like it back now, please." This time his expression was one of pure desire.

Seeing the fire in his eyes, she felt her blood ignite once more. "I guess you'll have to come and get it then," she whispered.

"With pleasure," he said, reaching out for her and pulling her in close.

Her last thought before complete surrender to the pleasure he offered her was that she should charge her phone. But then again, the only person she really wanted to have contact with was already deeply connected inside her and communicating in the most primal way possible. The outside world, with all of its conflict and dilemmas, would have to wait. For right now, Julie gave herself permission to live in the moment, consequences be damned.

Chapter Fourteen

BY THE TIME James dropped her off at home early Sunday morning, Julie knew that she was going to have to re-think everything. They'd spent all of Saturday on a wash, rinse and repeat cycle of intimacy. Aside from the sex being a mind and body bending experience, she found herself truly attracted to him. James was charming and interesting; he was well-read and well-traveled. They had a shared love of Ken Follet novels and of Paris, of dim sum and merlot. If she didn't know better, she'd say that he was her perfect match. Except for the part where he published a gossip machine that went against every principle she held dear; the right to privacy and the need to adhere to the basic rules of social etiquette. Julie believed that without strict guidelines there would be no grace left in the world; James' business represented the antithesis of that very thing.

Even though he told her over and over again that he wanted to change the direction of *Tell All,* to make it more legit and honest, she wasn't sure just how he would do that with his father still tightly holding the reigns with both hands. James had kept to his word and hadn't mentioned his original proposition again, however, she knew that he needed to present himself as a serious family minded individual if he was ever to gain control of the paper. His father had made that clear, and there was no way around it. She was just beginning to formulate a thought about just how she could help James achieve his goals without feeling like a fraud when she reached her front door. She took a deep breath and turned the key in the lock, knowing that her roommate would be waiting to hear all the juicy details of her night, much of which she simply did not want to share.

When she stepped into the apartment, the first thing she noticed was that it looked like a tornado had passed through. There were moving boxes and packing tape strewn around, stacks of books and sketch pads piled high in every corner of the main living space and half the pots and pans cleared from the kitchen cabinets and left out on the countertop.

"Caroline?" she called out. "Are you here?"

Julie heard what sounded like a muffled response from her friend's bedroom. She made her way across the apartment and opened the door. It was a wild scene. The closet was empty, but the bed was awash with colorful clothing. It was as if a bomb made of silk and lace had gone off leaving a hodgepodge of a wardrobe in its wake. Caroline was sitting on the floor in a frothy pink concoction of feathers and satin.

"What the hell happened?" Julie asked.

"What do you mean?" Caroline replied. "I have to pack, don't I?"

"Yes, but in an organized way, don't you think?"

"I have a system. I just have to remember what it is."

Julie looked more closely at her friend. Her eyes were blood-shot and she looked like she had been crying.

"Are you okay? Where's Stephen?"

"He's packing his place. And no, I don't think I'm okay." She sniffed dramatically.

"Why? Did you two have a fight?"

"Not exactly. I was worried when you didn't answer my texts. I wanted to go back to the marina and see if you were still there. Stephen told me not to go. He was sure that you were out with James and were fine." She looked up at Julie. "Are you fine?"

"Yes, yes, of course. My phone died, that's all." *Well, it did finally give out. I saw your texts, I just wanted to delay this moment as long as I could.*

"Julie. I'm not sure if I'm ready for this move. It seems so final."

"What do you mean?"

"I'm getting married. You know, like committing to Stephen for eternity."

"Are you getting cold feet?"

"It's not that. I mean, I love Stephen with all my heart. But I love our BFF life, too."

Julie left the doorway and went to sit down on the floor next to her friend, moving aside what seemed like six dozen pairs of thong undies.

"Nothing's really going to change," she said softly. "We'll still go out and have our own fun."

Caroline looked up at her. "C'mon," she began. "We live together and I can't get you to cut loose most of the time. What are the odds of me being able to do that once we're no longer roomies? You'll turn into a hermit for sure!"

"No, I won't. Besides, I went out with you and look what happened. I met James."

Caroline sat up straighter and pushed a stray curl out of her eye. "Yes, yes you did. Were you with him this whole time?"

"I was," Julie responded.

"And?" her roommate asked.

"It was truly something," Julie answered.

"O.M.G. I knew it. I just knew he was the real deal." She

pushed herself up off of the floor, instantly revived. "I want to hear everything. But I need coffee first. And a shower. I was up all night packing and worrying about you."

Julie looked around. It didn't appear that Caroline actually put anything into a box, but she wasn't going to argue the point, especially since she saw an opening.

"How about I run down to Viand and grab us each an egg sandwich and a large coffee? We can clear off the countertop and have brunch in the kitchen. I'll tell you what happened with James. Then I can help you pack."

"That's perfect. Our favorite NYC diner breakfast. Make mine with swiss cheese on a sesame bagel, okay?"

"Of course. I'll be back in fifteen minutes. We can hash all of this out then." *And I can figure out what to tell you about my night and what to leave out...*

On the two block walk to pick up their food, Julie decided that she had to come clean to Caroline about the fact that she slept with James. She had no real option because she knew that her friend would get the information out of her one way or another. She decided not to divulge the fact that she was developing true feelings for him though. For now, she would keep that to herself, her own personal secret, at least until she figured out the depths of her own feelings for him. Only then could she share this with Caroline. As for the man in question, she had some thoughts about him as well. What if she asked James for a loan in exchange for posing as his girlfriend for a night at his parents' home? She didn't have to tell him the exact purpose for the exchange of money or that her own mother was actually alive and extorting her; once she received the advance for her next book, she would pay him back. *This could work, right?*

Julie entered the diner and placed her to-go order with the cashier. Then she lifted her phone out of her bag. She still hadn't charged it and it was completely useless. She wondered if James had tried to call her. Highly unlikely, since they hadn't been apart that long. She sat down on one of the stools at the high counter while she waited, her mind drifting back to the early hours of this morning, to James' touch, to his tongue on her sensitive skin, to the way they could not seem to get enough of each other. She imagined what it might be like to actually be his girl-friend, to have access to his body whenever the mood struck her. It was a crazy thought, but one that lingered, or at least until her breakfast order was ready. The woman behind the register got Julie's attention by waving the check for the egg sandwiches in front of her face. Snapping out of the daydream, Julie paid the bill and went back to tell Caroline the version of the story that she felt she could share.

As they sat at their kitchen counter sipping the remnants of their coffee from blue paper cups with a drawing of the Acropolis on all sides, Caroline listened to Julie's recap of the night before.

"You slept with him? That's unlike you. I've never known you to fall into a man's bed so early into a relationship."

Julie tried to keep the emotion out of her voice. "It was our third date. Don't you always tell me that by the third date, you'll know if you want to have sex with a guy?"

"Yes, that's been my rule of thumb for years, but why did you take my advice this time? You never have before."

Julie was about to say something about how it was just an impulsive move on her part, but Caroline spoke first.

"Wait a minute, hold on. This is a different situation than the men you usually date. I know! You must like James. I mean really and truly like him. That's it, right?"

"I'm not sure that I'd say that..." Julie began, not wanting to give herself away.

"What else could it be? Besides. He's gorgeous, he's charming and his uber-wealthy. You hit the trifecta this time!" Caroline clapped her hands together in glee.

"Don't get ahead of yourself. I do like him, but I hate what he does for a living. I'm not sure how far this relationship can go when I think that *Tell All* is one of the reasons why our society has lost its sense of propriety. All the gossip and innuendo has such a negative effect on the way we see each other and the way we treat one another. I mean, who really needs to know about a celebrity's botched plastic surgery, or which one of the Housewives is getting divorced this time? Ugh!"

"So what? He publishes that rag but it doesn't mean that he's defined by it. He told us last night that he wants to change the direction of his business. I thought he was pretty sincere," Caroline said, taking another swig of the now cold coffee from her cup.

"I know, but his father has all the control." Julie stopped and chewed on her bottom lip, deciding just how much more she would let Caroline know. She decided to tell her just a bit more. "He wants me to spend the day with his parents, somewhere out on the east end of Long Island, next Saturday. Apparently they have a home there."

Caroline laughed out loud, then composed herself and said, "Of course they do. It's in Southampton, by the way, right on the ocean. That's where all the billionaires live. I mean, why waste time with the more pedestrian West Hampton or Sag Harbor when you can surround yourself with the absurdly wealthy crowd? Hmmph."

"Oh brother, how do you know all of this?"

"Really?!? Were we not just discussing his family's business? I've seen photos in *Tell All*."

"There you have it. We've circled back to my initial reason

for not wanting to have anything to do with James. I don't want to be in that tabloid ever again. That's the whole point."

"You have no choice. You like him too much," Caroline said with confidence as she nodded her head up and down.

"I like him, but not enough to take a chance with my future. I write etiquette books for a living. I can't associate with the rudeness exhibited by that paper!"

"Keep telling yourself that, sister. Just don't expect the rest of us to believe you." She stood up and began clearing the wrapping from their sandwiches, when she turned and asked, "By the way. How was the sex?"

"I'm not going to tell you that," Julie said primly. "It wouldn't be right."

"Okay. No need. Because you just let me know that it was good enough to consider doing it again, or else we wouldn't have had this entire conversation!" she declared.

"But you had to ask..."

"Of course." Caroline placed her elbows on the counter and leaned in. "Not that I expected you to spill any of his kinky ways. Yet."

"What does that mean?"

"Just that I will get those details out of you sooner or later. You know I will."

Julie hung her head and sighed. The truth was that she knew her roommate was right. The other woman would ultimately wear her down and she'd give up more information than she wanted to share. It was just Caroline's way. But that moment was not now. She changed the subject, "Let's get to the packing. There's a lot to do and not a lot of time to get it all done."

"We have another week here. The first of the month is still nine days away. And who knows? Maybe you'll find someone to rent my room. You posted your request, right? It just takes one person to say yes so that you can sign a new lease and stay."

"The odds of that happening seem to shrink with each passing day. I've tried everything and still no takers. So far the only people who are interested are creepy and sketchy."

"What are you going to do?" Caroline asked.

"Sleep in the guest room of your new loft until I figure it out, I guess."

"Well, that might solve both of our problems. You'll have a place to stay and we won't have to live apart."

"I don't know how Stephen will feel about that, Caroline. I don't think he had me in mind when he proposed to you."

"Don't you worry about Stephen. I can handle him."

"I bet you can," Julie smirked. "But how about we get these pots and pans wrapped up and into some boxes, huh? Let's be somewhat productive today."

"If we have to," Caroline agreed. She reached for the lid of a saucepan and began to cover it sheets of the previous Sunday's *New York Times*.

They worked in companionable silence for a while before Caroline asked, "So, will you go meet his parents? It could be interesting, and besides, I'd love to know what the inside of that house looks like."

"Why? The pictures in *Tell All* were only of the exterior?"

"The ones I saw were. The ocean is just mere steps away from their house. It's right there. So amazing."

Julie felt uncomfortable at the thought of seeing Ben Curran again, no matter how beautiful the setting might be, but she knew what she had to do. "I'm thinking that I might. I'm still not sure." *How else will I ask for a loan? I have to go.*

"I'll take that as a yes, then! How exciting. We'll really have to go through our closets for the perfect outfit. I can't wait."

"We'll be pretty much packed up by then. I don't even want to think about it. Too much pressure."

"I know. Just think about the hot sex you'll have afterward. That should keep you going," Caroline said with a wink.

"Is that all you can think about?" Julie asked.

"Until you fill me in on all the juicy details, yes! I'm making up scenarios in my mind. You might as well just set me straight!"

"Nice try, Caroline. But no. Let's just go fold all those clothes on your bed. We can pack them later. I need a nap."

"Ha! He tired you out! I knew it!" Caroline said as she bounded off toward her bedroom.

Knowing when to quit, Julie followed her friend, eager to finish what they started so that she could get some well-deserved sleep.

Chapter Fifteen

JAMES WAS SEATED behind the wheel of his silver two-seat Porche 911. He had the top down on this spectacular early summer morning and was on his way to pick up Julie for a day to be spent with his parents. He could not believe his good fortune. After the time they'd shared together on his boat, he could not stop thinking about her, the shape of her, her warm vanilla scent and the way she felt in his arms. There was something about her, something that made her stand out and apart from any other woman he'd dated. As he headed toward her apartment, he called Ryan to check in and give him an update. When the phone connected, he could tell that his friend was not at home; from the loud level of all the background noise, it sounded like he was in Times Square.

"Ryan? Hi. Is this a bad time to talk?"

"No, man. Actually, you're doing me a favor. I'm with Daphne at Buy Buy Baby picking out a stroller and some other things she feels are essential to have at home before this kid is born. I swear to you buddy, I've traveled the world for months at a time without all of this gear."

"I can't imagine. Sounds pretty intense."

"It is. But distract me, please. How's your life going?"

"Good. I'm on my way to the Hamptons. Julie agreed to come out there with me."

"To see your folks? Wow. That's big."

"I know. I don't want to mess this up. I can only hope that my dad doesn't scare her off."

"This woman sounds smarter than that. She can probably handle herself just fine."

"Let's hope so, but you know my dad."

"Take it slow and make sure your father's glass is always full. He's a lot easier to take after a few scotch and sodas."

James laughed out loud. "You remember that time we had half the cheerleading squad in the hot tub with us senior year of high school?"

"You mean the night we snuck out east and your parents came home early from the city? Oh yeah. I'll never forget how pissed he was when he found us all half naked in the tub."

"After a few drinks he wasn't angry any more. He almost got into the water with us."

"Oh boy. The good old days. Before adulthood and all the responsibility that goes with it," Ryan said wistfully. "I better get going. Daphne is headed my way with two shopping carts filled to the brim. Good luck today buddy."

"From the sound of things, you need it more than me. But thanks. I hope to hell that all goes well for both of us." James pushed a button on the display screen and disconnected the call. He turned the corner and pulled up in front of Julie's apartment building just as she stepped outside. She was wearing a tight white tee shirt and a short navy blue skirt and when he saw her, all the blood in his body seemed to rush to his groin. He drew in a deep, calming breath. *Don't get ahead of yourself!* he thought.

The doorman had run out behind her and reached around

her in an overly familiar way to open the car door. James felt an unexpected rush of jealousy.

"Have a nice day, Miss Julie," the other man said as he tipped his hat at James. Once she was seated, he closed the door and went back inside the building.

She turned and smiled. James could feel his heart beat faster in his chest.

"Hi," was all she said.

"Hello," he replied, silently chastising himself for reacting to the doorman's solicitous attention to Julie. Instead, he focused on her movements as she fastened her seatbelt and get settled in for the ride.

"Nice car," she commented.

"It gets the job done," he grinned. "Are you ready?"

"Hang on," she answered, opening up her purse and searching for something. "Here it is!" she said as she found a clip. She twisted her hair in a simple arrangement and secured it. "I think this should work. Caroline warned me that you might have a convertible. I figured that Charlie isn't always your means of transportation."

"Right. I do drive myself every now and then," he replied, pulling into traffic.

He head toward the Midtown Tunnel, all the while stealing glances at her. She looked beautiful and he had to truly concentrate on keeping his car on the road.

"How was your week?" he asked. They had not seen each other since the morning on his boat, although they'd spoken on the phone a number of times after their respective work days were done.

"Busy. Aside from the ever approaching deadline for my next book, Caroline and I finally finished packing. We move in two days. Or rather, I should say, she does. She and Stephen bought a loft downtown. Part of it will be living space, the other half a studio for Caroline's design team."

"Oh," he said. "Did you find a new roommate?"

"No. I'm going to crash in Caroline and Stephen's guest room until I'm finished with my book project. I'll find another place after that. I originally thought that I'd just get another roommate, but now, I'm not so sure. No one can replace Caroline. Absolutely no one."

"You're not thrilled by the thought of living alone?"

"It's not that." She shook her head and then said, "Manhattan is so expensive. I don't think I can afford it yet. Let's hope my book sales offer me some better options."

James hesitated before answering. Since money never factored into his decisions about where to live he realized that he had to be careful with his answer. He concentrated on formulating his words, not wanting to say the wrong thing. Then a random thought came into his head. *Maybe she'd consider living with him. No... it's too soon. Don't speak this crazy idea out loud, you'll scare her away for good.* Instead, he turned to her and said, "I'm sure it will all work itself out."

"Right," she replied as they entered the tunnel.

For the next hour as they traveled through Queens and out on the Long Island Expressway toward Southampton, he told her stories about his childhood and all the fun he used to have at his parent's summer home. As he did, he realized just how lucky he'd been to have those carefree times, when the season's long days would stretch on forever giving him time to chase fireflies and daydream in the tall grasses on the dunes.

"What about you, Julie? What were your summers like?"

She seemed to think about it for a moment then said, "I was the kid who enjoyed school, so once we were done, I was bored. I used to go to the library each week and check out as many

---

books as I could carry. I would read all day long while my mom was at work."

He glanced over at her. She was sitting with her hands together in her lap, her fingers tightly intertwined. She didn't seem to want to elaborate further, so he decided it was best to change the subject.

"When I told my father that I was bringing you out to the house today, he was thrilled. He really enjoyed meeting you at the gala."

"I'm happy to have another chance to get to know him. I feel badly that I walked away from you both that night. I was just so overwhelmed by the whole experience."

"Understood." He really didn't want to rehash that whole disaster of an evening again. He reached over and placed his hand over hers. "Besides. I'm all in on the concept of second chances."

"Me too," she replied.

James felt hopeful. Now he had to pray that his parents behaved themselves. He had a whole lot riding on the outcome of today's events.

❧

AS SOON AS THEY TURNED OFF OF OLD TOWN ROAD ONTO Meadow Lane, he could feel her body tense in the seat next to him. He knew that the homes were opulent and quite expansive, but it all seemed so familiar to him. He tried to see his surroundings through her eyes and realized that he had to say something to sooth her nerves.

"Did you like going to the beach as a kid? I used to love body surfing in the ocean."

"No," she said quietly. "Not really. It was always hot and sticky. I never truly enjoyed it."

"Oh," he replied. "That's a shame. Well, we don't need to go sit on the beach today. We can lounge under an umbrella at the pool." He glanced over at her and could see the panic on her face. Maybe this wasn't such a great idea after all.

And then it went from bad to worse. As they made their way up the long driveway, he saw a line of cars parked in the circle. His parents had a house full of guests. *Just great.*

James deftly maneuvered the Porche into a tight spot and turned off the engine. Then he said, "We don't have to stay long. I'd love to walk around town with you, Julie, just spend some time out here. Then we can head back to the city."

"Don't be silly, James. I'm a big girl. I can handle myself."

"I know that, Julie, of course! I just also know that the crowd my parents tend to surround themselves with can be kind of hard to take."

"Understood," was all she said as she opened the passenger door.

He scrambled out of the car and reached her just as she swung her legs onto the driveway. "Here," he offered his hand, which she accepted. Just the touch of her cool palm in his own sent sparks of unseen electricity up his arm and through his body. It was undeniable. When he looked at her face, he realized that she felt it too. He pulled her up into his embrace and whispered into her ear, "Just in case anything crazy happens in there," he nodded his head toward the house, "let me tell you how grateful I am that you agreed to be here at all."

"I'm glad to be able to do this for you, James," she murmured into his ear. He could not help but think that he'd rather hear those words whispered to him in his bed, with her there naked and willing, but for now, he'd accept her graciousness with a quick kiss. He leaned in and touched his lips to hers all too briefly. It was time to deal with his father. Grasping her hand tightly in his own, they walked into the house.

"Mr. Curran, sir! Good to see you!"

The booming voice with a distinct British accent came from his parents' house manager, the man who kept all of the Curran residences running smoothly.

"Greyson! Always good to see you as well. How are you?" James asked.

"Very well indeed. Your parents are out on the deck with some of their friends. Can I get you both something cold to drink?"

"Sorry. I didn't introduce my girlfriend." He reached around and put his arm on the small of Julie's back. "Julie Porter, meet Brian Greyson. He's worked for my parents since before I was born," he said. *Did I just call her my girlfriend? That's going to spread like wildfire in this crowd!*

Julie didn't react to the way he greeted the older man. She was composed as usual. She put her hand out, reaching for Greyson's. "It's so nice to meet you," she said warmly.

James watched as Greyson softened and clearly fell under her charm. The small gesture of a handshake was more respectful than she could have known.

"You as well, miss. Now, about that drink. If you'll allow me, I believe that the cook has just made a fresh pitcher of lemonade. May I bring you each a glass?"

"Yes, Greyson, thanks so much. We'll go find my folks."

"Thank you," Julie added as James guided her through the large great room to the expansive deck beyond.

As soon as James stepped outside, he knew that he had made a huge mistake by bringing Julie here. These people were certainly not the type of crowd that would make her feel comfortable, and to make matters even worse, he saw Delilah sitting under a large, striped umbrella with a man who didn't look familiar. He immediately decided to spend no more than an hour here; they'd make the rounds, he'd be able to show his father that Julie was a part of his life and they'd leave, hopefully unscathed. He scanned the group, spotted his mother and made his way over to where she sat, facing the ocean.

"Mom, we're here," he said, holding on tightly to Julie's hand.

"Darling, how nice of you to make it out," his mother said, smiling up at him from her seat, a large straw hat shading her eyes. "Introduce me to your date. We didn't have a chance to meet at the gala."

"Mom, this is Julie Porter. My girlfriend." He said it again. *Girlfriend.* Now he could only hope she didn't try to run. "Julie, this is my mother, Clara Curran."

Julie smiled.

"Girlfriend?" His mother extended her hand toward Julie. "Sit down next to me dear. Let's chat."

James felt his larynx constrict, making it difficult for him to speak. *Just what I need, for my mother to be the inquisitor.* He cleared his throat. "Actually, mom, I was going to take Julie down to the water. She's not been out this way before.

"That can wait, darling. I want to get to know her first."

His mother's tone left no room for argument. Thankfully, Greyson appeared with two tall, frosty glasses filled with lemonade. He nodded at the older gentleman and lifted the drinks from his tray, passing one to Julie.

"Go find your father," she said. "He'll be happy to see you. We'll be right here."

James looked over at Julie who had taken a seat next to his mother. She mercifully winked at him, giving him the sense that she was going to be fine. The problem for James was that Julie didn't have a true idea of how his mother operated. She could make his father seem to be a lightweight; his mother was a true force of nature.

"I'll check in with him and then I'll be back. Give me five minutes."

"Take all the time you need, dear. Don't worry about us," his mother said as he turned to go find his father. *Worry? How could he not? It was like he was leading a lamb to slaughter, leaving Julie alone with his mom,* he thought to himself as he scanned the outdoor space for his dad. Not finding him there, he headed back inside to his father's home office, where sure enough, the other man was on the phone in what appeared to be a serious conversation.

James waited for the call to be completed, scanning the bookshelves and sipping his drink. Finally, his father hung up and turned to him.

"I tell you son, I'm getting too old for this sort of aggravation."

"Something I can do for you, dad?"

"Yes. Settle down and get married. Make me believe that you can handle the business without me."

"I don't have to be married to do that. We've been over this."

"I need for you to have something bigger than yourself to work for, James. Nothing will do that for you like having a family of your own."

"So you've told me time and time again."

"I only repeat it because it's the truth." James watched as his father lifted an empty glass and stood. "I need a refill."

"Well, then come say hello to Julie. She's outside talking to mom."

His father's eyebrows lifted in surprise. "I'm glad you patched things up with that one. You must really think she's a keeper if you left her alone with your mother. Impressive."

"I had no choice. Mom insisted."

"Of course she did. Now let's go rescue your young lady before it's too late for you both."

They walked through the house and stepped outside where James scanned the crowd. There was no sign of Julie, just an empty seat where he'd left her. His mother was still there, though.

"Hey, mom. Where did Julie go?"

"Oh, James. She's really quite lovely. Polite. And smart. I approve."

"Great mom, but where is she?"

"The ladies' room? I think that's where she went."

He looked around and realized that Delilah was nowhere to be found as well. He could only hope that Julie had gone for a walk on the beach, but he knew that the odds of that were not in his favor. He quickly went off in search for them both.

Chapter Sixteen

As she head off in search of a bathroom, Julie thought back on her conversation with Clara Curran.

"Julie. Tell me. How long have you known my son?" James' mother asked.

Julie knew that this was only the first of a long line of questions the other woman would want answers to. She took a sip of the tart lemonade and paced herself.

"About two weeks. We've actually only been on a few dates, but we've gotten to know each other pretty well over the phone. We FaceTime each other mostly every night after work." *And I look forward to that time with James, more than he knows.*

"How quaint," his mother responded, lifting what appeared to be a glass of gin and tonic up to her mouth, draining it. "James tells me that you've written a book. Do you have plans to write another?"

"Yes, Mrs. Curran. Actually I'm in contract for a second title now."

"Please. Call me Clara. Mrs. Curran sounds so old and I don't like to admit to my true age," she said with a sly smile.

"Well, Clara," Julie began. "I write about etiquette, and the rules a proper society needs to follow in order to remain civilized.

"Is that right? Well, I often think that the world would be a nicer place if everyone played by the same set of standards."

"Of course," Julie agreed, noticing that she now had this woman's attention and maybe even a bit of her approval. She continued, "I think some of the politeness we've always expected from one another as a matter of course is gone. We just need to be nicer to each other in general."

Clara moved forward in her seat, clearly curious now. "Do you really think that you can make a difference?" she asked, a clear tone of doubt in her voice.

Julie nodded. "That's the goal. My first book is currently sitting near the top of *The New York Times* bestseller list, so I'm hoping that I'm making an impact."

Clara leaned in even closer then and asked, "Where did you grow up? Would I know of anyone in your social circle?"

Julie had anticipated this question and was quick to respond. "No. I'm from a small town in New Jersey, although I came to New York to attend Columbia and never left. I'm a true Manhattanite now."

"Delightful," Clara responded, moving on. "And what are your expectations for James? Where do you see yourself fitting into his world?"

Wow. This woman cuts right to it. Just stay calm, Julie told herself before speaking.

"Honestly, Clara, I haven't really thought about that. This relationship is very new. I have no crystal ball to see where it will end up."

"Yes, of course. And please, don't get me wrong. You seem lovely. Smart and beautiful, but you have to understand. I don't mean to pry, or be rude, but my son has a fortune to protect, a business to maintain. James has to be careful, you know."

"Are you asking me if I'm dating him for his money? Because I assure you, nothing could be further from the truth." *A white lie?* Julie questioned in her mind. *I do need a loan, but that would be between her and James, not her and Clara! Stay calm,* she silently admonished herself. *Don't let her trip you up!*

Clara smiled, her mouth lifting ever so slightly. "Well, in that case, you must send me an advance copy of your next book. I'd be happy to pass on my review and notes. I'm sure I can add something of value."

"Thank you so much," Julie said. *Just what I need. Notes from this woman.* "The next one is actually on wedding etiquette," she added, hoping to mask her inner turmoil.

Clara winked conspiratorially. "That's splendid. You can get all the dos and don'ts correct before you need the information for yourself someday."

"I suppose that's true. Although I have absolutely no plans to be married anytime soon." Julie hoped that her last statement would be enough to ease the other woman's mind. Clara had serious questions about her son, that was clear. He'd dated around and maybe his mother had her own worries about his choices. Julie could never blame Clara for having that level of concern. But for as much as Julie wasn't offended, she was simply getting tired of having to defend herself with these people. She smiled and stood. "Now, if you'll excuse me, I need to find the ladies' room."

"There's one over there, dear," Clara said with a wave in the direction of a large building near the oceanfront.

"Thank you. I'm glad we could get to know each other a bit better" Julie said.

"My husband was right about you, by the way. I like you too. You might just be the breath of fresh air this family needs."

Julie did everything she could to maintain her composure after Clara's statement. She nodded and stepped away in search of a small patch of quiet reflection. She felt as though she'd just cleared a huge hurdle. Clara Curran was no joke. *Just a few minutes to recharge,* she told herself as she went off in search of the restroom. *That's all I need. Then I'll throw myself back into the fray.*

⬧⬧⬧

AFTER WASHING HER HANDS AND SPLASHING COLD WATER ON her face, Julie stepped out of the overly lavish powder room in the cabana. Aside from the expensive marble fittings and the imported mirror that resembled a piece of fine art, it was larger than the apartment that she currently shared with Caroline. The cabana sat beside an Olympic sized swimming pool which was situated square in the middle of what looked like a meadow, but what was actually the very manicured backyard of James' parents' summer home. Even the Atlantic Ocean looked different here; bluer, cleaner, and more inviting than it ever appeared to her in South New Jersey. She was tempted to snap a picture and send it to Caroline, but she thought better of it; if she did, she'd be no better than the damned paparazzi that seemed to follow James around the city.

Halfway back across the expanse of soft, green grass between the ocean and the deck, she saw the figure she'd hope to never see again headed right for her. Delilah. Just about the last person who she wanted to face right about now. The woman was rapidly approaching and there was nowhere for Julie to duck and hide. She'd have to speak to her. Squaring her shoulders in preparation, Julie forced herself to smile.

"Hello, Delilah. Nice to see you again." *Another white lie,* she thought.

"Yes. You're Julie, right? It's so hard to keep track of James' women."

Julie couldn't help notice that Delilah's face barely moved when she spoke. She had heard about the effects of Botox, but this was the closest she'd ever been to someone who'd clearly been injected in what must have been the last few days. She tried not to stare. Then, ignoring that last snide comment as well as she could, Julie replied, "Beautiful party. And what a lovely setting."

"Oh yes. The Currans are fabulous hosts. My parents are dear friends of theirs. We've been here to celebrate lots of events over the years."

"That's great," Julie said, trying to slip past the other woman. "I'm actually on my way to go find James. If you'll excuse me..."

Delilah leaned in then, her overly cloying perfume invading Julie's space. She whispered directly into Julie's ear, "Listen. I don't know what your endgame is, but James is not meant to be with someone like you. He needs a woman who understands this world and that is clearly beyond what you could ever imagine. Leave him alone."

Julie drew in a breath. "As I said. Please excuse me, I'll be going now." She maneuvered around Delilah and walked quickly toward the house, seeing James on the deck. He broke into a wide smile when he saw her draw near.

"I've been looking for you. Where'd you go?"

"To use the restroom. But I got waylaid by Delilah."

"I was afraid of that. I was hoping to save you from her. And my mom? How was she?"

"Fine. She loves you, that's for sure. She just wants what's best."

"Right. But I'll determine what that means for me," he said, one arm circling her waist. "Ready to get out of here?"

"What? So soon? I'm not a quitter, James," she teased, then added, "let's stay a bit longer."

"You're too good to me, Julie. I promise to make it up to you later." He leaned in and kissed her cheek.

Julie felt her stomach flip at the thought of whatever "later" meant. If it was anything like the night they spent together on his boat, this afternoon's torture would be worth it. She smiled at him. "I'm going to hold you to that. You'd better come up with something very special if you plan on delivering on your word."

"Oh. Just you wait. I've got a whole lot up my sleeve. You haven't seen the best of me yet."

Well, since I've seen the most of you in resplendent, naked glory, she thought, *whatever is left must be pretty damned spectacular.* "I can't wait," she said with a smile, before leading him back into the thick of the crowd assembled on the deck.

JULIE WAS GRATEFUL WHEN JAMES INSISTED THAT THEY'D spent more than enough time at his parents' home. They'd made the rounds, meeting everyone in attendance and making enough small talk to have Julie feel like her head was actually spinning around on her shoulders. She held his hand tightly as he walked them over to where his mother sat, holding court among her guests.

"Mom," he said, "we're going to head back to the city. I'll speak to you later this week."

"Alright, darling. Just promise that you'll bring Julie around to dinner. Maybe we'll reserve a table at Le Bernadin. Yes, I think that would be nice, don't you?"

"Sounds great. I'll let you know when we're free."

"Thank you for having me here today, Clara."

"Of course," she replied before turning back to James. "Did you say goodbye to your father?"

"Not yet, but we will." He leaned down and kissed his mother's cheek.

"Drive safely, dear."

"Always, mom."

Julie watched as he scanned the crowd to find his father. Once James located him, he navigated them through the guests on the lawn until they stood before the man.

"Dad," James said, leaning in for a brief hug. "We'll catch up with you soon. Mom wants us all to have dinner together in the city."

His father's eyes shifted over to Julie. She felt as though he had some weird X-ray vision and it made her feel uncomfortable, but she offered, "It was lovely to see you again, sir."

"Come around any time you'd like, Ms. Porter. I hope to see you both again soon."

She could feel his gaze on them as they made their way back through the house and to the driveway. She almost held her breath the entire time, until they were sitting in James' car, heading away from his family home. They rode in silence for a while, but once they were in the middle of what appeared to be a cute small town, James pulled over and shut the engine.

"I want to take you somewhere. I think you're going to like it."

"Where?" she asked as he came around the front of the car and opened her car door.

"We're close. It will be worth the brief stop. I promise."

She took his hand and they walked to the end of the block, turning onto a tiny, winding street and stopping in front of an ice cream shop with a striped awning. The name "Cups and Cones" was painted on the door in big red block letters.

"This is the best treat anywhere!" he exclaimed. "Their peach melba is like tasting summer in a bowl!"

"I didn't realize that you were an ice cream connoisseur," she laughed.

"My friend Ryan and I used to ride our bikes here before we could drive. I love this place."

"I'm game," she exclaimed.

His eyes blazed. "I'm so glad you said that. C'mon," he said, pulling her inside.

The sweet smell of freshly baked waffle cones hung heavy in the air and the freezer was full of colorful selections.

"You can sample some of the flavors if you want to. I'm all in on the fresh peach," he told her.

"Hmm. Let me think," she said as she walked the length of the counter, taking in all the different selections. "Everything looks good to me but I think I'd like to try the strawberry, please." An eager young server by the register rushed over to give her a taste on a tiny pink spoon. As soon as the ice cream melted on her tongue she knew that James was right. This was a very special shop. "That's delicious. I'll have a small cup, please."

"Small? You're a lightweight. I dream about this stuff," he teased. Then to the server, he said, "A large cup of peach for me, please."

Julie watched as the young employee scooped what looked like a pint of the light pink colored ice cream into a container for James and a much smaller one of the deep red creamy treat for her. She accepted hers and put a spoonful into her mouth. There were large pieces of fresh strawberries studded throughout her dessert and she relished each bite. After James paid the server, they went back outside, and walked through the town for a bit, window shopping. They stopped in front of a very fancy boutique with a lovely navy blue and white linen dress on display.

"That would look great on you. Would you like to try it on?"

"No, James. First of all, who knows what it costs? Secondly, I'm enjoying my ice cream too much right now. But thanks."

"I'd love to buy it for you if you'll let me," he said.

"James! No! It's lovely that you bought me an ice cream, but that dress must cost a thousand dollars at least. I really wouldn't feel comfortable with that..."

"Ah, Julie. Sometimes you just have to live in the moment, you know?"

"Again, thanks but no." She finished the remains of her treat and walked over to a trash can on the sidewalk to dispose of her empty cup and spoon. *He is generous,* she thought, her mind racing. *How generous, though? Enough to help me out with my problem?* She pushed the image of her mother back down, knowing that it wasn't the right time to discuss a loan with James. She would avoid having to ask him for as long as she could.

He came up behind her and tossed his empty cup away as well. "That was every bit as good as I remembered it to be. Did you enjoy yours?"

"Yes, it was really delicious. Thanks for sharing your favorite spot with me."

He leaned in and gently kissed her. She could taste fresh peaches on his tongue, still cold from eating the ice cream. "Not as delicious as you taste," he said, looking directly into her eyes. She could tell that he wanted more of her, and she could not deny feeling the same way about him. "Should we head on home now?" he asked.

"Yes, it's getting late. I still have to finish packing."

They walked back together to his car and Julie couldn't help but savor these moments with him. She liked that they didn't have to fill every minute with idle talk, that they could sit in silence and still not feel awkward with one another. As they pulled onto the highway, he reached across and covered her hand with his, gently caressing the tops of her fingers with his thumb. It was heavenly. The smallest touch between them caused her entire body to react; heat blooming from deep in her core, spreading out to her extremities and making her heart pound a wild rhythm in her chest. It made it difficult for her to sit still in her seat; there was a growing ache that could only be soothed by him and all she could think of was being naked with James in his bed.

As if he could read her thoughts, he quietly asked, "Will you stay with me tonight? I really want you to..."

"Boy. You buy a girl an ice cream and you think that she'll follow you anywhere!" she teased him.

"I will buy you the entire contents of their freezer if you'll spend the night. I mean it."

Julie could see the seriousness in his eyes as he quickly glanced over at her while still keeping the car on the road. He meant what he said. It was a sexy move and she could not resist him.

"I don't know if I can turn down an offer like that," she answered. "But what would we do with all that ice cream?"

"I can think of lots of ways to make it melt and they all involve you and me naked and sticky."

That was it. Julie felt as though she would combust on the car seat. She turned to him and asked, "Are we there, yet?"

Chapter Seventeen

BY THE TIME they pulled into the garage of James' building, Julie felt as though her skin was on fire. Every fiber of her being was on high alert, just waiting for the minute when she could have him to herself and touch his naked body once again. All thoughts of her mother had been pushed into the recesses of her mind; she wanted one thing, and one thing only: James.

The elevator ride up to his apartment seemed to take forever. When it glided to a smooth stop, they stepped into the hallway and it registered in Julie's muddled mind that there were only two doors there. His home took up half of the top floor. *I am way out of my league. This is all too much.* He urged her inside and turned the lock behind them. Julie once again had to acknowledge that his world was so very different than her own. The quiet opulence of the space took her breath away. She didn't have very much time to take in all of the details as James pulled her in close and kissed her, blocking out everything except for the sensation of his lips on her own. She could feel her heart pounding in her chest as he explored the inside of her mouth with his tongue. She wanted him. Desperately. And when she kissed him back, she could feel a flame ignite between them that could not be ignored.

"Julie," he said leaning into her and taking a breath, his bold length trapped beneath the fabric of his pants, warm against her hip. "You make me feel so alive. I could stand here and kiss you all night."

"Hmm," she replied with a throaty sound that revealed exactly how much her body agreed with his.

He slowly walked her backward toward a low slung leather couch, gently lowering her without breaking their embrace. She felt a hunger she'd not experienced with anyone before him; as he unbuttoned her skirt she had to force herself to remain still; she could not wait for them both to be naked.

In one movement, he lifted her tee shirt up off over her head, leaving her in just her bra and panties; she quickly removed his clothing as well, running her hands along his bare back and over his smooth bottom. He was toned and strong muscled and felt so good to her touch.

"I want us to do this slowly," he whispered. "I want to feel everything."

Julie had no words for him, she just nodded in agreement.

James raised himself between her legs and up onto his knees, then very slowly removed her lacy undergarments. He pulled off his own boxers, his erection springing free. With one hand, he gently caressed one of her breasts while his mouth lavished attention on the other. Julie felt as though she might burst. Everywhere he stroked seemed to ignite with a longing that needed to be quenched. She forced herself up and pressed her lower body against his.

"All in good time, Julie," he murmured. "I want to taste you first."

With that, his lips trailed down, her skin burning under their light contact. He began to kiss her abdomen, flicking small kisses inside of her belly button. She was sure that he could feel her stomach flipping over and over again with each touch of his mouth, but if he could, he didn't stop. Reaching up with gentle fingers to caress her nipples, he moved his head lower until he was right at the apex of her thighs. She could feel his breath on the most sensitive part of her being and didn't know how much more of this exquisite torture she could bear without coming apart at the seams. When his tongue explored her there it was all she could do to remain seated on the couch; she felt as though she were levitating off of it.

"James," she said as she struggled to find her voice. "I want you. Now. Please."

"Do you?" he teased. "I think I can accommodate that request."

He made his way back up, kissing every inch of her torso as he did, and very slowly positioned himself at the entrance to her body. "If I didn't tell you this before, Julie," he said, extending the anticipation of their lovemaking even further, "I think you are the most beautiful woman I've ever met."

And with that, he buried himself to what felt like the tip of her core, overwhelming her with sensation. She could feel his strength, almost afraid that he was pushing her beyond her limit, overwhelming her in the best way possible. Together they moved in a rhythm all their own, taking from one another exactly what the other needed: they fit together perfectly. Julie closed her eyes and felt everything; when wave after wave of liquid warmth surrounded each fiber of her being, she knew that she could no longer deny that this man was special. As he emptied himself inside of her, he leaned in close to her ear and whispered, "Never, ever leave me."

Julie's eyes shot open wide. "I won't," she replied before she could stop herself, feeling a kind of contentment she'd not experienced before. She was surprised by her answer but not unhappy with it; she was being honest, even if she knew deep down she might not be able to honor what she'd just promised.

She could tell that it took him a minute to process her response, but when he did, he pushed himself up onto his elbows, their bodies still connected in the most intimate way possible. "I mean it, Julie. I truly do. Stay here with me. It would solve all of your problems."

How could he know that? He doesn't know the truth about my mother...

"That's not possible, James. We don't know each other that well. You might be sick of this after a few days and not know how to get rid of me," she replied in what she hoped was a teasing tone.

He rolled off of her just then and they lay side by side on the large couch. He lifted one arm over her shoulder and pulled her in close. "I'm serious, Julie. You need a place to live. Why not take a chance with me? You can always get another apartment if this doesn't work out. Let's give ourselves a minute to see if what we have here is real. I think it is, and by the way, just so we're clear, I will never be 'sick of this'. What we just experienced was mind-blowing."

"I agree, James. It's just that this is all happening very fast. It's overwhelming. I can't imagine living here, with you. It's just so, so..."

"Is it too much? We can get a smaller place, if you prefer."

"That's not it, no. This is your home. I'll figure it out. I'll be fine." She hoped she sounded convincing because she didn't even believe her own words.

"I want us to try, just for a little while. We can have a trial run. A month, maybe two if you're willing. How does that sound?"

A myriad of thoughts went through Julie's head all at once. *If I don't have to pay rent, I will have extra money to send my mother.*

Maybe then she'll leave me alone and I won't need a loan from James. It could work...

"It sounds too good to be true." She looked directly into his eyes. "Are you sure?"

He leaned into her and she felt his desire rising again. "I've ever been more sure of anything, Julie. Besides, at this rate, I may never let you leave." He pulled her on top of him and in a swift motion, quickly sunk back inside of her body.

She drew in a breath, both from surprise at the quick intrusion and the wonderful tingling sensation it created. It was hard to say no to the man when he made her feel this way. She had to consider taking him up on his suggestion, if only for the short time he had just offered. As they began to move in unison, bringing each other back to the point of no return, she allowed herself to empty her mind of all thought and instead focus on the pleasure he was providing for her. It was incredible to have every fiber of her being feel so aware and alive, and Julie wanted to stay in this particular moment forever. He felt so good, so right.

Now, the only thing left for her to do, she realized, was to pray that in the next sixty days she didn't lose herself to him entirely, because if this didn't work out, there would be no way back to any sort of life. He would have made it impossible for her to be with another man. In that moment, Julie realized, it might just be worth the leap of faith to have the memory of this feeling instead of never having known it at all. *And if it did work out? Wow. I can't even think about how wonderful that might truly be...*

AFTER A LEISURELY MORNING AND EARLY AFTERNOON IN BED together, Julie knew that she had to get up and head back for one last night in the apartment she'd shared with Caroline.

Luckily, most of what she had was packed for the move anyway. She'd given her bedroom furniture to her roommate to use in the guest room of her new loft, so all Julie had to take with her was her clothing. She had very few personal mementos; she turned away from her old life years ago and had taken nothing from her childhood along. The only photographs she had were ones of her and Caroline, and those she'd carefully wrapped and placed in a sole box that her friend offered to store for her.

James had insisted on driving her to the building she'd called home for the last few years, holding her hand for the entire ride.

"I'll be back in the morning to pick you up. What time should I be here?"

"Don't you have to go to your office? You know, go to work like the rest of the population?"

He shot her his mega-watt smile. "I'm the boss, baby. I can do what I want, when I want to."

"I see," she teased back. "If that's the case, see you at nine, sharp."

"Well now who sounds like the boss?" he laughed out loud as he pulled the car up in front of her building. He shut the engine and turned to face her. "Seriously, Julie, I'm counting the hours until I come back here for you. Enjoy your night with Caroline. Starting tomorrow, you're all mine."

His voice was low and sexy but his intonation was all business. His words sent a shiver of anticipation up her spine.

"I look forward to seeing you then," was all she said as she turned to open the door. She realized that he was still holding her hand. With a quick squeeze, he released her and quickly stepped out and around the front of the car to help her out. Once she was firmly on the sidewalk, he pulled her into his embrace for a long kiss.

"I'm going to miss you in my bed tonight," he whispered in her ear.

"I'll miss you too," she replied, almost wishing that she could just go upstairs and grab her bags, throw them in his backseat and go home with him now. "See you in the morning," she said instead as she broke away from him and went inside. Curtis opened the door and she walked through the lobby and into the elevator, pushed the button for her floor and tried to keep the intense longing she had for James down for a while. The time away would be good for her; she needed a moment to come back to earth after their incredible lovemaking anyway.

As she turned her key in the lock, she took a deep breath. It was the last time that she would do this and find Caroline on the other side of the door.

"Hey there," she called out. "Anybody home?"

"In here," a small voice replied. "I'm finishing up in my room."

Julie threw her bag on the empty counter with her keys and walked down the hall to find her friend. Once at the doorframe of Caroline's bedroom, Julie saw what looked like mountains of moving boxes piled high on top of one another in every direction. She said, "It sure looks like you're ready to go."

"I may be packed, but I don't feel ready," the other woman exclaimed as she lay face down on her unmade bed.

Julie walked over and sat down beside her. "Really? Aren't you excited to move into the loft with Stephen? It's going to be great, you'll see."

Caroline turned over and faced Julie, her eyes wide. "I think I am. Maybe I'm just nervous about the whole thing. Getting married is such a huge step. How can I be sure if I'm ready?"

"You are so ready. You were born ready."

"No. I mean, ready to settle down with one guy forever. Suddenly it all seems so final."

"It's a commitment, Caroline, one I think you're willing to make, right? You love Stephen!"

Her friend just shook her head back and forth. "I don't know," she replied. "I mean, I'm here watching you and James in the beginning of your relationship and it all seems so shiny and new. I miss shiny and new."

"That may be true, but I have some news for you. I'm going to move into James' apartment. We're going to give living together a try."

Caroline shot up to a seated position. "What?!? How did that happen?"

"He offered and I said yes."

"Seriously? You?" She motioned to her own huge diamond. "No ring on your hand and you're going to live with a man? This can't be happening."

"Why not?"

"Miss 'do everything by the book' will be living in sin?"

"C'mon, Caroline. It's not 1950 anymore. I think it's important to live with someone if the relationship has a shot of surviving past the hot sex stage."

"I can't believe what I'm hearing! And worse, I can't believe that you're not moving in with Stephen and me. How am I going to survive without you?"

"First of all, I'm a third wheel living in your guest room if I go with you. Second of all, I really like James."

"But you hardly know him. What if he turns out to be a serial killer?"

Julie laughed. "I think I'd know that about him already."

Caroline's eyes widened. "After all of the episodes of 'Dateline' we've watched together? You know it's always the guy you least suspect who turns out to be lying about his past and is someone other than who you think he's going to be."

Julie felt her blood run cold at her friend's words. She was the one lying about who she truly was, not James.

"You don't have to worry. I think he's a good guy. More than that, I think he's the one I might end up with forever."

"Wait," Caroline jumped up off the bed. "Just you wait a hot minute. You know this man for two weeks and you think he's someone you might spend the rest of your life with? What is happening here? I'm not comprehending this whole thing. My head is spinning."

"I know. Mine is too. It's all just moving so quickly. But he's really special, Caroline. I think I'm falling in love with him."

Her roommate stood still for what felt like a long time and then said, "I need a drink. Just wait here."

When Caroline returned, she came back empty handed. "I forgot. We packed the glasses and the tequila. We have to go out for some."

Julie looked at her wrist. It was only 4:00 o'clock in the afternoon. "We can't start drinking now. It's too early."

"We'll get some food with the alcohol if that makes you feel better. But we're going to drink," Caroline said emphatically. "And you're going to tell me everything."

For once, Julie didn't argue. "I'll get my purse," was all she said.

Chapter Eighteen

"I FEEL like this is deja vu," Julie said as she slipped into the booth she'd shared with James at Rye and Rum.

"I thought we were moving forward with that 'Dateline' vibe. Now you're moving into the area of psychic phenomenons," Caroline said.

They had ordered their drinks and a plate of spicy wings, deciding that calories were off the table for discussion this evening. As they waited for their server to return, Julie knew she had to delve deeper into her best friend's earlier words.

"Are you truly questioning whether or not you want to get married? It's not too late to call the whole thing off, you know. You've only ordered the invitations, you haven't mailed them."

Caroline let out a long sigh and then said, "It's not that simple. I'm just starting to wonder if I'm ready for this huge step."

"Then talk to Stephen. Postpone it. You don't have to get married if you don't want to."

"I know. I do love Stephen. You understand that, right?"

Julie nodded her head.

"I'm just not sure if I'm ready to tie myself down to one person for the rest of my life. And I certainly don't want to end up like my mother, bitter and angry when her marriage went south."

The waiter returned with their drinks and Julie watched as Caroline eyed him up and down as if he was a lush piece of fruit, ripe for picking. Maybe her friend wasn't ready to be married after all.

Caroline lifted her salt-rimmed glass and tipped it toward Julie. "Let's table this conversation for now and drink to us. The best roomies on the planet!"

Julie picked up her own margarita and touched it to her friend's. "To us, Caroline. Different zip codes are meaningless. We're always going to be BFFs."

As they each took a sip of their cold beverage, Julie couldn't help but think that maybe she should listen to what Caroline was saying. She was clearly doubting making a commitment to Stephen.

"Thanks for taking me out tonight, Julie, and for listening to me whine. I feel as if I've been carrying around this gigantic secret, like I haven't been totally honest with you. I hate that. I hate not telling you everything." She paused, then added, "And you're right, of course. I'm sure this will all work out. Besides, you'll make a gorgeous maid of honor."

Julie felt a cold chill creep up her spine. She was the one who hadn't been truthful. She had kept her own huge secret from her friend the entire time they'd known one another—her true identity. Maybe it was time to come clean.

"Well, if we're playing true confessions, then..." she began.

The waiter returned with a plate piled high with wings. It looked like twice the amount in a normal order. "A little something extra for you ladies," he said as he placed the food on the table with a flourish, carefully arranging a full bowl of ranch dressing on one side of the platter of wings and one of blue cheese dressing on the other. Before leaving, he winked at Caroline.

"Do you see what I mean?" she asked, lifting a piece of chicken from the plate and waving it in front of Julie's face. "Men. They're everywhere. Sheesh."

Julie realized that Caroline had not listened to the last thing she had said, so she thought better of revealing her own truth at the moment. Instead, she plucked a wing off of the plate and replied, "Only if you're not looking for one. Somehow they know. Men are mostly interested in us when we are unavailable."

"Interesting theory, Julie," Caroline said, taking a large sip of the contents of her glass. "Let's drink to that!"

The rest of the evening passed in a hazy cloud of spicy wings and too much tequila. Julie had to finally call it a night when Caroline decided that it might be a good idea to put some money in the juke box and find them a couple of hot dance partners. They both had a big day tomorrow, and it was time to go home together, one final time.

As they made their way out the door of the bar, Julie was careful not to bump into any of the men in her path. After what had happened on the last occasion she'd been here with Caroline, she was hyper-aware of each step. Once in the Uber, Caroline fell promptly asleep, her head resting on Julie's shoulder. *I'm going to miss this,* she thought to herself. *We've had so much fun over the years.* And then, *what would happen if I confessed to my true identity before the moving truck came in the morning? Would Caroline ever forgive me for not having told her all this time?*

The Uber came to a stop outside of their building and Julie nudged her friend awake, then helped her into the lobby. Once they were inside their apartment, Caroline made her way slowly to her bedroom under her own steam.

"Goodnight, bestie," she called out, her voice trailing down the hallway. "Love you lots!"

The awareness that this particular chapter in her life had come to an end hit Julie like a splash of cold water. The fuzzy effects of the alcohol dissipated and she stood alone, surrounded by moving boxes, tape guns and excess packing papers. It was time to come clean. She'd tell her friend the truth in the morning before they went their separate ways. Julie held out hope against hope that Caroline would forgive her.

⌘

WHEN SHE WOKE THE NEXT DAY AT DAWN, JULIE COULD TELL that it was raining just by the gray light seeping around the corners of her window shades. *Lovely. Weather like this just sets the mood for disaster.*

She quickly shed her pajamas and threw them into her open suitcase. She pulled on her favorite jeans and faded pink tee shirt, then went to wash her face and brush her teeth in the bathroom before packing what was left of her toiletries in her cosmetic bag. Once finished, Julie took the large case with her into her bedroom. Actually, her former bedroom, as she slept there for the last time the night before. Once there, she threw the bag into her suitcase and zipped it shut. She was ready.

When Julie came into the kitchen, she found Caroline sitting at the counter with two to-go cups of coffee and freshly buttered bagels, sitting on the waxy white paper they'd been wrapped in.

"You went out???" Julie asked incredulously.

"Nope. I called for delivery. It's raining."

"I know. How are you feeling this morning?"

"Not hung-over. I think my body knows that I have no time today for those sort of shenanigans. What about you?"

"I'm fine." Julie started to gather her courage. She sat down next to Caroline and picked up one of the coffees. "Listen. There's something I need to tell you."

"If it's that James is coming to whisk you away to Bali, keep it to yourself. I'm feeling vulnerable right now. I don't think I could take it."

"Nothing like that," Julie drew in a breath. "It's about me." She watched her friend's face, the worry lines between her eyebrows showing some strain.

"What is it?" Caroline asked.

"It's so complicated, that I don't know where to begin."

"Just tell me."

"I'm not who..."

The intercom buzzed and Curtis' voice came through, "Miss Caroline, Miss Julie. The moving men are on their way up."

Caroline jumped off of her stool and went over to the wall where the electronic device was connected to the lobby, pressed the button and replied, "Ok, thanks." Then she came back to where Julie sat.

"What were you saying?"

She lost her nerve. "Nothing, really. There's no time for this discussion now. We'll do it another time."

"Are you sure?" Caroline asked. "They can start without us, you know."

Julie just shook her head. "No. It's alright. We'll catch dinner later this week and I'll fill you in."

"If you say so," Caroline answered. Then she walked over to the front door and opened it wide. "Let's get this over with."

"Yes. Let's," Julie said, both relieved and disappointed that she hadn't crossed this hurdle with her friend. As three burly men filled the doorway of the apartment, she realized that it didn't matter. Her confession could wait. She kept the truth under wraps for this long, a few days more would make no difference at all.

. . .

TWO HOURS LATER BOTH WOMEN STOOD IN THE MIDDLE OF the empty apartment, crying in each other's arms.

"It's the end of an era for sure," Caroline said between sobs.

"On to bigger and better things," Julie replied.

"Promise me that we'll have dinner later this week. You can fill me in on whatever it is you were going to tell me."

"Absolutely," Julie said quietly. "Now hit the road. You want to get yourself downtown before the moving truck does."

"Right. I'm going," Caroline said, breaking the embrace. She lifted her purse off of the counter and was about to leave when James walked through the open front door.

"Take good care of my girl, Curran," Caroline said as she walked by him on her way out. Over her shoulder she added, "I'll send the truck your way with your boxes of winter clothing after they drop off my stuff." And then she was gone.

Julie looked up at James and wiped away what was left of her tears, managing a weak smile.

"Rough morning?" he asked.

"A little emotional. Caroline and I were roommates for what seemed like forever. It will be an adjustment, that's all."

He stepped in closer and kissed her lightly on the cheek. "I promise to distract you and make the transition as easy as possible. Let me grab your bags and we'll go home."

Home. Right now that word seemed like a foreign concept to Julie. James' eyes were warm and inviting and she knew that he wanted to make things perfect for her, but she also knew that her deception about her identity was something she'd need to address. Her immediate thought was to attack the issue by telling Caroline first when they met for dinner, then enlisting her friend's help in revealing her secret to James. That was, of course, if Caroline was still speaking to her at that point.

"Is this it?" James asked, lifting her large suitcase and smaller overnight bag, pulling Julie out of her swirling thoughts.

"Yes. The rest is on the truck. We have a while before it gets to your place."

"Let me correct you. It's our place now."

"That's so nice of you to say. I think it's more that I'm staying with you until I figure things out for myself," she replied.

"And I'm hoping that you never leave." He stepped in closer and leaned down to place another soft kiss on her cheek. "I think I have ways of convincing you that living with me will have its advantages."

Julie felt her stomach fill with butterflies. He made her feel sexy and special. She could only hope that he'd always want her at his side, especially after she revealed her truth. Shaking off her negative thoughts, she pulled herself up to her full height and replied, "Tell me. What do you have in mind?"

He smiled at her and she thought that she might just melt into a puddle on the floor of the empty apartment. "You'll never know if we don't get out of here. Are you ready?"

"Yes!" she replied, telling herself again that this would all be fine, that she didn't need to worry so much, that he was truly falling for her the way she was for him. "Just one last thing." She separated the key to the apartment from her others and wound it off the ring, leaving it on the counter next to Caroline's. "Done. Let's go."

With that, she walked out of the open door, waited for James to step into the hallway with her luggage and shut it behind him, heading off with him into uncharted waters. It was exciting and frightening at the same time, but when he reached for her hand, all Julie wanted to believe was that everything would be okay.

Chapter Nineteen

W HEN THEY ARRIVED AT JAMES' apartment, Julie couldn't help but feel anxious. She was here, with him, and she wasn't going anywhere. All of a sudden, reality seemed to be closing in on her.

He unlocked the door and they walked into the large entryway where he threw his keys into what looked like a very expensive crystal bowl on a side table sitting there for that purpose. He turned to face her and said, "I emptied out one side of the chest of drawers for you, and there's a second closet in the bedroom for you to use as well."

She froze for a moment and replied, "Wow. You didn't need to do that. I'm sure I can make do."

"There are two other bedrooms, and you're welcome to claim one of them. But I thought you'd like to share mine."

"I don't want to displace you. This is your home."

"Our home. It's our home now," was all he said.

She drew in a deep breath. "James. I so appreciate your offer to let me stay with you, but I want to be clear. I fully intend to find my own place. I'm just waiting to see what my next book contract looks like first. As you know, publishing is an up and down business. I can't even begin to plan my future without having an idea of my income for the next few years."

He stepped in close and ran his finger along her cheek. "I know, Julie. I'm just trying to nurture what we started here. I think you're special and this relationship of ours is the best thing to have ever happened to me." He paused. "I want you to stay for as long as you want. How does that sound to you?"

She could feel some of the tension ease at his touch. "It sounds so generous and kind. Thank you for saying that."

"I mean it, Julie. I really do. Having you spill tequila all over my shirt was the luckiest thing to ever happen to me." He leaned in and softly kissed her lips. "I'll bring your bags into the bedroom. You can unpack whenever you want." He lifted her suitcase and carried it down the long hallway. He quickly returned and said, "If you're hungry, we don't have to wait here for the movers to arrive. The doorman has the key. He can let them in."

"Or I can make us omelets, if you have eggs," she replied.

"I think that I do, we can look and see." He shrugged his shoulders and almost apologetically said, "I have a grocery delivery service. You can add to the list anytime, I'll send you the link."

Julie laughed as she walked with him toward the kitchen. She was curious because she hadn't seen it on her previous visit. "I think I can visit the market if I need some supplies," she said. When they turned the corner, Julie stopped short. She'd never seen an apartment in the city with a kitchen this large. Like everything else about him, this fully equipped space was spectacular. It had just about every appliance a gourmet chef would need. It seemed almost futuristic and was way over her pay grade. Creamy white marble countertops gleamed in the soft overhead light; stainless steel appliances dominated the room. There was an eight burner stove top and two separate wall ovens, as well as a microwave that slid out from a drawer. A small wine cooler sat beneath that as well. It was intimidating. *You can do this. Just ask for some navigational assistance.*

"Where do you keep the pans?" she asked, hoping her voice didn't betray her nerves.

"Right over here," he replied, bending down, opening a cabinet and pulling out a sliding shelf revealing an array of sparkling high end cookware.

"Perfect," she replied, grabbing a large skillet and placing it over a burner but not turning on the flame. She wasn't sure how and would need him to show her when she had everything ready to go. Then she turned to the massive refrigerator and opened one of the doors. Inside sat rows of perfectly stacked containers, each marked with a color coded label. There were a dozen eggs resting in a white ceramic carton on the door. She reached for those, pointed to the containers and asked, "what are these?"

"Pre-made meals. I don't actually do much cooking, but I'm great with the microwave," he said with a smile.

"I see. Well, I like to cook. Maybe we can compromise. Besides, I think that if I make some of our dinners at least, I'd feel somewhat better about staying here and not paying rent."

"You don't have to do that, Julie."

"I know. But I think I'd like to, at least a few nights a week. Now," she said, burying herself deeper in the cold, cavernous space. "Where can I find some cheese?"

He reached across her, brushing his arm against her breasts in his effort to open one of the many compartments under the main shelving.

"Here," was all he said, pulling back quickly and stepping around the large counter and out of her way.

She shook off the tingling sensation she still had from their brief contact and examined the contents of the drawer. "Cheddar sound good to you?"

He nodded.

She busied herself with the food preparation and once she was organized, she asked, "Do you know how to make coffee?"

He smiled. "Yes. I'm a master." He walked over to what appeared to be a very complicated machine.

Julie watched him for a moment and said, "I'm going to need a tutorial on that thing. It looks intimidating."

"So does what you're doing, at least to me. I think this is the perfect example of what a great team we make."

Julie felt warm all over from his words. Aside from Caroline, she'd never been close to any one person before. It would take some getting used to this arrangement.

"Do you want toast?" she asked.

"That sounds great," he replied. "And I know how to do that as well. I'll get it."

He walked over to the freezer and pulled out two bagels. Tossing them in the microwave to defrost, he said, "Let me show you where I keep the plates and silverware."

He opened some tall cabinets to reveal beautiful white plates, bowls and serving pieces. In a long drawer to the left of the sink sat dozens of shiny forks, knives and spoons, each in its own open bamboo box. Julie had never seen anything like this kitchen in her life and for the moment, she thought that she could get used to it.

"You could entertain an army with all this stuff," she said.

"I know. But I've haven't had a ton of guests here. And certainly no one special. Until now, that is, until you."

He looked at her with the most sincere expression she'd ever seen, and it made her heart melt.

"Really? No other woman ever stumbled back here with you after a night out?" Why is that?" she teased.

His gaze locked with hers. "I needed to have someplace that was just mine. This apartment has always been my sanctuary.

Somewhere to run and hide when the outside world got to be a little too much to handle. At least until now. But you, Julie? You make me feel like there's nothing I can't conquer when you're here with me."

She had to put the eggs down on the counter before she dropped them onto the floor. She almost didn't know what to say, but then she realized that she didn't need to reply with words. She walked over to where he stood and reached up to kiss him.

"I hope you always feel that way, James," she said, breaking their contact for a brief moment. *Especially after I tell you the truth.* Then she kissed him again.

"How long before those moving men get here?" he asked.

"Probably another hour or so," she replied, her breathing shallow.

"That's good to know," he said, lifting her up off of her feet and carrying her out of the kitchen, past the vast great room and to his bed. Food forgotten, they explored each other's body over and over again, making Julie wish that her past wasn't something that might come between them. She already knew that if that happened, she'd likely never recover.

LATER THAT EVENING, AFTER SHE'D UNPACKED HER SUITCASE and the few boxes the moving men delivered, Julie stood back from the closet and surveyed the contents. She really didn't have all that much, she realized. She worked from home, so most of the time she wore jeans. When she went out, she had relied on Caroline's clothing to help supplement her own. Now that she was living with James, she knew she'd need to buy a few pieces to fill in her wardrobe. There would be dinners and receptions to attend; she'd have to look like she belonged in his world.

She was making a mental checklist of what she might require

when James came into the bedroom. "Do you have everything you need?" he asked.

"Yes. I just have to get rid of the empty boxes. And go shopping," she added. "I think my clothing needs a slight update."

"Your wish is my command, madam," he said with a smile. "I'll take care of this garbage for you," he pointed to the pile of flat cardboard stacked in a corner of the room. "And anytime you need someone to take you shopping, just let me know."

Julie took a moment to compose herself before responding. He was so generous that she felt a little uncomfortable.

"I can shop for myself, but thanks. I'll look for what I need online, and if I don't find it there, I'll have Caroline help me. She's always been my fashion guru."

"I imagine that she does a great job of that, too. But don't let cost get in your way. I'm more than happy to help."

"I know you are, James." She smiled at him, hoping to convince him that she knew what she was doing. "I'm okay though. I'll work it out."

He nodded his head. "I'll be back in a minute. I'm just going to bring this to the recycling room in the hallway." He lifted the pile of discarded boxes and stepped out of the bedroom.

Of course this building has a recycling room! Not like my old building, where Caroline and I would load up our trash into the elevator and bring it to that creepy, dank basement for pick-up.

When he returned, he pulled off his tee shirt and threw it into the hamper that sat inside his walk-in closet, and stood bare-chested in front of her. "By the way," he said in a carefully measured tone, "while you were unpacking, my father called. He'd like us to meet him and my mom at my club for dinner on Friday night. Are you game?"

She sat down on the bed. "That was fast. He knows that I moved in?"

"Yup. And he's thrilled. He does like you, Julie. Maybe not as much as I do, but it's a start." He walked over to where she sat, and took her hand in his. "It's all good. I'm sure my parents will be on their best behavior."

She wasn't convinced, but replied, "If you say so."

He reached for her hand. "One day at a time, Julie. This will all work out, you'll see. I, for one, am so happy that you're here."

She looked directly into his deep brown eyes. They were intense and filled with longing. He was right. She was there with him and willing to take the risk of losing everything if this arrangement didn't work out.

"I'm going to take a shower before bed. Do you want to join me?"

She felt her knees go weak at his question. "Yes," she answered without hesitation. "I do."

He smiled and she felt her insides liquify. He then went into the large bathroom and turned on the water. Julie watched as steam began to fill the oversized stall. The shower was certainly large enough for two; the marble tiles seemed to glow as the warm water rained down on them. He quickly stripped off the rest of his clothing, his desire for her immediately apparent. He moved closer and lifted her arms. With one motion, pulled her shirt off over her head. He deftly unhooked her bra and threw it onto the smooth countertop before unfastening her jeans, unzipping them and pulling them down, along with her panties, very slowly over her legs. She stepped out of what was left of her clothing and let him lead her into the shower.

He had a variety of body washes and shampoos that sat neatly on a built in shelf. He lifted one bottle and a soft sea sponge, squirting some of the spicy scented wash on it. "Turn around," he said softly.

When she did, he began to rub it on her back. She felt her tense muscles relax as he washed away the stress of the day. He lowered the sponge and she responded, leaning back into his erection. He then parted her legs and dipped himself inside of her, so deeply that she didn't know if she'd be able to remain on her feet. He began to gently caress her breasts with the sponge. She reached out with both hands and braced herself on the slick wall, feeling the length of him stretch her fully and reveling in the blissful sensation he was creating for them both. The two of them shut out the world then; they moved with an ever quickening rhythm, remaining under the warm water of the shower, lost in each other. When he cried out her name, she felt wave after wave of electric pulses coursing through her body. It was as if they had been transported out of that shower to some higher plane of being; she could have stayed in that place forever.

A moment later, sponge forgotten, one hand on each of her breasts, he asked, "Are you still here with me?"

"Hmm," was all she could respond.

He shut off the shower and opened the large glass door, steam escaping into the room and fogging the mirrors. He grabbed a soft bath towel off the rack and wrapped it around her. It was warm. Julie felt like her body was made of liquid, as though all of her muscles had expended themselves and now needed to rest and recover.

"Time for sleep," he said, a towel draped around his midsection. He dried her off and brought her over to the bed, pulled back the blanket and tucked her in. She watched drowsily as he ran his own towel over his beautiful body before climbing in next to her.

"And to think," he whispered into her ear. "I used to hate Monday nights. With you here, I have so much more to look forward to."

She closed her eyes and drifted off to a peaceful sleep. Her true dream was resting comfortably by her side, and for tonight, that's all she needed to get some much deserved rest.

Chapter Twenty

WHEN JAMES WOKE the next morning, he checked to see if Julie was sleeping beside him. He wanted to be sure that he hadn't dreamt the whole thing. She looked so peaceful and angelic with her beautiful blonde hair fanned out on the pillow. The blanket had slipped off of her body and he had to tear himself away from her naked form now, he realized, or he'd never make it to the office today.

He walked into the bathroom and softly shut the door. Then he turned on the shower and let the water heat up while he brushed his teeth. Once he was done, he stepped into the stall, missing her presence there. Yesterday was truly memorable; he'd never felt this attracted to any other woman before. It was as if he couldn't get his fill of Julie, he wanted her to be in his arms always. Then he thought about Ryan and Daphne and was struck by the idea of marriage and children. While it had never appealed to him in the past, he could actually see himself settle down with the woman who was still asleep in his bed. It wouldn't be a sham, either, done just to deceive his father and further his own career aspirations. It would be real, if Julie would have him. They could live out their lives together bliss-fully, if she agreed.

He continued to process these new thoughts as he washed. He knew that he had to tread lightly; he didn't want to scare her away. But James also recognized that once he set his mind on a goal, he didn't shy away from it; he went all out, full force to guarantee that he'd succeed.

He'd need to start slowly. Make her feel comfortable here, assure her that this is where she belonged. As he massaged shampoo over his scalp, he had an idea. He would have one of the guest rooms turned into a home office, just for Julie. She could decorate it anyway she felt comfortable, a space where she could be productive and write her next book. That should make her happy and let her know how serious he was about having her stay here with him. James rinsed away the suds and decided to discuss it with her over dinner that night. In the meantime, he could have the woman who designed the interior of his place when he first moved in come back for a consultation with Julie. That could be the first step.

Feeling energized, James rinsed off his body with a shot of cold water and stepped out of the shower, toweling off before going back into the bedroom. Once there, he could see her beginning to stir.

"Hey there sleepy head," he teased. "Are you awake yet?"

"What time is it?" she asked, clearly stifling a yawn.

"Early. It's only 6:30. I have an important meeting downtown at 8. I have to hustle."

"Oh, okay," she replied, sitting up and pulling the sheet up over her breasts.

"I'll set up the coffee maker for you before I leave. It's the least I can do."

"Thank you, James. It's much appreciated. I never did get around to learning how to use that thing yesterday."

He could see a blush rise and cover her neck and face. "I guess we were too occupied with other, more important activities," he said with a grin. He walked into his closet, dropped his towel and pulled on some clean boxers. He pulled out his blue pinstriped suit pants and a white Egyptian cotton dress shirt, quickly working the buttons. Then grabbing a pair of gold cufflinks, he deftly fastened them securely through the starched fabric. Once done, he reached for a red and navy striped tie and fixed it around the collar of the shirt, checked his image in the full length mirror that leaned against the back wall of the walk-in, making sure the knot was even. Once satisfied with his work, he turned to pull the jacket from its hanger and stepped into the room.

"How do I look?" he asked.

Julie smiled. "Like the media mogul you are," she answered. "Very handsome."

"Well, this titan of publishing has to go, regretfully. There's nothing better I'd like than to climb back into this bed and do all sorts of fun things with you."

"That would be nice, but I understand. I have work to do as well."

He leaned over and kissed her, loving the feel of her lips against his own. "I'll see you here tonight?"

"Where else would I be?" she asked.

"That's the right answer," he replied. He began to walk out of the bedroom, but stopped short. "Julie. One more thing." He walked over to the dresser and lifted the top of a small, wooden box that sat there, a relic from a trip he'd once taken to Italy. He reached inside and pulled out a set of keys on a silver ring.

"Here. These are yours now. In case you want to go somewhere later, you'll have your own way to get back in the apartment." He handed them to her and watched as she pulled them in toward her chest.

"Thank you, James. Now I feel like an official roommate."

"You don't know how happy that makes me, Julie. Now I've gotta go."

He reluctantly turned and walked out of the room, knowing that he had the beginnings of a plan to make her stay, not just for now, but forever. As he head off to work, it was without his usual dread. With Julie in his life, everything had changed.

J AMES SAT THROUGH A DAY OF MEETINGS, GETTING A tremendous amount accomplished and feeling on top of the world. Even his assistant Claire had noticed the shift in his mood.

"What's next?" she asked close to five o'clock that afternoon. "Do you need a dinner reservation for tonight?"

It wasn't uncommon for him to escort one socialite or another out after work instead of going back to his apartment. But not anymore. "No, I'm good. You can go home. Thanks for today."

"You're welcome," she said, sounding somewhat surprised. "See you in the morning."

He looked up and smiled at the young woman. "Right. See you then." He noted the confusion in her expression and added, "It's okay, Claire, really. I'm good. Go on. Get out of here."

She disappeared quickly from his office and he could hear her rummaging around in her desk for a minute before all sound dissipated and it was quiet once again. He lifted his phone from the desk and dialed Julie. She picked up immediately.

"Hi," he heard her say. "How is your day going?"

"It was great. How was yours?"

"Productive," she said. "I finished an entire chapter on table seating charts. And you?"

"My meetings went well, thank you. So well, in fact, that I'm going to be leaving here soon."

"Wow, that's great," she responded. "I'm making dinner. I'm was the mood to experiment in that kitchen of yours."

"Of ours, Julie. Of ours."

"Okay, of ours," she laughed. "Any requests?"

"Just that you're there is enough for me. But don't ask me twice. I'm sure I can think of something..."

"I meant for dinner! Don't get any crazy ideas."

"Crazy ideas? I have lots of those. But as far as dinner goes, I'm sure whatever you make will be fantastic. I'll leave here in a few minutes. See you soon."

"Can't wait," was all she said as he hung up the phone.

James smiled to himself and realized that it was earlier than usual for him to call it a day, but he felt an undeniable longing to go home, to be with Julie, to have her to himself all night. This was all so new to him, these feelings about a woman that he had not known for very long. While he recognized that it happened very quickly, he also reminded himself that not everything in life went according to plan. As he shut down his computer and a random uncomfortable thought came to his mind. *What if this all didn't work out? What then?*

Aside from the fact that he'd be devastated if she left him, he'd lose all leverage he'd gained with his father for control of the company. Even though he'd started this relationship with Julie under false pretenses, thinking he could pay her to pretend to be his girlfriend to deceive his father, everything had changed. With her in his life, there would be nothing that he could not achieve.

In that one moment, James realized that he'd had enough of his dad's rules. He'd start a newspaper on his own, if he had to, and he'd convince Julie that there was no one she was meant to be with more than him. Feeling like he could conquer the world, he picked up his phone, tucked it away in his jacket pocket and made for home, looking forward to an evening with the very special woman who waited there for him.

JAMES COULD FEEL AN UNDENIABLE BUBBLE OF EXCITEMENT rise in his chest as he turned the lock and let himself inside the apartment, knowing that he had a whole evening ahead to spend with Julie. As he walked through the door, the air was fragrant, smelling like something wonderful was cooking in the kitchen. He could hear music playing and the table had been set with two gleaming white plates. A variety of glasses and silverware sat silently on the linen cloth that covered the table. Two silver candlesticks stood in the middle of it all, filled with cream colored tapered candles waiting to be lit. It was such a different scene than the empty, quiet, and lonely space it had been just a few days before now, that it actually took his breath away for a moment.

He shook his head to clear it, tossed his keys into the bowl on the table by the door and went looking for the woman who'd turned this place into a home virtually overnight. When he found her in the kitchen, she had her head bent over in a large stock pot, vigorously stirring the contents within.

"Whatever you've made smells fantastic!" he exclaimed as he walked around the large counter to take her into his arms.

"Well, I tried a new recipe. I hope it tastes good."

"I'm sure it does, but truthfully", he said, lowering his mouth onto hers for a kiss, "There is nothing that tastes as good as you do."

He heard her low moan as he dipped his tongue into her mouth. She had the same reaction to him that he had to her: pure desire.

"I'm going to go inside and change out of this suit, if that's okay."

"Of course," she replied, lifting the spoon into the pot once more. "Dinner will be ready soon, but formal attire is not required."

James glanced over at the simple yellow summer shift she was wearing. She looked so comfortable in her surroundings, and he felt his heart swell with happiness. He wanted her to feel at home, and it looked like she did. He quickly made his way into the bedroom and changed into a pair of worn blue jeans and a white tee shirt, leaving his feet bare.

As he approached the dining table, he saw her about to light the candles.

"Let me do that," he offered, reaching for the electronic igniter she held in one hand.

She passed it to him. "Great. I'll get dinner."

"Can I help?"

"Yes," she said. "Choose some wine and open the bottle."

"Red or white?" he asked.

"Surprise me," she replied with laugh. "I'm not one of those people who knows which wine goes with which type of food. I just know what I like."

"And what is that?"

"Something earthy, not sweet, please." She smiled and reached out to put her hand on his arm. He felt his skin heat up immediately under her touch. "Are you hungry?" she asked.

For as innocent as her question was, he knew that his answer was truly indecent, so he just nodded.

"Great. Everything is ready." She turned and walked back into the kitchen.

He went in after her, opened the wine refrigerator and pulled out a bottle of Far Niente Chardonnay. He'd visited the vineyard and had been mesmerized by the beautiful grounds and the old stone winery that had been lovingly restored by the owners and declared a National Landmark. It was a trip he'd love to take with Julie, he realized. He busied himself with the cork, smoothly removing it in one stroke and carried the chilled bottle to the table where he poured them each a glass.

"I hope you like gazpacho," she said, carefully balancing two bowls as she slowly walked them over to the table. "When I took a break from writing today, I went for a walk and ended up stumbling on a pop-up farmer's market in the school yard a few blocks from here. The tomatoes were calling out to me."

"It looks so good," he said, pulling her chair out for her once she'd completed her task.

She smiled at him and James felt the world outside the windows of the apartment fade away. It was as if they were in their own little bubble, no intrusions, no worries. He tasted the soup and remarked, "This is delicious." He raised his glass. "To you, Julie. Thanks for making me dinner."

She took a sip of her wine. "This is so smooth, perfect choice!"

"I'm glad it passes the test!" he teased.

"I hope you can say the same about my culinary skills. Just know that I enjoyed having the chance to cook in this kitchen. I found everything a chef could possibly need," she smiled and took another sip of wine. "I had fun," she added.

"Are you happy with the work you did on the book today?" he asked, changing subjects. "Were you comfortable writing here?"

"Yes. I sat at the counter. It was fine."

James drew in a deep breath. "I'd like to propose a different set-up. What if we turned one of the guest rooms into an office for you?"

She gasped and set down her glass. "Oh, no, James. That's

very generous, but totally unnecessary. I'm good wherever I can plug in my laptop."

"That may be true, Julie, but I'd like to offer you a more permanent solution. You can decorate the room however you'd like. We can upgrade your computer, as well."

She turned away from him for a moment, and when she looked at him again, there were tears in her eyes. He got up from his seat and lifted her out of hers.

"I didn't mean to upset you. It's just a thought. You don't have to..."

"It's not that, James. Honestly? I'm not sure how long I'll be here. I don't want you to rearrange your life for me."

He pulled her even closer. "Too late, Julie. That ship has sailed. I'll do anything to keep you happy and right here for as long as I can." She was trembling in his embrace, like a scared bird. He was afraid she'd try to fly away. Not wanting to overwhelm her further, he didn't verbalize his next thought: *Please Julie, please. Stay forever.*

Chapter Twenty-One

EARLIER THAT DAY, after James had gone to work and she sat behind her computer, Julie felt as if she'd been transported to some magical place where none of her problems could ever exist. James made her feel safe and protected; he didn't want her to leave and she didn't want to go. It was a perfect situation, if she left out the fact that she was lying to him about who she truly was. When the truth came out – and she realized that she had to tell him, and she had to tell him soon—she could only hope that he'd still care about her the way he did right now. Julie was feeling warm and fuzzy from all the wine she'd consumed, but it was a pleasant, liquid sort of relaxed sensation, as if her bones and muscles had finally found some peace as she sat with him on one of the couches in the great room, her body leaning into his. That morning, when she first sat behind her computer to work on her book with a large mug of the steaming coffee James had made for her, she had been so wound up and tense. Actually, each time she picked up her phone or opened her laptop, she worried about what the internet might have to say about her and James. Did the tabloids know that they'd moved in together? Would there be grainy photos of her slipping into the building where he lived? Did they find her shopping in the Farmer's Market? She'd taken care to pull a baseball cap she'd foraged for in the front hall closet low over her face, but she knew the paparazzi were a shrewd bunch. Most importantly, did her mother text her again and ask for more money? She sent a check with the amount she would have paid in rent for the coming month. Would it be enough to satisfy the other woman?

There had been nothing. No troubling pictures or requests. She had been able to write in relative calm, finishing a chapter early in the afternoon and making notes for the next one. She put away her work and roamed around the kitchen, running her hand over the smooth countertop and decided to experiment a bit by making James a meal. She went into the dining area to explore and found beautiful dishes, silverware, linens and glasses in one of the heavy sideboard buffet pieces there. She was excited to use everything she touched. She wanted to offer him something special to show him how much she appreciated being there.

Julie busied herself for the rest of the day, grabbing her keys, going to the market, returning to prepare a simple meal, nothing complicated. Some gazpacho, a green salad and baked salmon filets. By the time he called to tell her he was on the way home, she was done. She jumped into the shower and slipped into her favorite yellow sundress, added a touch of mascara to her lashes and returned to the kitchen to put the finishing flourishes on dinner. Now, in his arms, she was as happy as she'd ever been. She knew she had to tell him about her past, but it just didn't feel like the right moment. Especially when he began to run his fingers lightly over her stomach. She could feel the familiar butterflies spring to life.

"Dinner was delicious, Julie. Thanks for putting in all that effort. You don't have to do that, you know. I'm happy with take-out, or a sandwich. I just want to be here with you, that's all."

"I'm glad you enjoyed it, James. It was a great creative outlet for me today. I finished writing early enough to get it done." She leaned back and turned her face to his, placing a small kiss on one cheek. She watched as his warm brown eyes seemed to ignite with that spark of desire she'd come to recognize.

"Take me up on my offer, Julie," he whispered into the shell of her ear. "Let me make an office here for you. That way you never have to leave."

She felt so safe, so protected in that moment. She turned and pushed him down on the cushions, pressing her body on top of his. She could not stop herself from wanting him even if she tried. Julie knew one thing for sure: she was in love with James Curran.

He responded to her abrupt move by shifting himself more deeply into the couch so that he could slowly caress the exposed skin of her legs, deftly working his way up her thighs to the most sensitive part of her body. The heat between them was undeniable; his erection pressed against her belly and a moan escaped his throat as he kissed her neck. She fumbled to undo the fastening of his jeans, and when she succeeded, he shimmied them to his ankles as he lay beneath her. Then, in one quick move he pushed aside her panties and was inside of her, the two of them moving in perfect unison, finding each other in a burst of energy that made her heart race so fast, Julie was sure it would escape her chest.

A moment later, he asked, "Are you okay?"

"Yes. Are you?"

"I'm not sure," he responded. "That was…"

"Don't say it. Don't say anything. I know what you mean."

He lifted his head and she tilted her chin so that she was looking directly at him, her blue eyes staring into his brown ones. "You need to know this, Julie. I have never felt about anyone else the way I feel about you. What we have here is special. I'm not going to let you go, do you understand me?"

She heard his words, but they made her feel queasy. *Tell him the truth, Julie. Do it now.*

In the distance, she could hear something buzzing. She blinked and broke his gaze. "What is that?" she asked.

"Nothing important, I'm sure. It's just my phone. I put it on silent."

The noise stopped for a minute, then resumed.

"Maybe someone needs you. It could be important. Do you want me to get it out of your jeans pocket?" She motioned to his ankles and then looked down at herself. "I can't believe we did that without taking off all of our clothing."

He shrugged. "Sorry. No time. It would seem that I'm not able to control myself around you, sweetheart."

Julie laughed. "I think I'm the one who got us started. No apology necessary."

"Right," he said, lifting her up off of him so that they both sat next to one another on the couch. Shifting his feet to the floor, he kicked off his jeans and found the phone. It began to buzz again and he glanced at it. "My father. As you know, he wants what he wants when he wants it." He tapped the screen, lifting it to his ear.

"Dad," he began. "What can I do for you?"

She watched his face as he listened to the voice on the other end before he responded.

"Of course. Yes. I already told you we'd be there. See you Friday evening. Love to mom." He disconnected the call.

"His timing is impeccable. That was to remind me that we're having dinner with my parents later this week."

"I remember. And I'm meeting Caroline on Thursday night, so you're on your own. Don't do anything too wild."

"The only thing wild that I want to do is in the bedroom with you right now."

She felt her insides begin to quiver once again. "What did you have in mind?"

"Come with me and find out," was all he said, reaching his hand out for her to hold.

Julie said nothing. She put her hand in his, squeezed it tightly and followed him down the hall. If all her nights with James were to be as perfect as this one, she could only pray that he'd forgive her once he knew the truth. For tonight, she decided, she'd just feel, not think. It was better that way.

THE NEXT MORNING DAWNED BRIGHTLY. JULIE WAS OUT OF bed with the sunrise, determined to get at least one chapter done by lunch. She had made up her mind to go shopping for some new clothing, something she hadn't done in a very long time. In just two days, she and James had settled into a routine. He showered, dressed for the office and made her coffee; she kept him company and waited for him to leave before sitting down at her computer. Delaying opening her laptop meant that she could keep the outside world at bay for just a while longer, allowing her to remain in her little bubble of happiness for as long as she could.

Once again, she breathed a sigh of relief when there were no pictures or messages that she might find upsetting. She was able to get to work without having to worry about what type of bad news might come knocking on her door. Four hours later and half a chapter on the proper way to handle a guest who might have had too much to drink at a wedding reception, Julie raised her hands up over her head and stretched. She looked at the screen of her laptop and smiled. This project was shaping up nicely; her editor should be very pleased with the results. She lifted the now ice cold mug of coffee that James had made for her earlier and stood from her seat at the counter where she'd set herself up to work. Walking over to the sink to wash it, Julie thought about his offer of converting one of the guest rooms into a home office. She dried the mug and set it back in its place in the cabinet, rinsed out the coffee pot and disposed of the used grounds. *Which room would I choose if I were to let him do this thing?* She left the kitchen and walked down the hallway that led to the additional bedrooms. It was on the opposite side of the over-sized apartment, far from the space that she and James were sharing. This section of building was both quiet and removed from the more busy street-facing side; it would make for a perfect work area. She peeked into one doorway, then the other, trying to determine which would be best, ultimately deciding that it really didn't matter. If she were to accept his offer, either would work. It really made her happy to know that he wanted to make her comfortable here. Julie wanted to stay. She only prayed that he'd still want her after he knew the truth.

Shaking off the negative thoughts, she walked back through the apartment and went to get dressed. After a quick shower, she pulled a slim navy skirt and short-sleeved silk button down shirt off their hangers, slipped on her clothing and added a pair of wedged sandals. Once satisfied that her outfit would be easy to take on and off in a dressing room, she picked up her purse and the keys James had given her and took the elevator down to the lobby. She smiled at the doorman and he returned the greeting; then she head out into the bright sunshine of the early summer afternoon, walking down Fifth Avenue. James' apartment was well-located. It wasn't far from the famous museums a little further uptown or the pricey department stores just about a half mile in the other direction. Despite the calendar telling her it was summer, it wasn't that humid or hot; she decided to walk. Having lived in the city long enough to know when the major sales were scheduled at the more expensive shops, she knew that her timing was perfect and she could get lucky at Bergdorf's. With a spring in her step, she lifted her cell phone out of her purse and dialed Caroline.

The call quickly connected. "Hello, stranger," she said brightly.

"Hello yourself! How are you? We're still on for dinner tomorrow, right?"

"Yes, of course. Just checking in. Do you have some time today? Want to come shopping with me?"

"You don't know how much I wish I could say yes! I am swamped. I think I'm almost done with the new collection. I'll bring you some samples."

"Not necessary, but thanks. I'm in dire need of some new things. My wardrobe looks lonely without yours to fill it out."

"I told you you'd miss me," Caroline teased.

"More than you know," Julie answered.

"How's living with James? Hot sexy fun, I hope."

"It's working out for now."

"For now? What does that mean?"

"Just that he seems too good to be true, that's all."

She heard Caroline blow out a long breath before responding. "Julie. How many times do I have to tell you not to undersell yourself? You are pretty awesome. He's lucky that you spilled that drink on him."

"Funny. James said that same thing."

"Then believe him."

"What about you? How's living with Stephen?"

"Good, I guess. We really haven't seen much of each other. I've been so busy with work. I haven't even unpacked yet!"

"Well, let me know if you need help getting yourself organized. I can't wait to see the loft all set up!"

"Right. We'll have to have you and James over for drinks soon," Caroline said.

Julie heard a muffled crash from the other end of the phone. "All okay?" she asked.

"Um. Not sure. Gotta go. See you tomorrow. Text me a time and place."

The connection ended. Julie looked at the screen of her phone and realized it was later in the day than she'd first thought. She picked up her pace and walked a briskly, hoping to find a bargain or two in one of the high-end boutiques along the way.

Two hours later and multiple shopping bags in hand, she had spent more money than she'd wanted to but felt like she'd scored a few really good pieces of clothing: a halter top in a deep emerald green, two printed sundresses; a pair of designer jeans on the clearance rack that she could have never afforded otherwise and some strappy black patent leather sandals with sky-high heels that made her think of her best friend. Caroline would most certainly approve. She was on her way back to the apartment when her phone rang. Her heart leapt when she saw that it was James.

"Hi," she answered the call.

"Hi. What are you up to?"

"Heading home. I needed some retail therapy, so I went out for a bit."

"Were you successful on your quest?" he teased.

"Yes! I think you might say that I was." She looked down at the bags in her hands.

"Great! Dinner out tonight?"

"Or in. We could call for take-out. That might be nice."

"You don't have to convince me. The thought of sitting on

the couch with you, a glass of wine, and the cuisine of your choice sounds like heaven."

"Tough day?"

"I've had worse. Knowing I'm coming home to you makes it all feel okay."

She felt a rush of warmth course through her veins. "See you soon."

"Can't wait," he replied.

"Me too," she said as she hung up. Julie could not remember a time when she felt this content. She forced down the persistent thought that kept simmering on in her brain, the one where she knew that she had to tell James the truth about herself. Right then she decided to tell Caroline first, to see what happened when she revealed her past to her best friend. Once she cleared that hurdle, she'd tell James. She took one deep breath and allowed herself this time to be happy, for as long as it would last her.

Chapter Twenty-Two

BEFORE SHE COULD BLINK, it seemed to Julie, it was late Thursday afternoon and she was getting dressed to go and meet Caroline for dinner. Julie had been on pins and needles all day, knowing that it was time to confess everything to her best friend. Hopefully, Caroline would forgive her the huge omission. Julie truly wasn't sure if she could expect that from her friend. She convinced herself that if the situation was reversed, she'd let Caroline off the hook. But it wasn't. She was the liar, not her former roommate.

Julie thought about what she was going to say, had rehearsed it in her mind over and over again. She'd wait until they'd had some alcohol and then she'd spill the entire story. It was truly a big test, one she needed to pass, because after she told Caroline everything, James was up next. If her BFF accepted what Julie had to say, maybe he would too. At least that was her plan, one she felt shaky about, at best.

They had arranged to meet at their favorite sushi place near their old apartment. Julie put on the pair of the new jeans she'd bought yesterday with her tight pink tee shirt, then added a lightweight navy linen blazer just in case the air conditioning was running at full blast in the restaurant. She slipped on her wedged sandals and was ready to go. She reached for her purse and her keys, then lifted her phone out of her bag and dialed James. She waited a brief few seconds for the call to connect.

"You're a mind-reader! I was just thinking about you?" he exclaimed.

"I hope those were pleasant thoughts," she replied, holding her breath for a second longer. "I'm heading out to meet Caroline. Just thought you'd like to know."

"I remember. And don't you forget that we're having dinner with my folks tomorrow evening."

"Oh. I couldn't if I tried," she replied. "I'm prepared for an interesting dinner with them both."

"If I didn't know that you were kidding, I'd be concerned," he answered. "Be sure to have fun tonight. You've worked so hard all week. Take some time for yourself."

"I'll miss you," she breathed into the phone. "Make sure that you eat dinner."

"I did used to live alone, you know that, right? Besides, I plan to wait up for you. I have thoughts about what we can do once you get home."

A thrill shot up her spine. "You can convince me not to go. I mean it." *Please ask me to stay back. I really don't want to do this tonight.*

"Nope. You need some girl time with Caroline. Go and enjoy. I'll see you later."

She sighed. "Right. Later."

"Can't wait," he replied as he disconnected the call.

In the silence he left behind, Julie picked up her things and with a last, backwards glance, left the apartment, hoping that when she returned, she was in one piece and her friendship with Caroline was still intact.

. . .

JULIE WAS THE FIRST TO ARRIVE AT THE RESTAURANT AND SHE was able to ask for a table toward the back, a little more secluded than usual, but better for the serious conversation she knew she was about to have. She waited for a bit, scrolling through her phone, trying to distract herself. Then, in a cloud of the bergamot forward perfume that was her signature scent, Caroline was there, two small shopping bags in hand, all flushed as a result of the trip from the loft downtown. Julie stood and the two women hugged before settling down at their table.

"I'm so sorry! It took forever to get here. Don't you miss our old neighborhood? The cross-town traffic sucks at this time of day. Sheesh!!" She was rambling. "Oh, and, these are for you." She handed her company's logoed shiny red bags to Julie.

"No worries. I'm glad you made it. I've missed seeing you," Julie said sincerely. "What's in here?" She placed the bags down at her feet and reached inside.

"I miss you too, and that's some underwear from my new collection," she replied, scanning the room for their waiter. "Did you order a drink?"

"Not yet." Julie peered into the bag. It was filled with what seemed like scraps of lacy material.

"Well, let's do that first. Then I want to hear everything."

"About..."

"Don't be coy with me, Julie. About James. What it's like living with that dreamy man of yours."

Just then the server appeared.

"Two large Dassais, please," Caroline said. The man just nodded and left to fill their order.

Once he was out of earshot, Caroline asked, "How's the sex? It's different when you're under the same roof, isn't it?"

"What do you mean?" Julie asked, eyebrows raised.

"I mean, now that I'm living with Stephen, the bloom is off the rose."

"Huh?"

Caroline gave out an exacerbated sigh. "I feel like since I'm always there that he doesn't have the same urgency to fool around as he did when we lived apart and he had to go home. I don't know, it's just not the same. What about you?"

Julie didn't want to admit that she and James could not keep their hands off of one another. It didn't seem like an appropriate response. Instead, she said, "Things are fine for us. We both work long hours. The three nights I've been there, we've dozed off together on the couch watching Netflix."

"See what I mean? This level of commitment has some large disadvantages. I'm already missing hot, urgent sex. Not good. Maybe the contents of those bags I gave you will help. Not that it's done me much good."

The waiter returned with two green bottles and small drinkware on a silver tray. He carefully placed everything on the table and proceeded to open the caps, pouring some of the clear liquid into each cup. "Are you ready to order, or do you need more time?" he asked.

"We're going to drink this first, if you don't mind," Caroline said forcefully. The young man bowed to them and walked away quickly.

"Was I rude? I didn't mean to be rude," she put her head in her hands.

"You were a bit direct, but I'm sure we can make it up to him with a nice tip."

"Ugh," Caroline muttered.

"What's going on with you?" Julie asked, truly concerned.

"I'm not sure. I think that what it boils down to is that I'm beginning to feel as if I'm not really ready to get married. I do love Steven, but the whole wedding planning thing has me twisted in knots. We ordered the invitations, but how can I be sure that I'm truly ready for this step? And my mother? O.M.G. She's making me crazy. She's out of control."

Julie felt her stomach drop at the mention of the word "mother". She had to tell Caroline the truth. All of a sudden, it didn't seem like the right time.

"And to make matters worse, my dress is ready. I'm afraid to go try it on," Caroline added and looked directly at Julie. "Will you come with me?" She took a large swig of sake.

"Of course, you know I will. Isn't that my job as your maid of honor, anyway?"

"Whatever. This is crazy. Maybe Steven and I should just elope."

"And deny your friends and family the opportunity to celebrate with you?"

"I guess there's no real etiquette guide for my feelings, is there?" Caroline asked, taking another gulp of her drink and filling her glass again.

Julie looked at her former roommate and said, "Life is not always lived by the rules. You know that." She reached across the table and took one of Caroline's hands in her own. "And, no matter what you choose to do, I'm here for you."

Caroline's face crumbled and tears welled in her eyes. "I know that you are. I'm just so confused. What should I do?"

"I can't tell you that, sweetie. My advice is to follow your heart." *And in the spirit of that...* "I do have something I need to tell you, though." *Now or never.*

"If you tell me you're knocked up, I'm going to be sick all over this table."

"Really? Like I'm not the most careful person you know." She pointed to the slim stick implanted under the skin of her upper arm. The birth control device had another three years to go before needing to be replaced.

"True. I take it back. Now just tell me."

Julie drew in a breath. "It's not that simple."

"It can be. Talk to me."

"I'm not who you think I am," Julie said in a rush of words.

"Oh, please. None of us are, right?"

"I'm being serious," Julie said softly.

"What does that mean, exactly?" Caroline stared at her, eyes wide.

"For starters, my mother isn't dead. She's very much alive and living in a trailer park in South Jersey. And Porter isn't my real name. Delgardio is." *There it was. The truth.*

"What the hell are you talking about?"

Julie drew in a long breath and began to answer the question. "When got into Columbia, I decided to be an entirely different person than the one I was growing up. I wanted to be different, to be more refined than my roots would allow. So I changed my name, my attitude, my back story."

"What?? There was no accident? Your mom is alive?" Caroline was still stuck on the first of the details.

"Very much so. In fact, she's extorting me for money. She read about my relationship with James in *Tell All.* How's that for irony?"

"I don't think that's the definition of irony, by the way. It's just bad luck. But hold on. Why didn't you tell me this before? All that time we were living together, you could have confessed this. Why tell me now?"

"Because," Julie said softly. "You need to know the truth. And I have to let James know as well."

"Holy shit," was all Caroline said before draining her glass again. "I need a moment to think." She sat back in her chair. "For starters, you lied to me. All this time, and you lied. I don't know where to put that piece of news." Shaking her head, she continued, "And you say your mother is extorting you? That sounds even more hard to believe than the original story you told me about her being dead. I'm really not sure what I'm supposed to believe."

Julie sat up straight in her chair. "I know. I'm so sorry. You have no idea just how badly I wanted to tell you. I lacked the courage."

"What did you think I would do? Kick you out of the apartment? Not be your friend because of where you came from? I don't care about how shitty your childhood was. All that should matter is that you lifted yourself out of it."

Julie sat silently and let Caroline continue processing. "How do I know that you're even telling me the truth now? About your mother, I mean."

Julie reached into her purse and found her phone. She scrolled through her texts until she found the last thread from her mother. She turned the screen toward Caroline and watched her expression change as she read through the messages.

"Did you send her money?"

"Yes. I sent the cash I would have put toward our rent."

"And she hasn't contacted you since?"

"Not yet."

Caroline poured the remains of her bottle of sake into her cup then lifted Julie's almost full one. "Do you mind?"

"No. Help yourself."

Once she took yet another sip of the dry rice brew, she said, "We need a plan."

Relief flooded through Julie's body. She leaned in. "Does this mean that you accept my apology?"

"It means that I'm working on it. Besides, who knows what might happen tomorrow. You're my best friend. I need you."

"I love you, Caroline," Julie said, tears filling her eyes.

"Yeah. I know. And I love you too. Now. What and when are you going to tell James?"

Julie blew her nose into a paper napkin. "I was hoping you'd help me with that."

"I will. Right after we eat some spicy tuna rolls. I'm hungry, somewhat drunk, and I think my best friend told me that she's not the person who I always knew her to be. Oh. And I may not want to get married. That's a whole lot for an empty stomach."

Julie craned her neck and met their waiter's eye. "Let me do the ordering, okay?"

Caroline winked. "Sure thing, whoever you are. Just know that this dinner is on you." She sat back and downed the contents of her drink.

For the first time in what seemed like forever, Julie smiled and knew that even if she was left holding the check, she wasn't going to be left alone. She'd always have Caroline in her corner, and that was no small thing.

Chapter Twenty-Three

THEY SAT in the restaurant until the place emptied out entirely, save the staff who appeared very ready to go home. After she paid the bill, Julie stood, shopping bags firmly grasped in one hand, looked over at her friend and asked, "Do you need me to call you an Uber? I'm ordering one for myself. It's not a problem to do the same for you"

"No. I'm not as drunk as you think. I'm fine." She opened her own phone and scrolled through the program appropriately. "Are you set with the plan?"

"Yes," Julie nodded her head emphatically. "I hope it works."

"It will. Just wait until you're back home with him tomorrow night after dinner with his parents. He'll be so grateful that you're helping him win over his father that he'll forgive you anything. I'm sure of it."

She nodded. "And us. Are we okay, now, Caroline? I mean really okay?"

Her friend lifted herself off of her chair on shaky feet. She waved her hands in the air. "Yes. I'll get over this bombshell, I'm sure. I just need to sleep on it."

Julie grabbed onto Caroline's arm and walked with her outside to wait on the sidewalk for their rides home.

"You know what I really hate?" Caroline asked.

Julie was somewhat afraid to hear the answer, but replied, "No. What?"

"That we're taking separate cars home. I miss you. I miss our apartment."

"I miss you too," Julie answered, stepping closer to her friend and giving her a tight hug. "But I'm always here. Just a phone call away."

Then the car Caroline had ordered arrived. Julie helped the other woman navigate getting into the backseat on unsteady feet. "I'll call you in the morning," she said as Caroline settled into cushions. Julie closed the car door.

Her best friend leaned out the open window. "Not too early. You know me..."

"I absolutely do," Julie said with a laugh, feeling more light-hearted than she had in days. As she watched the car pull away from the curb, her only thought was *one hurdle down. One more huge one to go.*

"Did you and Caroline behave yourselves tonight? No flirting with the bartender, I hope?" James teased as she sat next to him on the couch. She had been dreaming of this moment of peace since she entered her Uber and made her way home to him.

"Yes. It was lovely to be out with Caroline. I really do miss seeing her every day."

"You should make it a regular thing, you know. Having dinner with your friends. I'm very capable of taking care of myself."

"I know that. I love being here with you, that's just the truth.

I will make time for Caroline, though. She's really important to me."

"Good. That's settled. By the way, what's in those?" He motioned to the shopping bags her friend had given her earlier.

"Some samples from Caroline's new collection."

"That sounds interesting. Can I see what she sent?"

Julie smiled. "I can model some of the pieces for you, if you'd like me to."

His eyes lit up. "A private runway show? I'd never say no to that!"

She stood up, a bag in each hand. "Pour yourself a drink and wait right here!" she exclaimed, taking her things into the bedroom. Once there, she dumped the lingerie onto the bed and realized that it might have been better to have looked them over herself first. Everything was sheer and very skimpy. She lifted a demi-bra, the matching thong panties and a pair of garters. *Well, if you're in for a penny, you're in for a pound.* She took off her clothing and shimmied out of her current undergarments, donning the frothy ones Caroline had made for her. Once she had everything on, she could see just how little coverage the scant material provided. Her nipples peeked over the lacy red fabric of the bra's half-cup, and the garters hung low on her thighs, grazing her skin and making her entire body feel overly sensitive. She was about to go out and model for James when she spied her gray high heels, the ones she wore the first night they'd met. She quickly slipped them on and made her way back into the great room.

When he saw her, James let out a long, slow whistle. "Holy shit, Julie. You look so amazing in that lingerie. Caroline really does know what she's doing."

"Does she ever. She's turned her small business into a huge company. She's got twenty-five employees, now."

"Good for her, but even better for me. Come here. I'd like to feel what's under that fabric."

She smiled at him and carefully walked over to the couch, turning slowly in front of him before straddling his lap, her breasts grazing his soft cotton tee shirt.

"I'll let Caroline know you approve of her designs. She'll be so pleased to hear it." She leaned in and kissed him, dipping her tongue into his mouth, enjoying the feeling of control the garments gave her. Caroline had been so right about feeling empowered by what you wore beneath your outer clothing.

When he came up for air, he said, "You should tell her that she's a genius. And here's the most important part," he remarked, deftly unclasping the hooks on the back of the bra, her breasts springing free. "It's even easy to remove." With that, the two of them quickly shed what was left of what they wore and made love long into the night.

AFTER ANOTHER PRODUCTIVE DAY AT HER LAPTOP, JULIE FELT on top of the world. There had been no new demanding texts from her mother or any new pictures of her and James together in the tabloids. She was easily adjusting to her new life in James' apartment and enjoying every minute of living with him. It all seemed too good to be true. She had spoken to Caroline in the morning while drinking the coffee he'd prepared for her before leaving for the office.

"Do you need to review our strategy? Do you have set what you'll tell James tonight after dinner with his parents?" Caroline asked.

"Yes. I'm feeling okay about this. I know I have to do it, no matter what. The time has come. I just hope he's as understanding as you were last night."

"I have a good feeling about him, Julie. I think he'll wrap his head around the truth and be fine with it. And if he's not, well then, he's just not worth your effort. My loft has plenty of space for you if you need to stay with me."

"You mean with you and Stephen."

"Of course, silly. That's what I meant."

"Let's hope I don't need to take you up on that, Caroline. I've fallen in love with James," she added softly.

"I can tell. It's nice to see you so happy."

Julie thought she heard a wistful sound in the timber of her friend's voice. "Are you okay?" she asked.

"Yes, yes," Caroline sounded stronger now. "Fine. Just busy getting ready for the new collection to hit the stores."

"Oh, and about that. James loved the designs. I modeled some pieces for him last night when I got home."

"I'm glad you did. It's great to get good reviews."

"Well, I promise you five stars on Yelp. We had a really good time."

"That's the whole idea. Okay. I've got to go. Call me from the bathroom of the restaurant tonight if you need a pep talk. But you won't. You've got this, Julie."

"Love you, Caroline."

"Love you too, doll." Then the line went dead.

As she carefully dressed in her emerald green halter top for dinner with James' parents, she slipped on another new pair of panties, this one with a dainty lace pattern across the top. She smoothed the fabric over the black pencil skirt she'd chosen to wear and felt confident and strong. They were all meeting at James' private club in an hour, and she still had to finish putting on her make-up. Rushing into the bathroom, she emptied the contents of her cosmetic bag on to the counter, reaching for her eyeliner. Once she carefully applied that, she took her mascara wand to her blonde lashes, giving them the volume and color they needed to be seen. Finally, she quickly brushed some blush across her cheeks and applied a deep red creamy lip gloss. She was ready to go.

Julie tugged on her black patent leather heels, happy in the knowledge that James would be waiting outside for her in his town car with Charlie at the wheel. *It's truly amazing just how quickly I am getting used to this lifestyle,* she mused. Then she sent up a quick prayer toward heaven. *Please let him understand why I lied. Please.*

She grabbed her evening bag and locked the door, taking the elevator down to the lobby. Smiling at the doorman as she passed, she stepped outside and saw the car idling at the curb. Her heart leapt in excitement knowing that James was inside, waiting for her. Just then, seemingly out of nowhere, a swarm of photographers descended from all angles, camera flashes blinding her for a moment. She heard them call out, "Miss Porter, look this way," then "Julie, smile for me" and she lifted her clutch up over her face to shield her eyes. Then she froze. The next thing she knew, James was by her side, guiding her into the waiting car. He slid her over the seat, got in and closed the door sharply behind them, ordering Charlie to drive.

"Are you okay? You're not hurt anywhere, are you? No twisted ankle?"

She just moved her head back and forth to let him know she was alright, but then her whole body began to shake.

He moved closer and put his arms around her. "I'm so sorry, sweetheart. I didn't see the bastards. I would have gotten rid of them if I did."

"How many of them? Were they yours? From *Tell All?*"

"If I find out they were mine, heads will roll. I don't think so. I've pretty much mandated that you're off limits to my people."

He held her tightly and kissed her cheek. "You're okay now. I'm here. They won't bother us again tonight. I promise."

"How can you be so sure? How did they know I'd be coming to meet you downstairs?"

"They probably waited outside the building all day for a glimpse of you."

Julie shuddered. She hadn't been out earlier, she'd been too busy writing. "Lucky for me, I guess. I was inside all day."

"We'll be at the club in a minute. Do you want to cancel on my parents? I really don't care if we just go home."

For a minute, Julie considered his offer, but thought better of it. "No. We have to live our lives, right? I'll be fine." She drew in a deep breath.

"Can I confess something to you, Julie?" he asked, looking into her eyes.

She smiled and hoped it hid her fear. *Was he hiding something too?* She watched as he drew in a deep breath.

"Julie Porter. I've fallen in love with you."

She shuddered when she heard him say her last name in light of what she was planning to tell him later. Maybe it was a bad sign that those photographers were there. Perhaps the universe was trying to tell her something. Maybe her plan to be honest with James later tonight was doomed to fail.

No. Wait. Back-up. Did he just said that he loved me? She straight-ened in her seat, knowing that she felt the same way. *I can do this. I have to do this.*

"I love you too, James," she replied.

The car slowed to a stop and he kissed her soundly. "Now I really just want to turn around and go home."

"We promised your parents..."

He blew out a breath. "Okay, okay. I'll get out first and be sure that there are no paparazzi here. Hang on a minute."

He exited the car and she could see him checking the corner

of the block and the shrubbery across the street before he returned. He opened the door and offered her his hand. "The coast is clear," he said lightly.

She reached for him, that familiar jolt of electricity running between them. She stepped out and into his arms.

"I swear to you that whatever happens in there with my parents, I'll make it all up to you later. Anything you want."

She could only hope that the promise he just made would be delivered in manner it was offered. She prayed that he'd still want her after what she planned to tell him before this night was over.

They hurried up the steps of the imposing brownstone building. It was familiar to Julie now, having been there with James after they'd left the gala together. That night seemed so long ago. He'd made an improper proposal and she'd walked away from him. She didn't think she'd possibly have the strength to do that again, now that she knew him better. Once inside, they were ushered to a table in the corner where his parents were already seated, a drink before each one of them. His father stood up as they approached.

"Mom, Dad. Good to see you," James said, pulling a chair back for Julie to sit on, then going around to kiss his mother on the cheek.

"Yes, son, happy you both made it," his father replied.

"How are you dear?" his mother asked James.

"Julie and I are both great, mom. We're finding out that living together has its benefits."

Julie felt his hand rest on her thigh and did her best to sit still in her chair.

"As long as you make a commitment, James, we'll all be happy," his father interjected.

"Julie, dear, how is that little book project of yours? Getting through it?"

"Mom!" James said. "It's not a 'little book project'. It's a pretty big deal."

His mother looked unphased. "I didn't mean anything by that, I just think it's a lovely idea and I'm sure it will find its audience."

Julie still hadn't uttered a word. She really didn't know what to say and was thoroughly distracted by James' light touch on her leg. Then she thought of Mrs. Tassen, her mentor. *When in doubt, talk about the weather.* "Have you been enjoying the summer, Mrs. Curran?"

"It's Clara, dear, remember? No need for formalities. You're living with my son, after all."

Julie regrouped, trying to be the polite person she prided herself on being. The woman sitting across from her was making that task feel like a huge mountain to climb. She drew in a breath and said, "Well then, Clara. Have you been out at the beach house this week? You look rested."

She watched as James' mother attempted a smile, or one as deeply felt as the Botox in her forehead would allow. "Yes. It's been glorious. Please, come out for a weekend with James. We should spend some quality time together as a family."

"That would be lovely." Julie hoped she sounded convincing as the waiter magically appeared with a bottle of wine and poured them all a glass of the deep ruby liquid. She certainly didn't want to be held captive at the beach house with these people. She realized that her words resonated when the conversation shifted to more impersonal topics, mostly business related. The inquisition seemed to be completed, at least for now. And as she mulled it over, she did hope there would be a next time, because that would mean that James still wanted to have her in his life. She raised her glass to her lips and sent up a silent prayer for her future, all the while hoping she still had one with him.

Chapter Twenty-Four

AS THEIR ENTREES WERE SERVED, Julie thought she heard her phone buzz in her clutch, which she'd placed at her feet. She ignored it, trying to concentrate on the conversation about advertising space and digital subscription services for *Tell All*. When it sounded a second time, she felt an unexpected rush of nerves shoot in all directions, stemming from her stomach and traveling through her bloodstream, making her uncomfortable. *It's probably Caroline, just checking in with me. She knows how nervous I am about this dinner and what I plan to tell James afterward.*

By the third time she heard the distinctive sound, she bent down to lift her evening bag on to her lap and excused herself. Having written chapter upon chapter on the topic of cell phone etiquette, she knew better than to look at her device at the dinner table. She stood and made her way to the ladies' room. Once there, she opened her bag and pulled out her phone. Julie felt a true jolt of fear when she recognized the area code, if not the actual number. 609. South New Jersey. There was a voicemail.

With a shaky hand, she pressed the icon to play back the recording:

"MISS DELGARDIO, THIS IS SOUTH JERSEY REGIONAL Hospital. Please call us back regarding your mother, Glenda Delgardio as soon as you get this message."

JULIE THOUGHT FOR SURE THAT HER RACING HEART WOULD escape from her chest. She redialed the number and waited for the call to connect. When it did, she said, "Hello. This is Julie Delgardio." The name sounded funny on her tongue. "I think my mother is a patient. I just received a message –"

"Hold please," the operator said.

The wait to speak to someone with more information seemed interminable and Julie's anxiety kept on building with each passing second. Her palms were sweaty, the skin on the back of her neck was clammy. Then someone answered.

"Miss Delgardio? Are you the daughter of Glenda Delgardio?"

"Yes," she answered, voice barely more than a whisper.

"I'm the nurse taking care of your mother. As her next of kin, I'm letting you know that she was brought in from the field with an opioid overdose. Narcan was administered by the Atlantic City police, an ambulance brought her to us. She's stable right now, but we're not sure how long she'd been down." The woman speaking was firm, but she had a kind manner.

"What do you mean?"

"She was found in an alleyway, Miss Delgardio, in a part of the city well known for drug dealing and prostitution. No one knows how long she'd been oxygen deprived before being revived. Right now she's in our ER and we're monitoring her. When can you be here?"

"Be there?"

"Yes, ma'am. We're hoping that when your mother wakes up that she has full function. But we don't know that yet, and she'll need to be convinced to go to a drug rehab if she does. If she doesn't, you're looking at long term care. There are many decisions to be made and those are best done by family."

"Family," Julie repeated, not truly processing the nurse's words. She had spent so long denying that she'd had a family, that this conversation didn't seem as though it could possibly be real.

"When you arrive, ask for me, Sarah McDougal. My shift doesn't end until 7:00 tomorrow morning."

"I'm in Manhattan. It might take a while for me to get there."

"Just be here before I leave. That would be best."

"I will," Julie said, adding, "thank you."

"Don't thank me, Miss Delgardio. This is my job."

The other woman hung up on her end and Julie stood in the posh ladies' room, with the overstuffed linen covered couches and gilded mirrors, wondering how it was that she was even there. She had fooled herself into believing that she'd left her past behind, but she hadn't. Once again, she acknowledged to herself that she had run away from a problem that was bound to resurface for one simple reason: she hadn't solved anything, but rather, she'd just denied its existence. That method of dealing with this issue, she realized, was truly never going to work. But for right now? She had to get to South Jersey, and she had to do it fast.

Thinking on her feet, Julie realized that Charlie was parked outside. She'd ask him to take her to the Port Authority station where she could catch the first bus to Atlantic City. She dreaded the company she'd be in; desperate gamblers, mostly, looking to score big in the seedy casino town, but it was her only option. As she opened the ladies' room door she was struck with the thought that there would be no explaining this to James. She had lied to him, plain and simple by not telling him about her past sooner. Then, there was the issue of his parents. Once they heard this, they would deem her unsuitable for their son and this blissful chapter of her life would come to a close. But there was nothing she could do about that, she knew it. Worse, she'd never get the chance to explain herself to James, and he deserved better from her. She'd text him from the car and say goodbye. At least that way she wouldn't have to look him in the eye and see the disappointment she knew she'd find there.

She quickly made her way out of the restaurant and escaped to the waiting car without incident. There were no photographers lying in wait and for that she was thankful. She opened the door and slipped inside. Charlie turned with a quizzical expression on his face.

"Miss Porter?"

"Hi. Can you drop me off at the Port Authority, please?"

"Are we waiting for Mr. Curran?"

"Um, no. He's having dinner with his parents."

"Well then, tell me where you need to be. I can drive you anywhere."

For the briefest moment, she considered telling Charlie the truth, but thought better of it. "No. The Port Authority is good."

"I can't do that, Miss Porter. Mr. Curran wouldn't want you roaming around there this time of night and he'd fire me for letting it happen. Let me drive you where it is you need to go."

"That's so kind of you, Charlie. It's just that..."

"I won't take no for an answer. Where are we headed?"

Tears filled her eyes. She had no real way to express her gratitude to this man, but she was going to allow him to drive her if it meant saving his job. "South Jersey Regional Hospital. It's in Atlantic City."

He picked up his phone, seemingly punching the name of the place into his navigation app. Then he turned the engine on and slowly pulled into traffic, heading toward the Lincoln Tunnel. "Why not close your eyes for a bit, Miss Porter. Looks like we have about two and a half hours before we arrive. You should rest."

"Thank you again, Charlie. I might just try and do that." She settled back against the seat and tried to slow her racing thoughts. All these years of telling people that her mother was dead, and now that might be actually happening. When Julie sent her mom the large check that would have been her rent if she'd been living with Caroline or on her own, she had hoped that the woman would use it for groceries or to satisfy some long standing debt. *How could I have been so stupid? Nothing has changed. Addiction is a disease and my mother is just another victim.*

She let out a sigh and knowing that she had to let James know where she was, she lifted her phone and sent him a text.

Please apologize to you parents for me. I had an emergency and had to leave. I'll fill you in later.

Realistically, she knew there would be no "later". When she had more information about her mother's condition, she'd text him again and let him know the truth. Then she'd end things with James forever. This was too big of a deception now. He would never forgive her for not telling him earlier, for playing at a game that she was not skilled enough to win.

Julie could feel the tears run from her eyes, soaking the fabric of her halter top, the one she'd chosen with care to present an image of someone she truly wasn't and sobbed. The rhythmic beat of the tires on the smooth highway pavement distracted her for a moment from what she imagined James' reaction to her text would be. She didn't have long to wait.

Emergency? What kind of emergency? Where are you? Are you hurt? I'm coming. Just tell me where you are.

She didn't even know how to answer him.

I'm with Charlie. I'm fine. It's a long story and I can explain it when I'm back in the city. I promise to fill you in as soon as I can.

She sat back to wait for his response.

Back in the city?!? Where are you going?

She grimaced. This was not how she wanted to have this conversation. Not seeing him, not being able to judge his reaction, it was all too difficult. But it was time. Heart breaking, she scrolled through her contacts, and found him in favorites, wondering just how long it would take before she removed him from that list. She touched her finger to his name and the call connected.

"Julie," he said, concern in his voice. "Tell me where you are. I will come and meet you."

"No, James. This is something I have to handle by myself."

"Are you ill? You seemed fine at dinner."

"It's not me, James. It's my mother."

"Your mother? How... isn't she... gone? Isn't that what you told me? I don't understand."

"I did tell you that, but," she drew in a deep breath. "I lied. I lied about everything."

There was a long silence on the other end of the call, then, "Why would you lie about that? Please, explain it to me."

"I can't. It's too long of a story and you deserve to hear it face to face. I promise, James, I will, as soon as I have more information. Once I get back to the city."

"Can I trust that you'll be back, Julie, or are you lying to me right now?" he asked, none of the typical warmth in his voice.

"It's the truth," she replied. "I will call you when I can, when

I have news to report. Please apologize to your parents for me." She disconnected the call. Closing her eyes once more, she drifted off to a place that was not either being asleep or being awake. It was the blank place in the middle where her worst fears took hold.

IT WAS DARK WHEN THEY ARRIVED. THE MOONLESS NIGHT SKY was inky black and felt foreboding, despite the warmth of the air that surrounded her as soon as Julie stepped out of the car.

"Will you be alright in there alone, Miss Porter?" Charlie asked, shutting off the engine. "Or would you prefer some company?"

"No, I'm fine," she said, through the open passenger door. "You rest. I hope we're not here for too long."

"Take all the time you need. I'm used to sleeping in the car," he said, patting the cushion of the seat beneath him. "Done it lots of times waiting for Mr. Curran." He pulled his ever-present cap down low over his eyes and tilted his head back, making himself comfortable while he waited for her and the return trip to Manhattan.

Julie shut the door and walked into the entrance marked "Emergency". Stepping up to the desk and squinting in the glare of the overhead fluorescent lighting, she asked, "Can I speak with Sarah McDougal? She's the nurse taking care of my mom."

The receptionist barely acknowledged her, but lifted a telephone handset and dialed a few numbers. "Sarah," she said. "Someone is here looking for you." The woman listened for a moment and put the phone back down.

"Have a seat. She'll be out when she can leave the unit."

Julie just nodded and found an empty chair in the waiting area. She didn't know how long it would take the nurse to arrive and looking at her phone she realized that the battery was running low. She didn't want to lose the ability to make a call if she had to, so she dropped it back into her bag, and took a moment to look around the space. It was a non-descript sort of place, with hard molded plastic chairs bolted to the worn linoleum floor, walls painted a sickly light green. There were a few posters tacked up here and there, warning against the dangers of street drugs and unwanted pregnancy. For as much as Julie thought she'd escaped this part of her past, it took no more than a few minutes for her to feel right at home. That thought depressed her. She had often thought of herself as the mythical phoenix who had actually risen from the ashes of her old life. She had worked hard to craft an image of the person she wanted to be, but it was all for nothing, really. Sitting here, dressed in expensive clothing, a handbag and shoes that cost more than most of the residents of this town made in a month, she felt like the imposter she truly was. Waiting for news of her mother was a painful reminder that one can run, but never hide from the truth. It will always track you down and expose you for who you are; her efforts to avoid it had been wasted.

A door at one end of the room opened and a middle-aged woman with silver hair wearing blue scrubs and running sneakers approached her.

"Miss Delgardio? I'm Sarah McDougal, the nurse taking care of your mom."

Scrambling to her feet, Julie asked, "How is she?"

"Better. Responsive. Not very compliant, however. She's threatening to leave."

Julie's eyes widened. "You won't let her do that, right?"

"Not quite yet. We need to monitor her oxygen levels and run some cognitive tests. But, we can't hold her here forever, especially not against her will if all of her brain function is normal, which at this point, I'm guessing it is. It's tough with addicts. They generally want to get back out on the street."

Julie felt a tiny bit of relief at the nurse's tentative prognosis. "How long can you hold her here?"

"Maybe 24 hours. She really needs to agree to go to a rehab."

"I don't think she will. She hasn't ever agreed before this."

"Well, maybe this time will be different. That's the hope, anyway, isn't it?"

Julie felt the nurse rest a hand on her arm.

"Talk to your mother. See if she'll listen to reason."

"I haven't seen my mother in over ten years. I doubt she'll even know who I am," Julie said softly.

"Mothers always know their children, Miss Delgardio. Give it a shot," she said with a small, knowing smile.

Julie could feel her body tremble slightly. She dreaded having walk into the ward that she knew sat right behind the swinging doors of the waiting room. Instead, she wanted to run back to James and into his arms, to pretend that all of the events of this night never happened. But she also knew that she had no option. She had to see her mother and James would not be by her side any longer. It was time to face the responsibilities she'd run from as a young girl, when she first got on the bus to Manhattan all those years ago.

"Okay," she said to the kind nurse. "I'm ready. Can you bring me in to see her now, please?"

"This way," Sarah McDougal said, turning and leading Julie to the one place she never wanted revisit: standing face to face with her mother.

Chapter Twenty-Five

JULIE WALKED past the curtained stalls in the emergency room behind the nurse until the other woman stopped at one near the very end of the cavernous space. Sitting up in the bed, an IV in one arm and an oxygen canular in her nose, was her mother. She looked older, more worn than Julie could have imagined. The time that had passed since they last stood before each other had most certainly taken a toll; the woman seemed smaller than Julie remembered.

"Mom," she uttered.

"If this is what it takes to get you to come home, maybe I should have done it sooner," her mother replied, voice curt.

"How do you feel?" Julie asked, trying to deflect her mother's anger.

"How do you think I feel? Like shit. I was fine, they didn't need to bring me here." Her mother picked at one of the many scabs on her arm, making it bleed. When she spoke, Julie could see that she was missing many of her teeth.

"Mrs. Delgardio, please," Sarah said. "Don't do that. I'll get the doctor to prescribe something to help those wounds heal. If you aggravate them further you'll end up with an armful of scars, and we don't want that now, do we?"

Her mother grimaced at the nurse. "Yeah. Like I'm entering a friggin' beauty pageant anytime soon."

"Mom. No need to be impolite to Sarah. She's only trying to help."

"Oh, Sarah is it? You would know, Miss High and Mighty. Look at you. All fancied up like you are. Too good for the rest of us now, I suppose."

Julie took a hard look at the woman in the bed. She was emaciated. Her hair was dyed an array of colors, and it was thinning, allowing large patches of her scalp to be clearly visible. Her face, chest and arms were covered with angry sores, some oozing pus, some leaking blood. Julie imagined that they were everywhere on her mother's body as well, adding to the woman's discomfort. She tried to not personalize her mother's angry tone; she knew that her mom was in pain and lashing out. She closed her eyes for a brief moment and when she opened them again she said, "I'm here now, mother. I just want to help."

"You know how you can do that, daughter?" the woman in the bed asked sarcastically. "Get me the hell out of here. Now. I'm fine. I just wanna go home."

"We're waiting for the doctor to come by, Mrs. Delgardio," the nurse said. "No one goes anywhere without official discharge orders."

"Hmpff," was Glenda's reply. "I'll give him thirty minutes to show up before I disconnect myself from all of these fancy wires and walk out on my own two feet."

"I don't recommend that, ma'am. Plus there's the little matter of the police officers who brought you in. One call to them and you'll have to deal with the consequences."

"Don't threaten me, lady. I know my rights."

"Yes. You have the right to be medically treated, she said

unphased by Glenda's rude tone. "Just rest until the doctor comes by," Sarah said. Then she turned to Julie. "May I speak with you privately, please?"

The two women walked away from the bed and stopped at the nurses' station in the middle of the ER.

"It's your job to convince your mother to enter a rehab. If she doesn't, the police will bring her to the county jail, where she'll detox in a very uncomfortable manner. I've seen this before. It's not pretty."

Julie felt her stomach drop. "Jail?"

"Yes. She broke the law. Illegal drugs and a concealed weapon. Not a good combination."

"Concealed weapon?" Julie knew she kept repeating what the other woman just said, but that was the most her brain would process at the moment.

"She had an unregistered handgun on her when they picked her up."

Julie felt dizzy. "I can try to talk to her. It's just that we have a very complicated relationship. I moved away from here a long time ago and never looked back."

"It's never too late to mend fences. Go on. Give it a try." She shooed Julie away as she walked behind the counter of the nurses' station.

Julie stood motionless for a brief moment, then nodded her head and went back to her mother's bedside. Once there, she said, "Mom. I'm so sorry."

"What for, Julie?" her mother asked with a gruff tone. "Abandoning me all those years ago or for showing up here tonight? I mean, why the hell did you come see me now?"

"You were found unresponsive on a street, mom. That's why."

"So what? You haven't shown any interest in me or my life. Hell, you ran from it."

Julie felt anger begin to build. "I did. But I'm here right now. How can we make this better?"

"Oh. I don't know. Where's your rich boyfriend? Maybe he can get me out of here."

"I don't have a rich boyfriend."

"Yes, you do. I saw your picture in the paper. You were with him."

"Don't believe everything you see, ma," Julie said, her carefully practiced diction slipping. "It's over."

"How'd you let that happen? You should have held on tight to that one. You could've spent the rest of your life on easy street with him."

"It's not that simple, ma. He's not like us."

"Well, daughter, you're not like 'us' anymore either, are ya?"

Her mother's words resonated. Julie felt like she was caught between two worlds, and she fit into neither one.

"None of it matters. The only thing that's important here is your health, ma. You've got to go to rehab."

"No." Glenda was emphatic.

"The nurse told me that if you don't, you'll go to County. Do you really want to detox in jail?"

"Wouldn't be the first time," her mother said in an even tone. "Lots has happened since you walked out the door."

"Don't you want to get better?" Julie asked, ignoring her mother's last jab.

"What for? What difference does it make to you? You've made it clear that you want nothing to do with the likes of me."

Julie had no answer for her mother. It was true. She left a whole life behind when she took that bus to Manhattan as a college student. Realization dawned. By not looking back, she made it very difficult for her mother to look forward. She swallowed down her tears and said, "How about this? I'll make a deal with you. Go to rehab, and when you complete the program, I'll come and visit you regularly. We'll figure out a way for you to get back on your feet. I won't disappear again. I promise."

"Why should I believe you? The only way I was able to get your attention was to almost die out on the street. Besides. Look at you, all gussied up. I hardly recognize you anymore. You're not the girl I raised." Glenda turned away and stared blankly at the wall.

Julie knew that there was a lot of truth to her mother's words. She had lived a lie for so long that she probably couldn't be trusted. She had abandoned her mother, and lied to Caroline, to James. Why should anyone trust her? "I'm still your daughter," she continued. "I want to help you. Will you let me?"

"Rehab's for wimps. I can do this on my own," Glenda said defiantly.

"Unfortunately, that's not one of the options here. Please. Go. Jail can't be the better way to handle this problem."

"I stopped being your 'problem' a long time ago. Now get out of here. I want to sleep for a while."

Julie backed up, feeling stunned and overwhelmed by the events of the night. "I'll let you rest. But just know that I'll be back. You better still be here in this bed."

"Yeah? Or what? Whatcha gonna do, miss fancy pants? Tie me down?"

"No, ma. Nothing like that," she said softly. She realized that her mother was coming down off of a dangerous drug that had almost killed her, that she must be uncomfortable and that her addiction was rearing its ugly head. "Just rest."

She walked back to the nurses' station and found Sarah. "Would you happen to have an extra phone charger and a place for me to sit? My mom is taking some time to think."

Sarah walked around to where Julie stood and put an arm around her shoulders. "Come with me," she said, leading Julie into a small lounge. There was a vending machine with candy and a coffee pot on a small table with disposable cups and spoons. "This is our little haven. Feel free to stay as long as you need." She then pulled a universal charger out of her pocket. "I keep this here for exactly this type of situation. Just return it when you're done."

"Thank you," Julie said, weakly smiling at the other woman. "I really appreciate this."

The nurse turned and left, heading back to work and Julie sunk down into an old and worn leather couch, feeling more exhausted than she could ever remember. It was too much to bear. First her mother coming close to death, then losing James, all in one night. She sent up a silent prayer to heaven asking to be spared any other calamity. She had lied, and now she'd paid the price. It was enough.

She pulled her phone out of her small bag and noticed that the battery had finally given up on her. She plugged the borrowed charger into the wall outlet next to where she sat and then connected the little metal piece to her device. A few seconds later, it sprung to life with multiple text messages from James and a couple from Caroline. As she read through them, she realized that he was trying to find her. Caroline's texts made it clear that he'd called her asking if she knew where Julie was, only to be told that she had no idea, and that she'd just heard the truth about Julie's past from her friend the previous evening.

Was that just last night? Julie questioned herself. Time seemed to be moving at breakneck speed. Once she had a bit of power back in her phone, she began to Google rehab centers nearby. A private facility would cost her every bit of her savings, but she had no other choice. Her mother had to get the help she needed to beat the opioid addiction she suffered; there was no one else who could help. She began to make some calls. An hour later and armed with information, Julie made her way back over to her mother's bed. Thankfully, she was still there, out cold, either from the combination of necessary drugs that the medical team had prescribed or sheer exhaustion. Julie pulled a chair over to sit and be ready for the conversation they needed to have. She closed her eyes and drifted off to sleep.

"WHERE IS SHE?" JULIE THOUGHT SHE HEARD JAMES' VOICE IN what she assumed was a dream. "Which bed?"

"Sir. You're not family. How did you get in here?"

"I need to see my girlfriend. Now!" he demanded.

Julie sat up straight, her muscles aching from hours spent sitting in the hard plastic chair. *Great. Now I'm the one hallucinating.* She shook her head to clear her mind, closed her eyes, and when she opened them again, saw James standing in front of her.

"What are you doing here? How did you find me?" she asked sitting up straight, stunned, not sure if she was happy to see him or not.

"Charlie. He texted me his location."

"Oh," she said in a small voice. "How did you get here?"

"Uber," he replied, "since you took my car, I had no other choice."

She didn't even want to think about what that had cost him.

"Do you want to explain this to me?" He looked over at the sleeping figure in the bed. "Is this woman your mother?"

She nodded.

His eyes rested on the small figure in the bed. Then he asked, "Can we go somewhere and talk?"

Julie knew that she owed him that at the very least, even if he hadn't ridden all this distance to find her. She nodded her head and stood on shaky feet. "This way," she said, leading him back into the lounge. Thankfully, they found the room empty.

"James. I'm sorry. I have nothing else to say, no real explanation to offer. I didn't set out to deceive you. I've been living this lie for a long time, you just became another piece of collateral damage."

"Collateral damage?" he spat out the words. "That's what I am to you? Collateral damage?" he let out a plaintive whistle. "Wow."

Julie's thoughts felt all scrambled in her head. "No. Ugh," she uttered in frustration. "That came out wrong. It's just a statement of fact. I've caused this disaster and I have no way to take back what I've done. All I can do is say that I'm sorry."

"That's not enough, Julie. You need to tell me the truth. All of it. Now."

"Can we sit?" she asked, afraid to admit that she felt wobbly on her feet.

"When was the last time you ate?" he asked in a moment of concern. "I don't remember if dinner had been brought to the table before you took off last night."

Julie's face crumbled. "Oh no. Your parents. What they must think of me now!"

With a raised voice he said, "I don't give a damn what anyone thinks. I want you to tell me how we ended up here Julie. One minute I think I've met the love of my life and then..."

He stopped talking. He stared at her for a long while as if she had an answer, but when she said nothing, walked over to the vending machine, looked at it and pulled a few dollars from his wallet. Then he put the money in the appropriate slot and pushed a button. He reached in and took out his purchase, coming back to sit down next to her, tearing open a small package of cookies. Somewhat calmer now, he said, "That's the best I can do." He handed her the food. "Talk to me."

She smiled weakly. "Thanks." She held on to one slim Vanilla Wafer and began to tell him the unedited version of her life story. The poverty, the uncertainty, the lack of parental affection, the difficult decision to leave it all behind.

"I can understand why you did it, Julie. What I still don't understand is why you felt you couldn't be honest with me. Did you think I would judge you?"

"Of course I did, James! And why wouldn't you? My real life is so far from your own. I can't expect that you'd get why I kept my secrets tightly guarded. Besides, I put all my effort into shaking off my past. I've worked so hard to change the path of my future. I mean, did you even see my mother? That could have been me!" It was not until she voiced those final words that she began to shake with her confession. *The truth. It was always hard to face the facts. And until this very minute, I'd never even admitted that last piece to myself.* Her fear was very real.

He moved even closer and put an arm around her, softening now. "Julie. I know that I'll never truly comprehend the depth of the obstacles you faced as a very young child. I had every material possession I ever wanted, and my father's name to open doors, that's a fact. But the one thing that we have in common remains the same. We doubted that we were given unconditional love from the people who matter most to children. Our parents."

She began to sob, tears flowing uncontrollably. "Right," she said between gasps for air. "And look where it landed us. I'm a mess and you're disappointed yet again."

"I'm angry at you, Julie. But I'm not giving up on us. I am deeply and madly in love with you. And what's more, I think you feel the same way about me."

She looked up at him, his brown eyes warm, his expression sincere. "I do feel the same. But how can you ever forgive me?"

"I'm going to make it my life's mission, if you'll allow me that one thing."

"Why are you being so wonderful right now? I don't deserve it."

"Never, ever undersell yourself, Julie. You deserve everything I have. I love you. I have no reason not to. I've told you this before. Meeting you was the best thing that ever happened to me."

With that, he leaned down and kissed her softly on the cheek. Julie felt opposing emotions in that moment: happiness, that he still wanted her in his life; grief that her mother almost lost hers because Julie wasn't a part of it. What she did know, though, was that she was in love with James. If he would have her, she was his, forever and always. Together, they'd find a way for her mother to be a part of their world as well.

Chapter Twenty-Six

TWELVE HOURS LATER, Glenda was checked into a private and discreet drug rehab program in Central New Jersey. Julie stood aside and marveled at his skill as James promised her mother the world in exchange for her agreement to remain in the facility until the doctors there felt she could safely be discharged to a step-down sober house, where she'd learn to reacclimate to a world free of drugs and alcohol. It would take a long time for her to get well, but James and Julie promised to visit as soon as the counselors there felt she was ready.

Julie had insisted that after settling Glenda into the rehab and before heading home, they stop by the trailer where her mom had been living the last number of years to gather up some of her clothing. It was old and rusty and very similar to the one she'd once lived in with her mom. The roof was halfway caved in on one end and the small box was sitting on cinderblocks that were crumbling beneath it. Looking at the dismal condition the place was in, Julie could feel her deepest and most damaging memories being triggered. In self-defense, she decided not to go inside, but instead to buy her mother the necessary clothing she'd need at rehab, along with any other items she requested instead of putting her own mental health in danger. It wasn't worth her sanity to save the few shabby personal articles her mother owned, especially when there was a Target store a mile from where the decomposing trailer sat. James offered to call a junk dealer in the morning and pay to have the whole thing carted away and once that decision was made, Julie felt as if a weight had been lifted from her shoulders.

After their essential errands were done and they returned to the rehab to drop everything they'd purchased for her mom at the main desk, Charlie drove them back to Manhattan. Julie closed her eyes and put her head down on James' strong shoulder as New Jersey began to fade from sight. By the time they reached the apartment it was dark outside. Julie was bone tired, barely able to put one foot in front of the other despite the brief rest she'd gotten on the car ride. James had to help her into the elevator and once he'd unlocked their door, lifted her into his arms and carried her the remainder of the way to their bedroom. He gently lowered her on to the mattress. She forced herself awake because she wanted to take a bath before resting between the clean, soft sheets.

"Would you mind turning the water on in the tub for me?" she asked him.

"Julie. You can't keep your eyes open. Just sleep. Bathe in the morning."

"No," she said, shaking her head. "I feel very grungy. First the hospital, then the trailer park. I have to take a bath."

He set his mouth in a firm line, but didn't say anything. He just went into the oversized bathroom and began to fill the tub. She could smell the lavender bath salts that she had purchased earlier in the week at the farmer's market as they dissolved in the steamy water. The beautiful scent soothed her ragged nerves. She began to pull off her clothing, the same outfit she'd worn for the last thirty-six hours, leaving everything in a heap on the floor in front of her. *I can deal with this mess in the morning.*

She walked naked into the bathroom and saw that James was busy removing his own clothing.

"What are you doing?" she asked.

"If you think I'm going to let you sit in a warm bath, fall asleep and drown while I'm somewhere else in this apartment, you are sorely mistaken."

She watched as he stripped down to nothing and then held out his hand for her to take. He helped her into the tub and then stepped into it himself, sitting down first and leaning back against the smooth porcelain. Julie slowly lowered herself into the hot water, feeling it soak into her bones, relaxing her sore muscles. It was blissful. James then maneuvered her body, so that her back rested against the front of him and she turned her head around to look into his eyes.

"If you think that this bath is going to be anything but thera-peutic, you're wrong. I'm too tired for sex."

"Do you really think that I have no self-control? You could barely walk in here under your own strength. Besides, we have the rest of our lives for all sorts of sexual escapades." He paused, then added, "I'm a grown man, Julie. I can delay gratification."

"That's good to know, James, but you need to tell that to your nether regions. I feel my ass being poked as we speak," she laughed, all of a sudden getting a second wind.

"Yeah, well, I can't stop my body from reacting to you, but I can promise not to take it any further tonight. It's simply mind over matter."

Julie closed her eyes and settled in while he ran a soapy loofah over her skin. She noticed that she had no control over her body, either, beginning to feel its familiar response to his touch. She smiled. If he could wait, so could she. Instead, she focused on something entirely different.

"What do you think your parents will say the next time we're all together? What did you tell them when I left the club at dinner the other night?"

"Just that you had an emergency and had to go."

"And they accepted my sudden absence, just like that?"

"Firstly, they had each had a lot to drink by then, but secondly, it really doesn't matter what they thought. Not to me, it doesn't."

She twisted around to look directly at him. "But it does to me, James. They're your parents. I want them to like me."

"Julie, half the time I'm not even sure if they like me, and I'm their blood."

"But you have to get along with them. You're a key player in the family business, after all."

"About that." He shook his head. That's a longer discussion, one we need to have when you're feeling one hundred percent. I have a plan, Julie, one that will change the dynamic of the relationship I've had with my father for a very long time."

"Can't you just tell me?"

"Oh, so I can delay gratification, but you can't, huh?" he teased.

She said, "Maybe not. What do you plan to do?"

"How about I tell you in the morning? After we both get some rest? It's complicated and you'll need your full power of concentration."

"Sounds a bit scary to me."

"It's all how you look at things, I guess. I think what I have in mind is very exciting."

"Now I won't sleep at all. You've got me trying to imagine what it is you have rolling around in that brain of yours."

"Well, if you don't want to sleep, I'm sure I can come up with a way to occupy us in bed without telling you my plan until the morning anyway..."

She stood up feeling wide awake and stepped out of the tub, reached for a warm towel on the heated rack and whispered, "Occupy me."

"With pleasure," was his low rumbled response. He accepted the towel she held up for him. "Are you sure that you're up for this?"

"It would seem that you are." Her eyes trailed down his taut belly to his overly evident erection. "I can rally," she laughed as she dried off with the fluffy oversized bath sheet. She finished, dropped it on to the floor and went into the bedroom. He followed. Julie knew he would. The James Curran she'd come to know and love never turned away from a challenge.

⚝

JAMES HAD GOTTEN UP BEFORE JULIE AND WHEN SHE OPENED her eyes, he was gone. When he returned, he brought muffins and jam, coffee and juice, all arranged on a beautiful ceramic tray that she hadn't seen before, with linen napkins, fine china and silver, and a bud vase bursting with yellow freesias. Their gentle scent, mixed with the smell of the strong brew, was heavenly.

"I could get used to this sort of service," she said, stretching her arms up overhead.

"I hope you can. I see many more mornings like this in your future," he replied.

"And how did you know my favorite flower? I don't think we've ever really discussed that topic!"

"Duly noted. I didn't have a clue, but now I do. I just know that freesias represent unconditional love. I wanted to pledge that to you, Julie. I promise that I will always love you for being who you truly are, forever."

She felt the breath leave her body at his sweet words. "I promise you the same," she whispered. "Better be careful, Curran. It sounds like you've been writing wedding vows."

"That wouldn't be the worst thing I could be spending my time on, would it?"

"What are you saying?" she sat up, pulling the sheet over her naked body. This didn't seem like a conversation she wanted to have with her breasts exposed to his view.

"Julie," he began as he carefully placed the tray on the bed and sat down beside her. "I know we don't know each other for very long, but I also know myself pretty well. I've never felt like this before, as if I can't breathe without you near me. I want us to be together. Always. Marry me, Julie."

Her eyes widened and she could feel a sharp twinge of tears beginning to form, not out of sadness, but instead, of happiness, in the corner of her eyes.

"After everything I've put you through, you want to marry me?"

"It's because of everything, Julie. We are more alike than either of us could have realized when you spilled your drink on me in that bar. We're both looking for the same thing. True love. I didn't know that about myself until I met you."

Her tears began to fall in earnest. "But my past. My mother. The lies I told you and your parents. They might not agree with you on this. I'm sure they'll find me unsuitable."

He took both of her hands in his. "That's part of what I want to talk to you about. I don't care what they think. I no longer want to be a part of my father's company. I want to strike out on my own. I'm done with the tabloid-type reporting that *Tell All* thrives on. I want to do something more important with my life than that."

"How?"

"I want to start a serious news magazine. I can ask Ryan to

join us. His gritty type of true journalistic photography is just what I'm looking for"

"Us?" she asked.

"Of course. I'm hoping you'll come on board as well."

"I don't think you need an etiquette columnist, James, but it's sweet of you to consider me."

"Don't sell yourself short, Julie. I want to explore the effects of social media on our society. I want you to head up that research. I see it as an ongoing series on how the digital world is effecting everyone, changing our norms and both bringing us closer and pulling us apart."

She nodded our head. "We most certainly could use some guidelines for that whole arena of life. But a magazine is a huge undertaking."

"All I can say is with you by my side, I feel like anything is possible. What do you think?"

She didn't hesitate. "Yes. To all of it. I say yes!" She let the sheet fall as she pushed him back on the mattress and climbed on top of him. The china clattered noisily on the tray, but she didn't care if the whole thing fell on to the floor. They could clean it up later, if need be. For right now, all she wanted was James. She pulled his tee shirt off over his head and began to work on the clasp of his jeans. He stopped her.

"Julie. One more thing. I love you. More than you can know."

She smiled. She was finally free of her past, of all the lies she'd told on the way to meeting the man of her dreams. "I love you too, James. I always will."

Just like that, breakfast was quickly forgotten. As the coffee cooled in its pot and the muffins sat uneaten, they remained, tangled in the sheets and in each other, until the sun hung low in the late afternoon sky outside the bedroom windows.

"Are you hungry?" he asked her.

"Starving."

"Should we order some food?"

"I guess we should. I just don't want to move. I like being here with you."

"I like it too. But we've got to eat." He shifted and lifted his cell phone. "How's Thai food sound to you?"

"Great," she murmured, closing her eyes. She heard him place an order for delivery. "I'll just rest until it gets here. I'm so tired."

"I bet. It's been a lot to handle these last few days. I'm going to shower. I'll come get you in a bit."

She felt him leave the bed and heard the water in the bathroom, but that was the last thing she remembered until he was back, gently shaking her awake. The only light in the room came from the small one on the side of his bed.

"Hey, sleepyhead. Time to get up now."

She looked around. It was fully dark outside.

"What happened to the Thai food?"

"Yours in in the refrigerator. I ate mine hours ago."

"Wow. I was out cold, huh?"

"You were. And you looked so peaceful I didn't have the heart to wake you. But I think you should get up for a bit now."

She nodded. "You go to the kitchen. I'll be there in a minute."

"Okay. But no going back to sleep. Not yet."

"Promise," she said, swinging around to put her feet on the soft carpet.

He left the bedroom and Julie took herself into the bathroom to brush her teeth and wash her face. Then she swept her hair into a high ponytail, threw on some sweatpants and a tee shirt, foregoing any underwear. She didn't see the point of being fully dressed when all she wanted was to be naked with James again soon. She padded down the hall into the great room and was shocked at what he'd done. There were bunches of colorful freesia everywhere, in vases, in glasses and in one enormous arrangement that sat fragrantly on the coffee table.

"What is all of this?" she asked.

"Let's just say that I was inspired earlier today. I realized that I proposed to you without the whole hearts and flowers aspect of the assignment."

She laughed. "I don't need any of that, James, when I have you."

"I know. But it's what I wanted to do. Now, if you'll join me over here," he walked to the wall that held a large stone fireplace.

Confused, she stepped across the room to meet him. Once she was there, he got down on one knee. She drew in a breath.

"Julie Porter. I want to spend the rest of my life with you. Will you say yes to being with me forever and always?"

"Yes, James, yes. I told you that earlier, didn't I?"

"You did. But I wanted to seal this deal." He reached into his pocket and pulled out a shiny black box with the insignia of Harry Winston printed on it. When he flipped the top open, she saw an enormous, Ascher cut diamond ring nestled in a bed of velvet.

She looked into his deep brown eyes. They were full of promise. "How? When? Where did you get this from?"

"I went out when you were asleep. If you don't like it, we can exchange it for any ring of your choice."

"No. It's so beautiful. It's everything I could have ever dreamed of and more."

He smiled, removed the jewel from it's nest and slipped it on her finger. It felt heavy on her hand but fit perfectly.

"And you guessed my size correctly. Amazing."

"Well, full disclosure," he smiled. "I measured your finger

with dental floss while you were sleeping. I'm good, but I'm not that good."

"James. You're my exact fit in every way imaginable. I love you."

"I love you, Julie. Now. Let's see just how well we fit…"

Epilogue

Six months later

THE SNOW WAS FALLING MORE HEAVILY NOW AS JULIE, STILL wearing the silky bathrobe with the title, "Maid of Honor" stitched across her right breast in neon pink thread, helped Caroline step into the frothy wedding dress of her best friend's own design. It had a lacy corset top that tied low across her back, very sheer but lined in a soft blush underlay. The skirt was voluminous, cascading down and billowing out around Caroline's legs, making it almost impossible for Julie to get close enough to the other woman to help pin the last of the pearl accessories in the arrangement of curls that kept threatening to escape the updo it had taken hours for a professional to complete. The whole time Caroline's mother had hovered over her daughter, until Caroline had to ask her to go downstairs and check that everything was in place. The woman was making matters worse, probably because her ex-husband was here with his new, young wife. Disaster felt like a short gasp away.

Julie couldn't help but share Caroline's nerves. It had been a rocky path on the way to this day. A New Year's Eve wedding. Nothing dramatic or overblown, just the event to cap off the year. There were times that her best friend threatened to pull out of the whole thing, only to crumble into tears and admit that Stephen was the love of her life and she couldn't go on without him. Julie had repeatedly asked Caroline if she was sure, reminding her that proper etiquette dictated that it was best to cancel before formal invitations were sent; then in the next breath reassuring her friend that everything would work out just fine. But today, with Caroline literally vibrating with anxiety, Julie wasn't so positive anymore.

"Is snow a bad sign?" Caroline asked, walking away from the full length mirror to peer out the window of the bridal suite of The Plaza Hotel. They were high above Fifth Avenue and if Julie was being honest, the thick bands of snow quickly covering the fabled sidewalk below did look ominous.

"No. It's good luck," she offered. Hoping her answer was enough, she kept her tone light and stepped into her own dress. It was a navy blue silk sheath that had jeweled bands criss-crossing each other in the back. It was a bit more revealing that she liked. She had to go braless and wore the smallest thong that Caroline could make for her to avoid ruining the lines of the garment, but she knew better than to argue. It was the bride's choice, after all.

"Isn't there a song about rain on your wedding day?" Caroline asked. "I think rain is good luck."

"Well, snow is just rain on steroids. Doubly lucky."

"I don't know, Julie. It just seems like the universe is trying to tell me something."

"You're nervous. That's understandable. There is nothing you need to know today other than this: You look beautiful and you love Stephen. It's all good." She could only hope that her friend would believe her.

Caroline turned and looked at Julie, coming over to adjust the thin straps of her maid of honor's dress. "Are you sure about marrying James? You haven't set a date yet. Makes me wonder."

"We've been busy putting the wheels in motion for the magazine. It's not easy getting investors for a project like this one."

"Right, of course. But what are you thinking? Maybe getting hitched this summer?"

Julie just shrugged her shoulders to signal her lack of an answer. What she didn't let on was that she and James had decided to elope. Even after talking Caroline out of doing that very same thing, telling her bestie that it wasn't fair to her family and friends, Julie had come to the decision that it would be better for all involved if she and James just ran off and got married. She had planned on telling her best friend all the details at the reception. They'd gone so far as to get a marriage license at City Hall earlier in the week and had plans to make a quick getaway to Barbados right after Caroline's wedding, barring this current weather catastrophe. They'd made arrangements on the small tropical island to tie the knot, just the two of them. Julie's mother was doing well in rehab but wouldn't be allowed to travel and James' parents were still miffed about him not wanting to head up the family business any longer. They didn't want to wait. They could always throw a party to celebrate their nuptials at a later date if they really wanted to.

"We haven't talked about this summer, Caroline. But besides, enough about me. Today is your day. Let's concentrate on you for now."

"C'mon. Indulge me. You have no doubts? Marriage is final, you know," Caroline said defiantly, hands now firmly placed on her hips. "No more thrill of a first date, a new relationship."

"Exactly. I've found my perfect match in James. I'm not

looking for anyone else. But this conversation is making me question how you're feeling today."

"I'm feeling like I'm about to make a huge mistake," Caroline replied matter-of-factly..

Julie felt a shot of adrenaline course through her bloodstream, leaving her on high alert. "Caroline. Talk to me. What the hell is going on?"

"Well, since you asked, I'm thinking I don't want to do this."

"Now? Now you come to this very important conclusion?" Sweat began to pool under Julie's armpits.

"I think I've always known it," her friend replied softly.

"What about Stephen?"

"He's better off without me. If I can't commit to him, let him find someone who will. He's a good man. He deserves better."

"Oh boy. Okay." Julie's brain went into overdrive. "How should we do this? Do you want me to find your mother and let her know?"

"Maybe that would be best. You go find her. I'll wait here."

"Alright. I'll think about what we can say to your guests." Julie made her way to the door of the suite before turning around and reaching out one arm to put on Caroline's shoulder. "Are you sure?"

Her friend just nodded.

"What do you want me to tell Stephen?"

"Nothing. I'll do it. I'll call him while you tell my mom."

Julie drew her friend in for a hug. "I want you to be happy. Always. If this is what you need to do, I'm right here with you."

"I know. That's why we're best friends. You've got my back and I have yours. Now, go. You've got the tougher assignment. My mother."

"Right. I'll be back when I'm done." Julie crossed the room and opened the door of the suite. "See you soon." She stepped into the hallway and walked over to the bank of elevators. She pushed the call button and magically an empty car appeared. She rode it down to the lobby and went off in the direction of the Terrace Room where the ceremony was to be held. Just as Julie reached the doorway, James appeared, looking so handsome in his tuxedo, the same one he'd worn to the gala all those months ago, his bow tie perfectly arranged.

"Hey," he said. "What are you doing down here?"

"You won't believe this. Caroline just decided to call off the wedding!"

"I'm not that surprised. She's been hesitant all along."

"Seriously? Have I been living in a sex-crazed state all this time? So out of my mind with lust that I didn't notice?"

"Pretty much," he replied in a teasing tone.

"Great. Now I have to let her mother know."

"You got tasked with telling Angela? You are a good friend."

"Someone's got to. Maid of Honor duties, I suppose."

"Can I help?"

Julie looked up at James and smiled. "No. Just wait here. If you hear loud screaming, come rescue me."

He did as he was told and she opened the door to the room only to find Caroline's mother arguing with the florist about the color of the hydrangeas she'd had specially flown in from Florida for today. "I said pink, not blue!" Angela shouted. "This is a disaster!"

Nowhere near the level of unhappiness I'm about to bestow...

"Angela," Julie said, interrupting the other woman's rant. "I need to speak with you."

"Not now dear. I'm dealing with a crisis."

"Um, Angela. It has to be now. I'm so sorry."

The florist took that as his cue. He scampered away, seemingly happy to be out of shouting distance.

"What's so important that you needed to interrupt me? Did Caroline spill something on her gown?"

"No." Julie drew in a deep breath. *Better to just say it.* "She's decided not to go through with the wedding."

"What are you talking about?" Angela asked becoming pale while putting her hand over her heart. Julie was worried for a minute that the older woman was about to pass out. She was silently reviewing her CPR skills in her head when Angela shifted gears.

"I need to see my daughter. NOW."

"Let's go upstairs together," Julie said, watching as the woman hurried out of the room, pushing past the waiting James as she went.

Together, they caught up to Angela at the elevator. She was stamping one heeled foot impatiently. When it finally arrived, the three of them rode up together in silence. Once outside the bridal suite, Angela knocked on the door. There was no answer.

"Did you grab the keycard before you came downstairs?" James whispered in her ear.

Julie just nodded yes, then stepped in front of Angela to disarm the lock. Caroline's mother burst into the suite, with Julie and James behind her. A quick check of the bedroom only proved what they all knew to be true. It was empty, and Caroline was gone.

"This is my worst nightmare," Angela said, collapsing on the couch, tears streaming from her eyes causing her mascara to run down her cheeks.

"If Caroline thinks that this is all for the best, then we have to accept her decision," Julie said, as gently as she could. "I, for one, am happy that she didn't do something that she would live to regret."

"What about the two hundred and fifty people downstairs waiting for her? Huh? What do I tell them?"

"The truth," Julie replied, looking up at James. "I've learned that it's always best to lead with the truth."

"I agree," he said, locking his eyes with hers. "Would you like some help with all of this? I can make the announcement, if that is something that would make this easier on you."

Angela just shook her head. "What a shame. All those months of work arranging everything so that it would be a perfect wedding. I had to convince the Mayor to officiate. I made a huge donation to his war chest just so he'd agree."

James' head shot up and he smiled. "Well, Angela, maybe we can salvage some of this planning, or at least the ceremony piece of it."

"How?" the older woman asked.

He turned to Julie. "What do you think? Should we do this thing? Looking at the weather, Barbados might not happen in the next short while."

"Do you mean what I think you mean?" she asked with a wide-eyed smile.

"Yes. Marry me. Today."

"What are you talking about?" Angela interjected. "You two can't get married right now. There's a lot more to it. You need a license, you need a wedding planner, you need…"

"Actually, Angela," James stopped her from continuing. "We can. And we want to, if that's alright with you."

"I think that Caroline might get a kick out of knowing that we picked up on what she started. She was grilling me about when we were going to tie the knot just before she made the decision not to do it herself. I can't wait to tell her all about it, once I find her, that is," Julie added.

"What about Stephen? His family?"

"Caroline plans on telling him herself. That's the right thing to do. And if his family chooses to stay, well, that's okay too," Julie said with an air of authority. *Thank you Mrs. Tassen,* she thought to herself. *Another valuable lesson learned…if you sound like you know the answer, people will believe that you do.*

They both waited as Angela processed their request, finally wiping the last of her tears away and nodding. "But you don't know any of my guests in that room downstairs. It will be strange, don't you think?"

"We're okay with that," James said.

Julie nodded. "We don't care, Angela. We're happy to salvage whatever we can today."

"What about the reception? Should I go forward with that as well?"

"You know what, Angela?" James began, "I think we should make that a party to celebrate you. After all, you worked so hard to put it all together for your closest friends and family. And the weather outside is terrible. It will give people something fun to do today in the storm."

Julie and James both held their breath as they watched the woman process the information.

"Yes," Angela said, nodding her head. "Okay. Let me just fix my face. I'll be down soon."

"James. Go let the wedding guests know that there's been a slight change of plans. I'll help Angela and meet you in a few minutes."

He leaned down and kissed her softly. "This day is turning out to be perfect, wouldn't you agree?"

"I do!" she said.

"Hold that thought for a bit. You'll need to repeat those words very shortly." He winked and ran off to inform the large gathering of what was to happen next.

Julie turned around and walked into the bedroom. Seeing the bathroom door shut, she decided to give Angela a moment to gather herself together. It was then that she noticed Caroline's coat, still draped across the desk chair. She got up and lifted the outer garment and a piece of paper fluttered to the floor. She picked it up and recognized her friend's handwriting:

. . .

JULIE,

One last thing, and I hope you don't mind. I've turned the tables on you and borrowed your coat. It has a better hood and a warmer lining, and since I'm not too sure where I'm headed, I took it as insurance against the storm. Love you. I'll be in touch when I'm ready.

XO, CAROLINE

JULIE SMILED. SHE'D BORROWED ENOUGH OF HER FRIEND'S clothing over the years to have owed her this favor. She sent up a silent prayer that wherever Caroline was going, she'd find herself happy there.

As soon as Angela emerged from the bathroom, her face camera ready once again, they left the suite and together got into the elevator to return to the Terrace Room. On the short ride, Angela turned to Julie and asked, "Do you need help walking down the aisle? You're the closest person in the world to my only daughter. It would be my honor to stand at your side, especially since your parents are gone."

"Oh, about that," Julie began. "My mom's alive. But that's a whole other story for another day. For now, I'd love for you to walk with me." She linked arms with a confused Angela and made her way to the Terrace Room. Caroline's party planner was standing there waiting and silently put a bouquet of pale blue hydrangeas in Julie's hand. Julie just figured that James had filled her in on current events.

"Sorry about those flowers," Angela whispered as the double doors opened, a roomful of people sitting there, most of whom Julie had never met. "They were supposed to be pink."

"They're perfect," Julie said, looking up to see James at the other end of the aisle, grinning from ear to ear. She couldn't help but do the same. She was about to marry the man of her dreams while wearing a navy blue dress instead of a white gown in the middle of the biggest Nor'easter her adopted city had experienced in over a century. *As a matter of fact,* Julie thought with each step toward her future, *nothing could be more perfect than this!*

Hey there happy reader!

I hope you enjoyed reading "Perfectly Polite" as much as I did writing it. The whole idea came to me after both of my sons decided to get married ninety days apart on two separate continents! I was thrown into a frenzy of wedding planning and had to learn fast on my feet. Julie Porter popped into my mind fully formed and things snowballed from there...

Did you know that I have a fun newsletter where you can catch up on all of my antics, including these upcoming nuptials?!? I hope you'll join in on the fun:

https://hilaritcohen.com/newsletter/

And in case you were wondering what happens next for Caroline, you can read the first chapter of her story, "Fabulously Flirty", just by clicking the link below:

https://hilaritcohen.com/fabulously-flirty-bonus/

Keep your eyes open! That madcap rom-com will hit your inbox soon!

    xoxo,
    Hilari

About the Author

Hilari T. Cohen is an award-winning editor who has worked and consulted in the publishing field for over twenty-five years. She built brands for Berkley, Harlequin and Zebra Books as well as edited many New York Times bestselling authors and titles in both fiction and nonfiction categories. However, she always harbored a secret ambition to write a novel of her own, and she did, successfully publishing *The Lyric of Memory*, *Adjusting the Rear View*, *Perfectly Polite* and the romance series, *The Gypsy Moth Chronicles*. She lives in suburban New York with her husband, loves to bake, drink red wine and read voraciously when she's not writing!

Photo credit: Leslie Magid Higgins

Also by Hilari T. Cohen

The Lyric of Memory

Adjusting the Rear View

Quarantined By Love, a novella

The Gypsy Moth Chronicles:

June

July

August

September

October

Made in the USA
Coppell, TX
16 November 2021